# FIRST LOVE

"Stevie, you really need to talk to the boy. Remember at luncheon when he said you wanted him to be perfect? You know you never felt that way, but he *believes* it. Worse, he believes he cannot possibly live up to your expectations, so he despairs. He needs to know how you really feel. Stevie . . ."

Cartwright ran his fingers through his carefully arranged hair, allowing a thick swath to fall down over his forehead in a way that would drive his valet to distraction when he saw it. "Speak with him," repeated his lordship slowly. "Talk to him. . . . Di, I haven't a clue how a man goes about talking to his son. And that is an admission I would make to no one but you," he added, turning and putting his hands on her shoulders.

He stared down at her as she looked up at him. The odd light gave a sense of isolation. In that false solitude, each looked deeply into the other's eyes. Questions passed between them—silent, unspoken, but real. Real—but unanswered and perhaps just yet unanswerable.

Still, there was something. . . .

Slowly he bent his head. Slowly she rose to meet his lips with her own. Gently, carefully, they kissed. A brief kiss. A hello kiss. A kiss full of hidden meanings. . . .

Published by Zebra Books

# THE HOUSE PARTY

## JEANNE SAVERY

ZEBRA BOOKS
KENSINGTON PUBLISHING CORP.
www.kensingtonbooks.com

ZEBRA BOOKS are published by

Kensington Publishing Corp.
850 Third Avenue
New York, NY 10022

All Kensington titles, imprints and distributed lines are available at special quantity discounts for bulk purchases for sales promotion, premiums, fund-raising, educational or institutional use.

Special book excerpts or customized printings can also be created to fit specific needs. For details, write or phone the office of the Kensington Special Sales Manager: Attn. Special Sales Department. Kensington Publishing Corp., 850 Third Avenue, New York, NY 10022. Phone: 1-800-221-2647.

Zebra and the Z logo Reg. U.S. Pat. & TM Off.

ISBN 0-8217-7817-X

First Printing: July 2005
10  9  8  7  6  5  4  3  2  1

Printed in the United States of America

# PROLOGUE

Miss Francine Witherspoon stared at her father. "*Two weeks*," she repeated. "A dozen guests and a pair of *thespians* will arrive in only *two weeks*?"

His lordship nodded several times, his head bobbing enthusiastically and his hands rubbing together with the bubbling exuberance so much a part of him. "Think of it, Francie. All those people interested in my theater! It is so exciting."

"Two weeks?" said Francine again, but rather faintly this time.

"Yes, yes, two weeks," he responded impatiently. "Will you stop saying that?"

Francine turned on her heel and headed for the door, doing her best to suppress tears of rage.

"Where are you going?"

She turned and, with a chill in her voice, asked, "Has it never occurred to you that one must *prepare* for houseguests? That rooms must be cleaned? Beds aired? Food must be ordered? That there is a great deal to do and that two weeks is *not* enough time in which to do it?"

"Pooh. Nonsense," blustered her father, growing faintly red around the ears. "Jenkins will help."

"*Jenkins*," exclaimed Francine, making no attempt to hide her loathing of the one-time actor her father had hired as butler—his incompetent and untrainable butler.

Francine left the room. It was bad enough her father could think of nothing but the theater. She had accepted that, but he had infected Richard with his passion, and *that* she could not bear. That she never had her father's attention . . . Well, that was one thing. If *Richard* also turned from her . . . The thought was intolerable.

The tears would no longer be suppressed, and Francine turned into the first door she came to, shutting and locking it behind her. However much she had to do in the next two weeks, she would, just this once, indulge in a good cry. Perhaps—she pushed aside a long-standing doubt as to the efficacy of tears—she'd purge herself of some of the pain . . .


"What is it, Euphrasia?" Morningside itched to get his hands into Eustacia Fairchild's unmanageable red hair, ached to pull out the pins she'd stuck in randomly, was painfully aware of how she'd look with it down . . .

Rafe Trent, Lord Morningside, pushed aside the unacceptable notion. Miss Fairchild was not available for such fun and games.

"Euphrasia?"

"Don't call me that," said Eustacia, but it was an automatic response with no heat behind it. All her attention was on the engraved invitation she held between finger and thumb. "Tell me why a man I barely know has invited me to a summer-long country-house party?"

Rafe's gaze sharpened. "Who?"

"Lord Witherspoon . . . ?"

There was a faint query to that, and Rafe hid a smile. It never ceased to amuse him, whom Eustacia knew and whom she did not. "He's a longtime theatrical aficionado, my dear, and has just completed the construction of a private theater. I presume his lordship is collecting together anyone he thinks might be as fascinated as he, asking them to come and act in it."

Eustacia's frown deepened. "But I don't know him."

"Unnecessary. He will have sent invitations to anyone who ever showed interest—which you will admit," he finished on a dry note, "you *have* done the past few months."

Eustacia blushed, embarrassed by her extravagance. Renting a theater box had long been a dream, and, a spinster and bluestocking left alone by the death of her cousin and one-time guardian, she'd finally been free to do as she pleased. A theater box, of all things. A box she too often occupied.

"So I have," she said, pretending an insouciance she did not feel. "He will have us take parts? We will put on a play?"

"Very likely more than one."

Eustacia thought about it. She glanced at Rafe, who sprawled in the most comfortable of the chairs in her small salon, playing with his riding crop. "I've no desire to go to Brighton for the summer," she said. "I have never liked it there." Then, slowly, she nodded. "I'll accept." She tipped her head, considering, and a curl dropped from the insecure top-knot to lay against her throat. "*If*," she mused, "it turns out that I find it tedious or discover that I dislike the company, I may always say I've received a message of disaster here in London . . . yes." She nodded once more, this time decisively. "I *will* accept."

Rafe nodded in response and made a mental note to send Lord Witherspoon an acceptance to his own invitation. He stood, picking up her pert riding cap and holding it out to her. "The park should be fairly clear of others at this early hour, and if we hurry we might manage something more than a strict trot. Do come, Euphrasia, my dear. Our horses await us."

"That is *not* my name, Rafe." But she wanted to ride and, although angry, allowed him to lead her from the house.

Sir Cyrall reread the square of engraved paper and lifted his gaze to stare out the window. He was alone and, with no one to see, had donned none of his many affectations.

Quietly, he spoke to the empty room. "Why not?" he asked it.

A vision of the beautiful but unobtainable Madeline Winthrop filled his mind. It was essential that he remove himself from London. He could not bear to watch his older brother wooing the woman with whom he'd fallen deeply in love.

"If only I'd nerved myself to approach Lord Winthrop before Primus discovered I'd an interest in Maddy. . . ."

But he had not, and Primus, as was usual with him, had instantly decided that he wanted for himself what Cyrall wanted. Primus, the ton's Golden Adonis, the heir. Lord and Lady Winthrop were unlikely to look kindly on a mere second son when the *heir* showed an interest.

A pang squeezed Cyrall's chest. If only their middle brother had not died. Primus had more or less ignored the much younger Cyrall before Secondus broke his neck in that curricle accident. . . . A muscle rolled over in Cyrall's jaw, and then, resigned—as he'd been resigned from nursery days to his eldest brother's difficult nature—he did his best to put aside his dislike.

But a deep, dark pain filled Cyrall, something that felt as if it were choking him. "It hurts to think of sweet Miss Winthrop bound to a cur like Primus. . . ."

Young Steven Cartwright, newly arrived on the ton, read the invitation once again. Something inside him expanded. Lord Witherspoon had noticed him. Lord Witherspoon thought

him worthy of an invitation to help inaugurate his new theater. As he wrote his acceptance, Steven felt warmth fill him
and anticipation of nothing but pleasure.


Diane Runyard paused by the desk, picked up the contract she'd just signed, and reread it. She laid it down and
crossed the room, turned and paced back. "It is a wonderful
way to fill the summer months, is it not?"

Roger Brown looked up from the play he studied. "Of
course it is." Something about the actress facing him caught
his attention. Perhaps the unusual disarray of her walnut-
colored hair. Perhaps the fact her usually serene nature was
troubled. "What is it, Di?"

Diane paused in still another transit of the theater's office
and frowned slightly. "I don't know. I've been so restless."
Suddenly, anxiously, she turned toward her colleague. "Roger,
am I getting too old to play comedy roles?"

Roger barked a short, sharp laugh—but when she remained
sober, his humor turned to a frown. "Nonsense. You are loved
in such roles. The ton would be angry if you ceased to play
the comic heroine."

Diane turned to the mirror, studying the fine lines radiating from the corners of her eyes. She sighed softly. The time
*was* coming, whatever Roger claimed.

And then what would she do?

A memory burst into her mind. A young blond godling
watching her smear on paint before a performance. He had
promised her she must not worry about her future, that he'd
see her secure. . . . And in an exceedingly odd fashion, Stevie
had done just that, had he not? The ancient pain throbbed and
faded. After all, the wonderful months they'd had together
were ended nearly twenty years in the past. . . .

So why had that old ache, the feelings of loss, become
sharp and new again?

# CHAPTER ONE

The door slammed shut and Diane Runyard crossed the room to her bed. Half laughing, half crying, she threw herself onto it and beat her fist into the coverlet. Its silky softness made that unsatisfactory, so she turned over and, reaching for the pillow, hugged it.

" 'Twarn't no blidy ghost," she growled into the fat cushion.

She rolled over, curling around it, as still another emotion was added to the cauldron bubbling and boiling inside her. This new one was nothing more or less than the purest embarrassment. She'd learned to speak properly more than a decade earlier, and that she should revert to old ways, even in this situation, steadied her.

Incipient hysteria faded, and, sitting up, she clasped the pillow to her chest, resting her chin on the firm end. "I've been an actress for near to two decades," she muttered. "Surely I can understand how I feel."

She attempted to separate the wild sensations roused by the young man who had entered Lord Witherspoon's salon a handful of minutes earlier. His appearance shocked her, and she'd wanted nothing but to escape, *needed* to escape. Now, safe behind a closed door, chaotic thoughts faded into a vision that slid into her mind. The image of this young man was laid over that of a nearly identical man—a man perhaps half a dozen years older and dressed in a style twenty years out of date.

A man who held a small, very private piece of her heart, who always would . . .

So *many* years since that original man looked across the green room of the theater in which she'd worked. Their eyes met, held, and, as if drawn by a string, they walked toward each other. What followed, their weeks and months together, was the most wonderful time of Diane Runyard's young life.

Steven Cartwright dined her. He wined her. And, soon, he rented rooms for the two of them. . . .

*Gently, his fingers pushed damp hair back from her temple, tucking the strand behind her ear. "I didn't believe it possible to love as I love you," murmured the blond god leaning over her in the bed they shared.*

*"I will love ye feriver," she responded fervently, running her hands up his back, loving the feel of warm, clean skin damp from their lovemaking.*

The only cloud on the horizon of their young and heated love had been the disapproving physiognomy of Steven's toffee-nosed, monkey-faced valet. Diane lay back against another pillow and, ignoring the well-appointed room that only a few hours earlier had delighted her, sighed.

"What *was* that stiff-rumped, disapproving bastard's name?" she muttered.

All she could recall was the glint of satisfaction in the man's eyes when he informed her the flat's rent was paid until the end of the quarter. At that time she must have a new protector to support her—or she must depart. . . .

*"They have arranged a marriage for me, Di. What am I to do?"*

*Diane felt her heart breaking, but she dared not allow Stevie to see it. She had always known nothing could come of their love, had known it could not last . . . but she'd hoped for more than eight months.*

*"What are ye to do?" she asked. "Why, 'tis simple, my love. Ye know 'tis. You've a duty, haven't you? To family. To your future." She could no longer control her features and ducked her head in under his neck, speaking into his shoulder. "We knew this was a dream, only a little bit of borrowed Heaven." She held him, keeping her face pressed to his shoulder so he could not see it. "Ye'll go home, Stevie. Ye'll meet your wife-to-be, and ye'll treat her with the respect she deserves."*

*She drew in a deep breath and finished, speaking more to herself than to him. "Of course ye must." Inside, where he could not see, she felt as if a part of her had died.*

*"You'll stay here," he murmured into her hair. "You'll be here whenever I can see you."*

*She shook her head against his shoulder. "Can't. Ye know we can't. 'Twouldn't be right. Ye know 'twouldn't."*

*He'd groaned, holding her so tightly he'd left bruises. "I cannot give you up."*

*Diane knew him. She knew his idealism, how honorable he was. He would endure the worst sort of guilt if he came to her while married to another. She called on every bit of training her theater-bred parents had given her and pushed away from him.*

*"'Twon't do, Stevie, lover. Ye know 'twon't. Ye wouldn't be you, Stevie, if ye thought it right, and I 'twouldn't love ye so much if ye were different." Distinctly, each word pushed from*

*her mouth with an effort she hoped she'd never again need,
she added, "You go on now." She'd forced herself to stand
firm, straight backed. "You do what you have to do."*

*It was still harder to raise her chin, to smile, to add, "I'll
be all right . . . and so will you."*

Diane hugged the bolster still harder at the memory of
one final distressing scene. Some weeks later, an older gentleman came to the theater where she worked. He ordered the
owner to send for her, that they were to be allowed to speak
privately. . . .

*"Miss Runyard?" he had asked, his back stiff and his
eyes cold—but touched by a hint of curiosity.*

*She ached at how much this man resembled her Stevie. An
older, silver-haired Steven. And then fear filled her in a rush.
Something had happened. . . .*

*"Yes, m'lord?" she'd asked, her heart beating hard. "My
Stevie . . . ?"*

*"My son is fine. Not happy, but behaving like the gentle-
man he is." He paused before adding, "The thing is—"*

*Was that embarrassment she read in his expression? Surely
not.*

*"—I discovered he was not a gentleman when he gave
you your conge." He handed her an envelope, which, without
thinking, she took. "That should be sufficient."*

Diane lay back, chuckling. Perhaps his lordship was embarrassed to admit his son had forgotten to, hmm, *reimburse*
her for their fun and games. She was never certain about
that, but she knew he was utterly *betwattled* when, realizing
what he'd given her, she'd thrust the money back at him.

What had she said to him? Softly, Diane quoted her much younger self: "Thank you, my lord, for the thought, but what your son and I shared is not something which can be bought and paid for. Good day."

Diane stared up at the ceiling with a smile on her lips. That boy downstairs in the Witherspoon salon . . . Was that Stevie's son?

" 'Course it is," she muttered with self-directed scorn.

Looking the image of her Stevie and a much softer version of the tall, hard-eyed gentleman who had been his grandfather, this boy *must* be the current Cartwright heir. She remembered reading the announcement of his birth one year, six months, and nine days after she'd last seen her Stevie. She'd cried one last heartrending bout of tears . . . and gone onstage an hour later to play her very first speaking part—a pert maid with laughing eyes that shone less from the merriment she was supposed to be projecting than from unshed tears.

A bone-deep sadness flitted in and through Diane. Very softly she mumbled into the pillow. "This youth might have been mine. *Ours* . . ."

Diane wanted to cry. But there were no more tears. There would be none. Instead, she rose to her feet and went to the dainty little dressing table. She assured herself her face showed nothing of the emotions that raged within and then prepared to return downstairs, where she must play a harder role than ever—the part of a woman with a job of work to do while ignoring pain. Pain very nearly as sharp and more bitter than that she'd known two decades previously. Thanks to that boy who might have been her own, a *lot* more bitter.

But then another bitter memory overwhelmed her, and, her hand on the door, she discovered she *wasn't* ready to face anyone. Wasn't ready to join the others and pretend nothing had changed. Too many memories still swept through her troubled mind. . . .

*"For me? But where's it from? Who . . . why . . . ?"*

*"You've no need to know any of that," said the stern-visaged clerk who brought her the first quarter's income. "You are not to know it."*

*Life had been hard just then. She'd been out of work, had sold very nearly everything she had to sell. Not the necklace with Stevie's portrait painted on it, which she would never sell, but everything else.*

*Worst of all, just the day before she had looked at Tower Bridge and—shame filled her—considered whether she'd the courage to end it all.*

The income she received quarterly from that "unknown source," beginning a month or so after her Stevie became Baron Cartwright, had only added a shameful, acid-sharp bite to the feelings of loss that never quite left her. It stung her pride that she couldn't turn it down as she'd turned down the money Stevie's father had tried to give her. Times *were* hard. Although shamed by it, she'd not rejected her lost love's belated generosity. . . .

Diane paced. *It would*, she thought, *have been nice if he had come to me, explained why he would do such a thing a good eight years after our little interlude ended*. She wondered if she'd been wrong about him—because the man she thought she'd known *would* have come to her, *would* have explained. . . .

She pushed the thought away as she'd often done before and, for distraction, stared into the mirror. She noticed there were a few gray strands among the dark and made a note to apply more walnut stain the next time she washed it. She leaned nearer and touched the lines at her eyes, sighing.

There was no forgetting she had reached her thirty-seventh year, that she was well beyond her prime as an actress. Still, she had more than a bit of a reputation. Nothing like that of

Sara Siddons or Dora Jordan, of course, but anyone who went regularly to a London theater knew her, liked her, and applauded her.

She pushed at the skin at her temples and glared. Perhaps it *was* time to give up her traditional roles, time to think of taking only secondary comic roles or—dared she? Might she try more serious dramatic roles? She'd never played a truly dramatic part. . . .

Diane stared around the pleasant room, a room that would be hers for the weeks she'd stay at Lord Witherspoon's estate. Such a lovely room . . . and there was no reason to spoil her pleasure in it by worrying about decisions about her future.

Right now this minute she must rejoin the guests. She had been hired to help Roger Brown direct the first amateur performances to be staged in Baron Witherspoon's brand-new private theater and perhaps to take a part in one or another play. She must remember how grateful she'd been for the opportunity to spend the summer months here at Lord Witherspoon's favorite estate, far from London's heat and summer stink. Not only was she out of London, but there was this wonderful room, a guest room and not, as she'd expected, a tiny space shared with one of the maids—or, if she'd been lucky, perhaps a slightly better room near where the upper servants slept.

"I *am* grateful," she said.

Diane nodded once, a sharp little nod of the head, took one long last deep breath and, again calling on ingrained stage presence, returned to the salon.

She would not look at that boy and think of her Stevie. She would *not*. . . .

# CHAPTER
# TWO

"What is the matter with you?" Roger Brown asked, leaning near Diane Runyard's ear so no one would hear his scolding tone.

It was after dinner, and the men had joined the women in the Witherspoon main salon. Roger brushed fingers through the silvery white hair sweeping back from his high brow, erasing a frown as his hand passed over his face.

"You are as tense as the string on a wound-up crossbow," he added chidingly when she didn't immediately respond.

"It shows?" she asked, turning a startled glance his way.

Roger shrugged. "I know you. I doubt anyone else has twigged to what is obvious to me. So?"

Diane sighed. She turned back to the window out which she'd been staring. "The boy. Young man, I suppose I should say. . . ."

Roger glanced around. The only really young man among the guests was a slender blond youth, newly come among theater enthusiasts and, thanks to that interest, invited when Baron Witherspoon gathered friends and acquaintances for this house party.

"Steven Cartwright?" he asked. "A nice lad. A bit lost among the older gentlemen but well behaved and not pushy nor so impolite that he shows that other thing a boy on the verge of manhood always has."

There was humor in both his voice and the subtle expression. Diane flicked a look at him, one brow arched in query.

"That utter certainty indulged by young men," explained Roger, "that they are the very first ever to feel strange emotions and discover odd facts of life."

Diane smiled, restraining an unkind chuckle. Not that young Cartwright was so near he'd overhear them, but the boy had turned one or two speculative looks her way during dinner. And once the gentlemen joined the ladies, he'd stared continuously in the most heated of fashions. She suspected Roger was incorrect that Steven was blasé toward his newly adult emotions—even if he hid those emotions reasonably well.

So far.

"Have you met everyone?" she asked, seeking distraction.

"Most of them. It is too bad we aren't putting on *A Midsummer Night's Dream*. Sir Cyrall—" He directed her gaze toward a slender, rather foppish, man. "—has that elvish face and mischievous nature that makes a perfect Puck." He frowned. "Since we are *not*, I fear we will find him a bit of a troublemaker. . . ." His voice trailed off for a thoughtful moment as he glanced around. "Then, over there—" Roger thrust his chin toward the fireplace, where a tall, saturnine gentleman stood, his arm laid along the mantel. "—you'll see that Lord Morningside has arrived." He grinned at her moue. "I think, my dear, you convinced him you are not interested. It is several years since he last pursued you."

"Who said I wasn't interested?" she retorted. "I have been *interested* in any number of men."

Roger's warm chuckle drew a number of eyes, but his manner toward Diane, one of friendly intimacy, turned them away. "Have you *ever* succumbed to one of your pursuers?" he asked softly.

"I have this odd belief," she evaded a direct answer, "that lovemaking requires that one be in love with the other—not merely in lust."

His heavy lids lowered and a faintly sardonic expression warned Diane that he was not satisfied—or perhaps it was merely that he thought her a fool for holding such a belief. Not wishing to discover which it was, she asked, "And that man beside Lord Morningside?"

Roger glanced back toward the fireplace. "Sir George Allingham. He stutters. Badly."

Diane's brows arched. "Yet he is here . . . ?" she asked.

Roger shrugged. "Perhaps he is merely a friend," he said. "Over there, that striking woman? The tall one with red hair?" Diane nodded. "That is Miss Fairchild."

"*Miss*?" Diane was startled that the woman—richly gowned and revealing a great deal of poise, to say nothing of strong character—was unwed. Although her looks could not be considered beautiful, exactly, they were such that they should have drawn a court from among the discerning. Then too she wore valuable jewelry, and her gown had been made up by one of London's leading mantuamakers, which suggested she was well dowered. So why was she unwed at an age where she'd be called spinster by the kind hearted, an ape-leader by those who were not? "Did you speak with her?"

"An intelligent woman, but a bluestocking, I fear." Roger frowned, rubbing chin with forefinger and thumb. "I'm uncertain as to her first name. The women call her Eustacia, but Lord Morningside quite distinctly called her Euphrasia." He shrugged slightly. "I don't suppose it matters. . . . Who else? You met Miss Witherspoon, did you not? I have wondered about her and the neighbor lad, Richard Coxwald. There is that special coolness between them that requires that there was once heat." Roger was amused.

Diane was not fond of gossip. Especially not the salacious sort of gossip Roger loved. "Tell me," she demanded, turning fully toward him and firmly changing the subject, "how soon do we cast the first play?"

Roger, who was not always so obliging, allowed the change of topic. "Our host announces our first meeting any minute now and will explain how we are to go on." He grimaced, his mobile features momentarily expressing his suspicion it would not be so easy as that.

"And the play?"

"That is the problem." He sighed, an overly dramatic expression of sorrow—or perhaps disgust? "The neighbor, Coxwald. I am informed he is a, umm, budding playwright?" His brows arched suggestively. "He has, I am informed, written his own particular version of the Oedipus story."

"Have you seen it?" asked Diane, wondering how awful it would be.

"No. Copies are to be handed around tonight. I dare not hope that he has managed to restrain himself. An amateur is too enamored of scenes impossible to stage. You know the sort I mean."

Diane shrugged. "If necessary, I will, as tactfully as possible, explain the difficulty and help him rewrite it. I have done so before."

Roger laughed, and again his deep, warm chuckle drew eyes. Especially *feminine* eyes. "Yes, you've a talent in that direction," he said and referred to her work on one particular play. "You'll recall what a *melo*drama it was, although the writer considered it serious drama?"

She repressed a chuckle. "How could I forget that difficult gentleman?" she asked. "He was convinced that changing a single word of his masterpiece would ruin the whole. But even he conceded that a raging storm with trees crashing about the stage and a house falling around the ears of the heroine was a bit much—"

Roger shuddered.

"—to say nothing of the scene in which the hero was to save the heroine from the back of her runaway horse as they galloped across the stage."

"You saved that particular scene."

"Yes." She made a graceful movement with her hands, indicating the sweeping back of a curtain. "We opened the act with the sound of galloping hooves *off*. Horse, complete with hero, *on*. Heroine clutching hero around the waist, her legs dangling and draped in the skirts of her habit in such a way they'd trip up his steed—or would have done if the poor beast had moved a single hoof! But it worked—you must admit it worked, even if he did have to cut all that bit about the hero actually catching her up and pulling her from her mare."

"What I freely admit is that you rewrote that poor playwright's play from one end to the other without damaging his self-respect and, at the same time, improved it so that it actually played reasonably well. Far better than *I* ever expected." He eyed her, something akin to curiosity in his gaze. "I wish I knew half your tricks," he said. He stared down at her with a serious and, for once, perfectly sincere expression.

"Hush. You have earned a well-deserved reputation for getting a decent performance from amateurs. If you rub Witherspoon's guests up the wrong way—as you will—then I am here to apply the necessary oil and smooth the rough spots. Ah. I do believe the baron is about to make an announcement."

"Friends! Friends, *quiet*. Please."

After only one or two more such exhortations, the room stilled and Lord Witherspoon, rubbing his hands together, grinned broadly, his excitement catching. "Tonight! Tonight we begin. If everyone will go to the music room and find their seat, then we will tell you about our first play and how we are to proceed. Come along, then. Come along." He looked around. "Mrs. Runyard? Mr. Brown? Are you ready to begin?"

Roger offered Diane his arm—only to discover that the lad, Steven Cartwright, had appeared at her other elbow and was offering his. Roger bowed to the boy and walked away. Diane cast a half-rueful, half-glaring glance after him.

"Miss Runyard?" asked Steven politely. "May I take you in?"

"It is Missus. *Mrs*. Runyard," said Diane softly.

She hoped the young man would believe her married and unavailable for what she feared he wanted of her. Diane had adopted the title soon after her interlude with this boy's father ended and had never regretted it. Quite often it was sufficient to turn off attentions such as young Steven had in mind. As she put her fingertips on his arm and allowed him to draw her from the room, she hoped it would in this case as well. Once in the music room, she excused herself and rejoined Roger.

"Don't," she said in a low but fervent voice, "do that to me again."

Not pretending to misunderstand, Roger grinned a sardonic grin before turning his attention to the front of the room. Another man, enjoying only a handful more years than Steven could own to, was seated there, a pile of paper on the table before him.

"Our playwright," said Roger softly, watching the man fiddle with the script he held in one hand. "I bet you a guinea his sweaty hands will pulp the paper on that side."

"Done," said Diane and turned mischief-filled eyes up toward Roger as, almost instantly, the script was laid down and patted into a neat pile. "I knew he'd not ruin his hard work." She looked around the room.

Rout chairs were set in three erratic rows, small rout tables near many of them suitable for a gentleman's drink or a lady's cup and saucer. Before the chairs was the oval piecrust-edged table behind which Richard Coxwald, the playwright,

sat. Richard continued fiddling nervously with a corner of the play.

"I'll win yet," whispered Roger.

The door opened, allowing Francine Witherspoon, their host's daughter—and, as she made no attempt to hide, their reluctant hostess—to enter. She stalked in, a grim look about her mouth and disdain in her eyes. Avoiding the rout chairs, she sat, her back straight, on the edge of an armless chair placed near her harp. Diane watched as Richard Coxwald cast the baron's daughter a pleading look. She grimaced and turned her head. Their playwright sighed.

"He's wondering exactly when, why, and how he lost the chit's affection," guessed Diane, who often attempted to interpret little scenes such as they had just witnessed.

"Something of the sort," murmured Roger, far more interested in their host—or, more accurately, their employer—than the trials of young love. "Where's Witherspoon gotten to?"

Lord Witherspoon bustled in behind the last of the guests, rubbing his hands in that way he had and grinning widely. "Everyone here? Good. Good. Let us begin." He reached the chair beside Coxwald's and seated himself. He half turned and looked expectantly at his young friend. "Well, Richard? Ready? What have you done for us?"

"It's the Oedipus tale. You know. The Greek tragedy of a princely family?"

Richard Coxwald was interrupted by a rather prissy but teasing voice. "No, no . . . not a *tragedy*! Please!" Sir Cyrall Jamison, baronet, waved a hand in a weak fashion before his elfin face, his thin lips pulled into a tight little V-shaped smile. "A nicely bawdy Restoration play?" he suggested on a hopeful note. His thin brows shot up. "Now *that's* the ticket. And may I be the . . . the *gardener*, please? And Miss—" His gaze passed quickly over the group turned to stare at him. "—Fairchild my *rose bush*? May I pluck all the *buds*? Make the roses *bloom*?"

Beside the baronet, young Steven Cartwright blushed.

Sir Cyrall, noticing, laughed. "Oh, dear. I seem to have discomposed the wrong person. Why, Miss Fairchild, are *you* lacking roses in your cheeks?" he asked in a falsely interested tone.

Miss Fairchild, spinster, merely blinked at Cyrall's comment.

Sir Cyrall chuckled softly. He knew that Miss Fairchild recognized the double entendres strewn through his teasing little monologue. He'd been present at her intellectual cousin's table when she was hostess on a night that Restoration plays were the subject for the evening's discussion. The scholarly gentlemen gathered around that board had not spared their hostess's blushes as they discussed the freer speech and still freer behavior of their ancestors.

It occurred to Sir Cyrall that it might prove interesting to discover just how far Miss Fairchild could be made to go, interesting to discover exactly *when* the roses would appear . . . and *digging in her garden* would be a distraction from his problems!

"Hmm?" he asked brightly, pretending to become aware that Lord Witherspoon had been roundly scolding him. "Did you say something?"

"I said," sputtered his lordship, "that you know very well we cannot put on such a play. 'Twouldn't be at all the thing! Don't know what those people were thinking of."

The baronet opened his mouth to explain exactly what had been in their forefathers' minds, when he caught Rafe, Lord Morningside's, expression. The irritation he read in his friend's face brought faint roses to his cheeks. He hid his embarrassment by smiling one of his suggestive little smiles and batting his long, golden eyelashes at Rafe.

Lord Morningside grimaced.

Richard Coxwald grasped the opportunity engendered by the gentlemen's silent exchange to begin a summary of his play. He finished and asked if anyone was interested in a particular role.

Roger Brown, hearing his cue, cleared his throat. He rose and moved forward a step or two. The playwright's gaze was drawn to him as Roger had hoped. "May I speak?" asked Roger in his most sonorous tones.

He was asked to come forward.

"Mrs. Runyard and I have been asked," he said, once he had everyone's attention, "that, as professionals, we take a hand in helping you to the very best acting you can manage. Do you truly wish that?" asked the actor, the deep, bell-like tones rolling over his audience.

Heads among the assembled guests nodded, including enthusiastic head bobbing from Lord Witherspoon. Roger took that as permission to continue.

"In that case, my lords and my ladies, we must begin as we mean to go on. Mr. Coxwald will distribute copies of his version of the Oedipus tragedy, which, if you would be so kind, you will read. *This evening.*"

Knowing how amateurs tended to put off such things, Roger glanced around, catching and holding this blank gaze, those raised eyebrows, another frowning stare—and one glare. Francine Witherspoon made no attempt to hide *her* dislike of the whole situation.

"It is normal in a group of players," he continued, his voice hypnotic in its smooth, rolling tones, "that several will be interested in the same part. Tomorrow morning, in the hall outside the breakfast room, a schedule will be posted."

Past experience with amateur players at country-house parties had taught Roger that that was the best place to put notices he wished everyone to read.

"Each hour, in the order listed, we will hold trials for a particular role. Anyone hoping to be given a certain part must appear at the theater at the hour posted for that role. After a trial, the best performer of any particular role will have won it." Once again he looked around. "That is why you must read and study the play tonight—so you will know which role or roles you wish to try for."

He bowed and made a smoothly professional exit, taking two copies of Coxwald's play with him. One was for himself and one for Mrs. Runyard, who, with no more than a look, he drew out the door with him.

"I'll take my guinea now," she said when the door was closed behind them. She held out her hand, knowing from old that Roger made a habit of forgetting such things.


The meeting over, Rafe, Lord Morningside, rose to his feet and moved toward Eustacia Fairchild. Sir Cyrall reached her a moment sooner. Eustacia, who had no taste for the games men play—and angry with Rafe for other reasons entirely—took a step toward George Allingham, hooked her hand through his arm, and, without a by-your-leave, strolled off with the bemused gentleman as, red faced, he stuttered assurances to her question that of course he had no other plans.

"Well," said Sir Cyrall, hands on hips, confusion making him blink his eyelids in a rapid fluttery fashion.

"Not at all well," said Rafe, his tone stern.

Cyrall cast him a curious glance, his long, pale lashes veiling his eyes. "An interest there, Rafe, old friend?"

"Perhaps." He cast a quick glance at Cyrall. "Or again, perhaps not. But a *definite* interest in *George's* well-being. Eustacia Fairchild is not the woman for a man of George's cut."

"No, of course not. A man of *my* cut, perhaps," teased Cyrall, his lips trembling at the corners with suppressed humor.

"No." Rafe studied his old friend. "You don't know her, Cyr," he said after a moment. "She'd have you in knots in less than a week. It will take a man like *me* to tame that virago."

Cyrall's mobile expression changed to one of disbelief that anyone could think him unable to handle a woman of any sort.

"Don't attempt it," warned Rafe. "Believe me, you'd get your fingers burned. You assume you'd not become seriously involved, but there is something insidious in that woman, something that draws one in. . . ."

Lord Morningside, fearing he'd revealed too much, moved to the table and picked up a copy of the play. His lordship then went to his room, meaning to read it through immediately. If it chanced that there was a part in it for Eustacia, he wished to make it an absolute certainty that it was *he* who played opposite her!


"No, nononono," groaned Roger, his hands in his hair and his head bowed. "No! It is not a comedy," he said more moderately, lifting his gaze to stare at Sir Cyrall.

Sir Cyrall's mouth was in that little V-shape Diane already realized meant he was in a funning mood. "But," said the baronet from the stage, "you have not tried me in a love scene. Ah!" He kissed his fingers as might a Frenchman. "You would see how perfect I am when allowed to make desperate love to my lady mother."

"I think not," said Roger dryly. "Besides, if you read the play as you were supposed to do, you know that Oedipus and his mother have no knowledge of the relationship. Nor does she know her son killed his father, her first husband. Nor," he added sternly, "is there any actual lovemaking between them—at least, not on stage!" Roger waved his hand. "Next?" When there was no movement, he added a trifle testily, "Come, come. Someone. Anyone. We haven't all day for this one role."

Steven Cartwright rose from the chair in which he'd been seated about halfway up the theater aisle. "I would like to try," he said softly.

"Hmm? What?" Roger turned in his seat. For a moment he stared, and then he relaxed, a rather curious expression on his face. "You are a trifle young perhaps," he said slowly. "Have you done any acting?"

"At school. And then again at my aunt's last house party. The school play was *Julius Caesar,*" he finished with more enthusiasm.

As the youth strode down the aisle, Roger watched with narrowed eyes and was pleased by the lad's unconscious grace. Steven moved to the side where there were stairs up onto the stage and came to the center. "What should I read?" he asked, clutching his copy of the play.

Twenty minutes later, when one other would-be Oedipus had had his try, Roger consulted with Diane. "No," he said, disagreeing with her comment on Steven's age. "Now I've thought about it, I see no reason why Oedipus should not be young. His killing his father, who would be a far more experienced fighter, could be played as a bit of an accident. Perhaps his father steps on a stone, slips, even falls, making it easy for the boy—" He waved his hand dismissively. "—to end it. Something of that sort. And if the boy is young, then his mother need not be so old as to make their lust for each other ridiculous." His mouth firmed, his eyes narrowed, and he looked, for a long moment, at nothing at all. He nodded. "Yes. I'll give the part to Cartwright. Who have we interested in the part of Laius, his father?"

That and several other parts were easily filled, but neither of the two women who, hesitantly and after encouragement, tried the role of Oedipus's mother were satisfactory. Witherspoon's feminine guests found the notion of even a pretend son making love to their pretense of being his mother far too outrageous, far too shocking, to contemplate. They could not put their heart into the role

Roger pointed to Diane. "You."

Diane's brows arched. She had feared it would come to this, which was the main reason she'd objected to giving the Oedipus role to Steven Cartwright. She glanced to the side where the lad sat. He hadn't been far from her the whole of the morning, and she was finding his hovering a trifle wearing. "You cannot do that to me," she whispered and stifled a groan at Roger's quickly hidden grin. "Or to him. You *know* how it will end."

"So the boy will think himself hopelessly in love with you. That isn't altogether a bad thing. He must suffer his calf love soon in any case, and, at the least, you are too honorable to take advantage of him."

"You enjoy seeing me beset by problems, do you not?"

Roger sobered. "In actual fact, I *do*. I learn from watching you and, because of it, know a great deal more about emotions and the ups and downs of human nature. It is a convenient and enjoyable method of learning."

"*I* find it neither convenient nor enjoyable."

Diane thought of the complications of this particular problem. In particular, there was her history with Steven's father. But that history was something she'd no intention of revealing. To Roger or anyone else. *Most definitely not to Steven.*

Steven's youth was a second complication. There was the difficulty of not harming his image of himself.

And last, but certainly not least, her years of celibacy sorely tried her. Whenever she looked at Steven, she saw the man with whom she'd fallen deeply in love, with whom she'd tumbled into bed, and with whom she'd learned all she knew of passion. She wondered if she could remain unaffected, *could* keep her head. . . .

A touch of panic had her demanding, "Surely there is *someone*."

But she knew there was not. Diane sighed. Roger grinned. She seemed to collapse a trifle into herself, and he folded his arms. They stared at each other. He nodded. She nodded as well. Once. And, leaving her seat, headed up the aisle.

She heard Roger stop Steven, speaking to him about the Oedipus role, telling the lad it was a heavy role for an amateur, explaining what would be wanted, his voice rolling out in those long periods that, Diane knew from experience, could go on and on and on. . . .

She smiled a quick smile that her old friend felt a need to atone a trifle by assuring that the lad did not immediately follow after her, but the humor faded just as quickly and she went directly to her room.

Once there she wondered why she hadn't taken herself somewhere more interesting. But where . . . ? Nowhere. Besides, it was the loveliest room she'd ever had for her own use, which was reason enough for coming there.

Then, because she did not care to flounder about, drowning in a sea of memories, she took her copy of the play to the window seat, tucked her legs under her, grasped an ankle with one hand, and, concentrating hard, began the well-known chore of memorizing a new part.

It would be a good part, she realized as time passed and the lines slowly seeped into her. The emotions ran the gamut. There was the resentment over the loss of her child when the oracle predicted the baby would grow up to be the father's bane—resentment tempered by fears for her husband's life. Then, later, grief at the death of that husband soon followed by the birth of a new love and its fulfillment, and, finally, the abject horror of discovering she loved her husband's murderer, who—still worse—was her own son.

*My horror when that knowledge comes, and then my death*

*in this, merely an amateur play, may be one of the best scenes
I ever play*, she thought judiciously.

She raised her head and stared across the room.

*There is that notion I had that I might turn my hand to
more serious roles*. After a moment, she nodded. *This part
will reveal, rather painlessly since it is not on the London
stage, if I've any talent for drama. So*, she concluded, *perhaps it will not be so very bad, this playing opposite young
Steven. . . .*

She thought about that.

*Yes it will.*

# CHAPTER
# THREE

Six days later, after rehearsal ended, Roger walked with Diane toward the house. "You've been spending an awful lot of time with the boy," said Roger, watching her narrowly.

Diane shrugged. "His is a difficult part. I have coached him."

"And," asked Roger with a touch of slyness, "is that *all* you've done?"

"I listen." Diane felt a touch of warmth in her neck and ears. A trifle defensively, she added, "He talks. About his mother, mostly. She died. It was a number of years ago, but he still misses her." She put her foot on the first step up to the terrace and turned to Roger. "Why the sudden interest?" Her eyes widened as his expression forced a guess. "There is talk." She stood a step above him, her eyes level with his. He turned away so he would not have to look into hers. "So." Resigned, Diane sighed. "What do you suggest?"

Roger's shoulders shifted in an uncomfortable fashion. "Perhaps . . . stay where others can see that you behave innocently."

"We do. And then the *others* go off and leave us. I am to drag him after?"

Roger turned back. They continued up onto the terrace. "So I've noticed—"

He shrugged. Now he was assured she was aware of it, he lost interest in the problem and put it aside. It was, after all, *her* problem.

"—but enough of your trifling predicament. You'll deal with it. We've another, far more important problem. Think, instead, of that."

Diane grimaced but knew Roger sincerely believed her situation with Steven nothing more than a minor irritation. After all, it had nothing to do with the play—or so he thought! So she asked, "The man playing Laius had to leave? I hope the gentleman finds that his wife was not badly hurt in that accident."

"Rumor has it that there was no accident. She has, it is said, lied more than once in order to draw his attention," said Roger in his driest tone. "But never mind that. *Our* problem is filling that particular role with someone who can take it on at this late date. Who would you suggest for Laius . . . Diane?" he added when she didn't respond.

"Not another blidy ghost!" she whispered, her tone intense.

"There are no ghosts in this play," he said with false patience.

"Steven's father."

"No, no, Diane," he said impatiently. "It is *Oedipus's* father we discuss."

Diane stifled a half-hysterical laugh. "*I'm* not. He is here. *There*, I mean." She pointed surreptitiously, one finger slightly raised. "Talking with Lord Benningcorn. I cannot meet him in company, Roger. I *will* not." She bit her lip, ignoring the questions she could tell were on the tip of his tongue and thinking quickly. "If . . . anyone . . . wishes to find me, I . . .

I mean to ask for a tray. In the conservatory. I'll remain there for a time." She turned on her heel, returned back down the stairs, and moved quickly into the gardens.

"Stevie," she murmured, her chest tight and her eyes burning with unshed tears. "The changes the years make! Ah, you've grown so very like the gentleman who tried to give me money, tried to bribe me into leaving you alone. As if a bribe was necessary!" A touch of outrage filled her, faded, and the panic returned. "Ah, my dear, that silvery white hair— when, my love, did *you* grow to be a silver fox as your father was before you?" She went on murmuring words to a man who was not there to hear them, walking beyond the garden and into the orchard, where she paced back and forth between two long rows of trees heavy with young fruit.

At the far end of the orchard was a stone fence and, eventually, Diane seated herself there to look out over the meadow beyond. She drew up one knee and clasped it, laying her cheek onto it. A long, slow sigh escaped her.

"Life gets so blidy complicated," she muttered.

After a moment she heaved a self-consciously melodramatic sigh and, taking herself firmly in hand, returned to the house. Since everyone was changing for dinner, the halls were quiet. She found the butler and requested a supper tray in the conservatory before she went up to wash away the dust of the day and don a more formal gown.

And, she realized a bit later, do her best to make herself look as young and innocent as she was when Stevie and she first met. Instantly she went to her washbasin and washed away the paints. She was who she had become, and so he must find her.


Diane had finished her meal when she heard a sharply barked, "Aha! There you are. Heard I'd come and thought you could hide, I suppose."

Very slowly Diane laid aside her copy of the script and even more slowly stood, staring curiously at the man who had once meant absolutely everything to her. And still meant more than she cared to admit.

"Hello, Stevie."

He halted in midstride and then, more slowly, drew closer, peering at her. "Di?"

"You look just like your father. I thought perhaps you would. Someday . . . Not so soon. . . ."

"My *father*?" The anger he'd expressed before recognizing her had faded into bemusement. Bemusement grew to utter bewilderment. "What has my father to do with anything? Di? It is *you*?"

"Oh, yes. Unlike you, the changes in me are *not* an improvement. Women don't age as well as men do. You look wonderful, Steve."

His eyes widened and outrage returned. "You? *You* seduced my son?"

"*Seduced* him?" She tapped his chest with a reproachful finger. "*To the contrary*. I have been doing my best to avoid being seduced *by* your son." She compressed her lips, and her eyes twinkled. "It would be ever so much easier, Stevie, if he didn't look so exactly as you did back when we . . . knew each other. And besides, there is the other problem in the way of seduction in this case." She sobered. "Seeing him is too much like looking at a boy who might have been mine. I'm not about to bed my son—whatever happens in the play we are staging."

Lord Cartwright relaxed. "I should have known you would not. But just for a moment there . . . and the tales Lord Benningcorn wrote . . . well . . ."

She nodded. "You arrived an avenging father to have words with the aging actress who was drawing your innocent boy into sinful pleasures. Which," she added thoughtfully, "must have made you feel a trifle hypocritical, recalling your own youthful folly."

"Folly?" he asked, the word formed with some care.

"Is that not how you thought of it? Afterward? Ah, well. A very long while ago," she said, and tried to read the emotions he hid so well.

"Yes. Long ago." And then even the little emotion he'd revealed faded into nothing. "Well, well."

She discovered she didn't like the forced joviality in that. So," he continued. "How *are* you, Di?"

"Very well." She didn't want to talk of herself and hurried on. "I was sorry to read of your wife's death some little while ago." When he only stared at her, she added, "Five years now?"

"Four." His eyes sharpened before his lids dropped, hooding them. "A good woman, Di. A, um, decent wife. We trotted along in harness fairly . . . smoothly."

"Good," she said, distraction making her less perceptive than usual. "I'm glad. For you."

"Hmm."

He ran his fingers through his hair, drawing her attention to his hands. Hands she remembered perfectly. Long-fingered, strong, gentle hands.

"So," he added again after another moment's silence.

Diane, suddenly very much afraid of what he might say, interrupted. "Now you are reassured I am not corrupting your son, what do you mean to do? Will you leave? Return to wherever you spend your summers?"

His eyes narrowed. "I *meant* to gather him up and take him away from your evil influence, of course," he said with dry humor. "Perhaps to Bath, since I think him too young for Brighton. Or perhaps a tour through the Lake District . . . but instead—" Once again those fingers ruffled through his hair; humor disappeared. "—I think," he continued slowly, his eyes narrowing, "that I will stay on. Old Witherspoon has talked of nothing but this theater of his for months. I meant to wait until the newness was worn off and he might talk of something else before I visited, but, since I am here, I find I'm curious."

"Young Steven has a major part in this first play. I'm glad you do not find it necessary to draw him away. We'd be in total disarray." She forced a smile. "You see, the man playing the part of Laius was called home, and we are already left with a hole to fill."

"You are staging *Oedipus*?" he asked, recognizing the name.

"Not Sophocles' version." She saw he looked confused by that. "This is a surprisingly well-written amateur effort. Roger is pleased with it."

Something seemed to fade in the figure looming over her, and somehow he looked ... older? Whatever it was, however he did it, somehow he withdrew from her, and, more surprising, he managed the trick without moving a muscle.

"Ah." He frowned ever so slightly. "Roger ... Brown?"

"He's directing. Do you know him?"

"Know ... of him. As who does not if they ever attend the theater?" He eyed her. "Yes. Hmm. I see." He backed off a pace or two. "Sir Cyrall mentioned something about a tournament in the billiards room," he said in a different, still more distant, tone. "I think I'll just go have a look. . . . Good evening, Di. Mrs. Runyard, I suppose I should say?"

"Di, surely. I cannot be formal with *you*, Stevie. At least not when we are alone. . . ."

He smiled, but it was only the ghost of the smile she remembered. He nodded, turned on his heel, and disappeared among the greenery. Diane looked down. Found her hands clenched. After a long moment, she looked up, stared toward where he'd disappeared.

"I forgot to ask," she said to no one at all, "why he made the decision, so belatedly, to arrange for that annuity."

\* \* \*

Roger and Lord Witherspoon conferred up near the stage. A handful of amateur actors stood to one side, the soft laughter suggestive of their mood—except for young Steven, who remained apart, his eyes never leaving Diane.

Diane herself, conscious of the elder Cartwright's presence at the back of the theater, pretended to listen to the discussion between his lordship and Roger.

"So?" asked Roger, turning toward her. "Have you no suggestion, Diane? We must have a Laius. We cannot continue until we do, and it looks very much as if one will have to appear from thin air." There was just a touch of irritation threaded through his attempt at humor.

With difficulty, Diane drew her mind back to the discussion. "Conjure from thin air? You have, Roger, managed to work miracles on occasion, but this one might be beyond you."

"Never say so," he bantered.

Diane felt the approach of the elder Cartwright and wished she'd better control over the blood rushing up her throat and into her face. She turned slightly and looked at him. "Perhaps your miracle arrives," she said softly, so that only Roger would hear her. She turned. "Good morning, my lord," she added, keeping her voice polite.

He ignored her, a rather sardonic gaze directed toward Roger. "Brown," said Lord Cartwright, "did I hear correctly? You are in need of a king?"

Roger grinned, revealing excellent teeth, an asset of which he took great care. "A Theban king, my lord." The two had been introduced the evening before, and Roger had been much impressed by the man's poise and intelligence but had wondered at the touch of animosity he'd sensed. "Have you indulged in a bit of acting, my lord? It isn't a huge part, but—"

"The king dies in the second act, so it could not be, could it?" interrupted his lordship.

"—it *is* important," finished Roger. "And we are desperately in need of someone who will take it up now, after we are well into production."

"If Mrs. Runyard is willing to help me learn my lines, I will be happy to step into the role." He turned his gaze toward Diane, who tipped her head, her look one of suspicion. "Will you help me—"

One brow quirked in a way she remembered, and Diane could not help but wonder if his seeming innocence was tainted by some plot. One designed to see she did not spend too much time with his son, perhaps?

"—become a proper Laius of Thebes, Mrs. Runyard?"

"Delighted," she said but could not keep a certain dry note out of her voice that had Roger casting her a quick glance.

Roger, however, didn't pursue his suspicions. The play was the important thing, and he had his new king. He nodded and handed Lord Cartwright the script he'd wrested from the departing actor minutes before the distracted husband had left Lord Witherspoon's house.

"You will find," said Roger as he moved toward the seat he occupied during rehearsals, "that this version begins earlier than Sophocles' classic play of *Oedipus Rex*. It is the whole of his life in one play. The first act presents the oracle's dire predictions concerning Laius's fate, after which the king deems it necessary for a son of such ill omen to die. That decision results in conflicting emotions in Jocasta, of course—fears for her husband set against her love of the babe. Not that she has any real choice. The king is king, and his orders are to be obeyed. Except that the shepherd given the babe to expose on a hillside does *not* obey. The child's life is saved, and the king of Corinth adopts him, giving him the name Oedipus." He broke off. "But *you* know the tale," he added somewhat apologetically.

Roger had recalled that he dealt with an educated member of the upper classes, not a man reared in the theater, one who could know little more than what he'd learned while treading the boards. Still, it was his habit to outline a part for a prospective actor, and he continued.

"Later there is a scene with his adoptive father and mother when Oedipus leaves Corinth, meaning to go to Thebes. The young prince has just learned of the curse. Desperately, sincerely, he wishes to avoid fulfilling the fate laid upon him before his birth. Unfortunately, he is unaware that the man he has grown up calling father is not his true sire. He kills a man chance-met on the road when an argument arises between them, and the first half of the prophesy is fulfilled, ending your part in the play, my lord. The second half of the curse is fulfilled when Oedipus reaches Thebes, outwits the Sphinx, and is raised to the throne by the populace—inheriting not only throne and associated wealth, but his father's wife, Laius's queen and Oedipus's mother. The play concludes with more tragedy when Oedipus and Jocasta learn of their sins, but you will know that as well. Perhaps you could begin studying your part while we rehearse the third act."

Lord Cartwright ignored the hint that he go away. "I understand you rehearse in the mornings and again in the afternoon after time for lunch and rest. I will stay and watch how you go on and begin work after lunch, when Mrs. Runyard is free to help me."

"I will help you." The voice held a faint touch of belligerency.

Lord Cartwright and Steven faced each other. "Very generous of you, Son, but I think the help of a professional will be more useful." He nodded what was obviously dismissal and turned back to the others.

Young Steven glowered at his father and then turned a heated look on Diane. That look softened when she smiled slightly, but she too turned away. Steven, disconsolate, wandered back toward the stage and only occasionally glanced toward the group he'd left behind.

"Young pup," said his father softly, with the barest hint of disparagement. On the other hand, he spoke loudly enough that Diane overheard.

"An unhappy boy," she said. In *her* voice was a hint of a scold.

# CHAPTER
# FOUR

Lord Cartwright watched the woman he had once loved to distraction walk away from him. She joined the others, appearing to be completely unaware of his presence. He found that more irritating than his son's behavior. He laughed wryly at the feelings raging through him for a woman who had been free of him for nearly twenty years and derided himself for the unreasonable conviction that she was still *his*. The illogical certainty that he possessed her, heart, soul, and body, bothered him a great deal.

His lordship sat halfway toward the back of the small, dark theater, his eyes never leaving Diane. He stared hungrily as she moved around the stage, going through her part, helping other actors as they stumbled through theirs.

*She is more beautiful than ever*, thought Cartwright and allowed his mind to drift back to those months together. *She was so very special. Her heart was three sizes too large to have held all that love and generosity*.

His lordship sighed softly. Leaving her, going home to the woman chosen to be his bride, had been very nearly the hardest thing he had ever done. Leaving Diane and then, for his sanity, going to great lengths to make it impossible to learn further of how she went on, fearing to hear of another man in her life, never seeing her, struggling hard to forget her existence . . .

"Ah! But however hard I tried," he murmured sadly, "it was never good enough."

Then, something more than a decade after his marriage, he'd traveled to York to look at a horse he'd heard was for sale. A notice outside his hotel told him Di would be on stage that night, and, certain his emotions were under control, that he felt no more than a nostalgic recollection of the woman who once held his heart, he'd gone to the theater.

It was a hot July evening, and he'd sat through *The Irish Widow,* growing more and more uncomfortable and thinking he should leave. Then, just when he was certain he could bear no more, there she was, performing the lead in *Laugh When You Can.*

He'd been astonished at how much she'd changed. She was older, he'd reminded himself. But, he'd decided, maturity suited her. She was more beautiful than in the days of her innocence.

Now, his eyes on the stage, Lord Cartwright shifted in the chair, one of fifty Lord Witherspoon had purchased for the audiences he hoped to entertain in his new theater. Lord Cartwright's uncomfortable body was there, but his mind was elsewhere—back a decade earlier in that York theater.

He'd yearned to go backstage, *ached* to see Di—for old time's sake, of course. Not to renew their relationship. Never that. But to see her again, maybe take an hour or two to reminisce. Just talk. Have supper, perhaps, but only talk. . . .

He'd dithered, but finally he'd gone around to the back—and arrived just as she entered a small carriage drawn by a single horse. He had drawn back, appalled at the jealousy raging through his soul. Someone had her in keeping, *must* have her in keeping. Actresses did not enter private carriages unless going with, or to, some man. They could not, on their own, afford such comforts—not with the cost of stabling. And one mustn't forget the wages for a coachman or the heavy taxes imposed on a carriage—to say nothing of the original cost of the carriage itself. Not on what an actress earned.

But hiring such a rig for an hour or two . . . ? No. There was no reason. . . .

His eyes on Witherspoon's stage, Lord Cartwright felt his teeth grind together at the memory. On the other hand, he also found himself wryly amused. With himself. *Two decades,* and he still felt as if the woman was his and his alone, that she had no right to a life without him.

"*Ridiculous*," he muttered. "I left her. I went home and wed another woman, a woman with whom I managed to live a more or less peaceful, if unexciting and not particularly satisfying, life." Cartwright glanced around, embarrassed, and was relieved that no one was near.

*Someone might have heard me*, he silently berated himself. He'd no desire to reveal his feelings for Diane. *My Di. Mine.* "Mine?" he whispered.

The thought brought his lordship to his feet. He left the theater abruptly, angry and unsettled. She was *not* his. Had not been his for a very long time. Worse, she encouraged his *son* to pay her attention, to sit at her feet and offer up his adoration. And she had known. Oh, yes, she knew very well whose son she played with. . . .

Lord Cartwright stalked off toward the orchard at the back of the house, finding the long stretch of grass between two rows of fruit trees an excellent place for pacing. He was making his third turn before he managed to bring his temper under control.

With renewed calm, rational thought returned and he admitted that Diane Runyard had *not* toyed with Steven. She was *not* seducing the boy. He must remember that and *not* allow his jealousy to come into play.

"And besides—" He stopped short and spoke to a perky little robin sitting on a nearby branch. "—what did she mean, that Steven is unhappy?"

He stared blindly at the bird, which head to one side, stared back. He considered.

"Bah," he said. "Nonsense. The boy has everything he wants, everything he needs. . . ." He thought a bit more and then shook his head. "Di is a brick short of a wall if she imagines the boy has the least reason for unhappiness."

His lordship pulled his watch from his fob pocket and opened it. What had Witherspoon's daughter told him about a luncheon? Food, she'd said, was set out about this time for those who wished it. Yes, exactly—but had she said *where*?

He strolled back to the house, took the stairs to the terrace two at a time, and stepped into the house through an open low-silled window. *Ah. The library. I'll explore it later*, he thought as he crossed to double doors that opened onto a hall. But once there, he hadn't a notion which way to turn.

"The right," he told himself and set off, hoping it would take him to where a servant could guide him.

*Witherspoon does himself very well*, the wry thought crossed Cartwright's mind, *if he calls this a small estate*.

The house sprawled in all directions with intersecting hallways. Cartwright turned a couple of corners, went up a few steps and, not much later, down three—and then, after a lucky guess and still another hallway, found himself in the mansion's entry, where a footman stood to attention.

Given directions, his lordship made his way to the small dining room, where he hoped he'd find Diane, who, if he recalled correctly—and there was very little he'd forgotten—ate at midday. His son did not.

More exactly, in the past he had not.

Lord Cartwright frowned when he saw that not only was Diane at the table as expected, but she was surrounded. Steven, who never ate in the middle of the day, was seated to one side, his plate well filled. On Di's other side was Sir Cyrall Jamison, showing off and, as usual, making an ass of himself.

Cartwright moved to the sideboard where food was laid out for those who wished to eat. Another who required nothing in midday, he chose just enough to make it reasonable that he seat himself and did so across from the others, where he could listen but need not participate in the chatter.

"Oh, but you will make a delightful Jocasta, my dear," purred Cyrall.

"A perfect Jocasta," said Steven, obviously not to be outdone. "You are perfect in every way."

"You both exaggerate outrageously," retorted Diane. "I will do an adequate job, I hope, but playing tragedy has not much come my way, and I doubt I've the experience to fill the role as it should be played. We've an excellent new playwright, have we not?" she asked, attempting to move the subject away from herself. "Have you noticed how professional his work is? I was startled to find it so. Most young writers have such grandiose notions that it is impossible to stage their early attempts. Some never outgrow that fault."

"It is an interesting interpretation of the Oedipus tale," agreed Sir Cyrall. "But—" Mischief gleamed in his eyes as he returned to the original subject. "—how can you think you'll be less than perfection as Jocasta?"

Diane turned a look of disbelief his way, and Cyrall chuckled in that softly suggestive way he had. Lord Cartwright ground his teeth.

"*I* think you perfection," repeated Steven, which garnered a snort from his father. Steven heard and glanced across the table toward his lordship. Preoccupied, he had not noticed his father's entrance. Reddening, his gaze fell to his plate.

"Thank you, Steven, for the compliment," said Diane, carefully but with a glance toward the elder Cartwright that should have burned him, "but you know it is nonsense. No one is perfect. It is not possible."

"My father has always expected *me* to be perfect," mumbled Steven, his resentment clear.

Lord Cartwright was among those who overheard his pettish if low-voiced words. He frowned. Where had his son come by such an odd notion? Of course, he wished the boy to do as well as he was able, but, as Diane pointed out, no one ever reached such an exalted state that it might be labeled perfect.

"I doubt that. He cannot be so silly," said Diane and echoed, if she'd but known, the father's thoughts. "Perhaps you have misinterpreted his desire that, in everything you do, you do as well as you are able and not just enough to get by."

Steven shrugged his shoulders, resettling his coat. Pretty obviously he was unconvinced, as revealed by a pout he'd have hated if he'd realized it had settled onto his features.

"You could ask him," suggested Diane softly.

The youth's expression made clear that this was something else that had never crossed his mind—the notion he might discuss such things with his sire.

Diane stifled a sigh, finished her last sip of tea, folded her napkin, and rose to her feet. More observant than one might have expected of him, Sir Cyrall also rose, forestalling a footman who came to pull back her chair.

Steven stared at his plate. It held a great deal of the luncheon he'd chosen. He was too young and insecure to simply abandon it. Irritated, he watched his father follow behind the woman with whom the youth had convinced himself he was in love.

Sir Cyrall, in the spirit of mischief that ran strongly through his character, chuckled. "He is far nearer her age than *you*, my young buck."

Steven glared at Cyrall Jamison. "You know nothing about it."

"I suspect," said Sir Cyrall, suddenly sober, "that I know far more than you. Ask his lordship when he first met Mrs. Runyard." He had not seated himself after rising to act the gentleman for Diane, so it was simple for him to depart before Steven could frame a retort—or a question.

Steven looked once again at his plate, glanced at Sir Cyrall's and then across the table at the place his father had deserted. He discovered neither man had finished what he'd chosen. He looked again at his own plate, and, a rather mulish expression of rebellion settling onto his features, he too rose and exited the room . . . and then hadn't a notion where to go.

Where he wished to go, of course, was wherever Mrs. Runyard had disappeared, but the footman stationed in the hall could not tell him. Disconsolately, he went up to his room, where he settled himself to studying his part. He was determined to do such an excellent job in the role that Diane would turn admiring eyes his way and reward him in the fashion in which he'd like to be rewarded. That thought embarrassed him, and he immediately pushed it from his mind. Mrs. Runyard was, he'd decided, much too much the lady to behave in the fashion expected of most actresses. Too pure. Too perfect . . .

But there was his part to learn. Steven forced himself to concentrate.

Elsewhere, Lord Cartwright held Diane's arm just a trifle more tightly than he'd have done if he'd noticed what he was doing. He drew her down one hall and up another, opening a door here and then there, until he found a small sitting room tucked away far beyond the part of the manor in which the company congregated.

"This will do," he said and waited for her to enter the door he held open.

* * *

"Francie, please don't run off!"

The young mistress of the Witherspoon estate stopped, her head rising and her spine stiffening. "What can I do for you, Mr. Coxwald?" she asked, her voice so chill it might have iced over the small pond in which the two had once, long ago, attempted to teach themselves to swim—and come too near for comfort to drowning.

"You can stop acting as if we were strangers who had never before met," scolded Richard. "You can explain to me why you are angry with me instead of behaving as if I had insulted you beyond bearing when I know I have not."

"I never suggested you insulted me," said Francine. She glared.

"But you *are* angry."

"Not at all," she said, tossing her head and turning away.

"Francie, don't lie to me." His voice sounded tired, dispirited. "You hurt me terribly when you act this way."

"*I* hurt *you*!" She swung back, her face reddening with emotion. "You know nothing of hurt. *Nothing.*"

"I do," he insisted, but still in that quiet voice. "Once we promised each other—"

"Stop." She held up her hand. "We were children," she interrupted, the mottled red of anger fading to a mere blush of embarrassment. "We didn't truly know each other. You cannot hold me to that childish nonsense."

He frowned. "Francie—"

She held up her hand again. "Not a word. You cannot have known one thing about me, Richard. If you did . . ." She straightened, her chin rising. "Never mind. You do not, and that is that." She shrugged. "Excuse me," she added, once again in that chilling tone. "I must have a word with the laundress. She must hire more help for so long as this benighted party continues, and I forgot to order it so."

Richard ran his fingers through his hair, staring morosely after his love. "Women," he muttered.

Sir Cyrall, leaning against the wall a short distance away, grinned. "Only now discovering they are the most irrational of creatures?" he asked.

Francine had never been irrational, but Richard was forced to admit, if only to himself, that recently she appeared exceptionally soft in the head. He turned on his heel, tearing his mind away from his woes. "Sir Cyrall. I was unaware anyone was near."

"I am often where I'm not supposed to be. Your Miss Witherspoon giving you trouble?" he asked sympathetically, coming along the hall to link his arm with Richard's. He walked the younger man off toward a door to the terrace. "Is she stubborn? Uncooperative? Unwilling to talk to you?"

"All of that," muttered Richard.

"And cold? Very cold when once she was warm and friendly and—"

Richard's head came around, a glare daring Sir Cyrall to make any sort of insulting comment about Francine.

"—generous and kind and . . ."

Richard relaxed.

". . . *giving*?"

Richard pulled his arm free. "What do you mean by *that*?" he asked, fearing he knew.

"Giving?" Cyrall's eyes widened in pretend innocence. "Why, that she would help you, listen to you, be with you when you needed a friend. . . . What else could I have meant?" asked Sir Cyrall. His brows arched high.

Richard rubbed a hand over his features. Sir Cyrall was not only older than he was himself, but the man had Town bronze to a degree he was never likely to achieve. *Mainly*, he realized, *because I will never find in myself that cynical edge that seems to cut every thing Sir Cyrall says or does.*

"You know exactly what you wished me to think,"

Richard said in a quiet voice. He caught and held the teaser's gaze. "Why do you do it?" he asked.

Sir Cyrall blinked, startled by the bluntness of the question, a method of communication he avoided if at all possible. "Do . . . it?" he asked, regaining some of his insouciant manner.

"Why do you always do your best to get a rise out of everyone? Do your best to stir up trouble. Attempt to set one person against another?"

Sir Cyrall blinked again. And then grinned. "You are far more intelligent than you look, are you not?"

"I don't believe that is an answer," said Richard, eyeing him thoughtfully.

"Is it not?" Cyrall sobered, frowned. "Well, it is all you'll get." He turned on his heel and stalked off toward the orchard, where, as had others before him, he discovered the long strip of grass between the trees a perfect place to walk off irritation.

"That young pup! How dare he ask such a question?"

Sir Cyrall discovered a strong feeling of distaste for being on the receiving end of the treatment that he usually handed out to others. He scowled. Richard had only seen the half of it, really. Whatever he did or said, however it looked to others, his intention, always, was to make his prey think. In his own way, an odd way to be sure, he only wanted to help.

But there was something Cyrall had not previously known. He only now discovered that *thinking* could be a trifle distressing—at least, when it was one's own thoughts in question.


At the far end of the terrace, Rafe, Lord Morningside, grinned. "I think someone finally got Cyrall's goat, rather than Cyrall getting theirs."

Eustacia watched Rafe's friend enter the orchard. "He did look a trifle put out, did he not?"

"That he did, Euphrasia, my love."

She stiffened. "Rafe, I swear, the next time you call me by that absurd name, I will hit you."

"Euphrasia?" He looked at her thoughtfully. "It is not absurd. It is the name you should have been christened." When she turned toward him, obviously angry, he lifted his hand to her chin, grasping it firmly. "I wouldn't try it," he said softly. "I just might hit you back."

Her eyes widened. "You wouldn't."

"Would I not?" He studied her classic features. "Perhaps not." His gaze dropped to her lips. "Perhaps I would punish you in some other way." Then, his gaze meeting hers, he spoke abruptly. "The name is *not* an insult." He turned on his heel and walked away.

Eustacia ground her teeth, clutching the railing so firmly her knuckles turned white.

"Lord Morningside has hurt you, has he not?" asked Francine, coming up behind Eustacia. "Is it not terrible that someone you like has so little understanding of you he cannot see how badly he hurts you? I am very sorry for you."

Eustacia blinked. "Someone *you* like? You mean our author, do you not? Richard Coxwald? What has he done to you?" Eustacia's eyes narrowed slightly, and she smiled a slow smile. "Did the young fool attempt to steal a kiss?"

Francine drew herself up. "You jest, of course. I had thought perhaps, since *you* are hurting, that you would understand my pain, but I see that it is not so."

Before Eustacia could decide what part of that stern comment she should respond to first—the notion she was hurt rather than angry, or the idea she could not understand if given a clue or two—Francine's quick steps had her disappearing inside the house.

Eustacia returned to clutching the railing as she wondered why her world was so complicated. Had it been only months since the death of her elderly cousin, at one time her guardian, the man with whom she had continued living as his hostess even after she had come of age?

His will, which left her well provided for over and beyond what she had already inherited, forbade her to go into any sort of mourning, and she had obeyed. Eustacia had thought that, at long last, she might organize a life of interest to herself. For the first time ever she'd felt she was free to live in a manner pleasing to herself, and she'd set out to achieve that goal. She'd not come near it. First she discovered that her obedience to her cousin's wishes set tongues wagging. Other errors of judgment kept them wagging. . . .

Actually, if only he would cease to tease her, she could find it in her heart to thank Rafe for his help in her difficulties. He had done far more than anyone knew—since it was inappropriate for him, a gentleman unrelated to her, to do some of the things he'd done. It was he who found the house she now rented, and he who located the intelligent but indigent widow she hired as companion. After all, a young unmarried woman, if she were to retain any pretense of propriety, could not live unchaperoned, however much she wished to do so. But if Rafe's actions became known, the woman would be thought his tool. . . .

Still, with all he'd done, one thing he could *not* do for her. She found it difficult—was, in fact, near to deciding it was impossible—to find congenial friends. Worse, the strain of behaving in such a way that she would not become a further object of gossip and conjecture was, she had almost concluded, not worth the effort, and she rued the fact she was not older so she could do as she pleased and be called an eccentric.

Rafe had offered no solution to either problem, or, if he did suggest something, did so in such a teasing fashion he only roused her ire. She had *never* liked his teasing.

She had joined this house party in the hopes of finding a few congenial friends and, so far, had irritated her hostess and insulted her closest friend—and *not* acquired the hoped-for new friends.

But friendship? Was *Rafe* her friend?

She thought about it. Yes. He was. Even before she put up her hair and let down her skirts, he'd been there when she needed advice and rescued her when—once or twice—curiosity or naïveté led her into a situation where she'd needed a man's protection. And besides that, he was always ready for the exchange of lively banter.

On occasion, when he was in the mood, he even indulged her in more serious discussion.

She hated to be on the outs with him, but she hated even more that he would not call her by her name. That he insisted on that awful Euphrasia when Eustacia was bad enough.

Eustacia sighed. She must do something other than fret about Rafe's stubbornness, so she searched her mind for distraction, and, realizing she'd packed nothing to read, she wondered what sort of library Lord Witherspoon might have. She found a footman, who directed her, and managed to forget her latest bout of verbal fisticuffs with Rafe by dipping into old favorites and exploring unknowns. She was moving slowly along the shelves, debating with herself about one particular history of early England, when she found George Allingham skulking in a corner, a copy of the play in his hand.

"George?" she asked, surprised.

He looked up, turned a painful red, and stuffed the script partially behind his back. He cleared his throat. "M-m-Miss Eusta-sta-stacia!"

"Is that a copy of the play?" she asked, curious, ignoring his difficulties forming his words.

He nodded, the fading red returning.

"Are you just reading it . . . or"—a sudden notion struck her—"were you learning one of the parts?"

He hung his head.

"You were. Which one, George?"

"La-la-*Laius*."

"Why?"

His tongue brushed over his lips. Carefully, slowly, he said, "For fun?"

"I don't think so." She waited, but he merely looked miserable. A sudden, utterly astounding notion entered her mind. "George, would *you* like a part in one of the plays we do this summer?"

He looked in every direction but toward Eustacia.

"*Is* that what you'd like?"

"In school," he said. "Pl-pl-played a part. D-d-didn't st-st-*stutter*."

Eustacia nodded slowly. "That makes sense, actually. You learned the words beforehand, and, besides, you could pretend to be someone else."

He looked surprised and then smiled. He nodded. "That's it."

"George, I will talk to Mrs. Runyard. Explain. Perhaps they can find you a part in the next play, one you needn't try out for. If it is a smallish part, you can learn it quickly and need not worry when we begin to rehearse."

He looked extremely gratified.

"I'll help you learn it," she promised. "Now . . . I wonder where Mrs. Runyard might be . . . ?"

"Earlier. Saw Cartwright walking off with her. Away from the small dining room," said George helpfully—and not stuttering at all when talking about someone else or something unimportant to himself. "Had her arm in a tight grip. Thought at the time she'd have bruises. . . ."

"Young Steven was hurting her?"

George shook his head. "His lordship."

"*Lord* Cartwright?" Eustacia frowned. "Why? I thought he'd realized she wasn't running after his son. So what reason can he have had for . . . I mean, is it possible they *know* each other? No, never mind. The talk I must have with her will wait until later. Perhaps when everyone goes to the theater for the afternoon rehearsals. Have a good day, George," she said, nodded, and went off to her room, forgetting she'd meant to find a book.

# CHAPTER
# FIVE

Out of the corner of her eye, Diane glanced at the tall, silver-haired man walking so calmly at her side. They had worked for two hours on his part, and her curiosity was roused by how quickly he learned. She'd known actors who could memorize a new part in only a day or two and be word perfect, but to find a man who made no pretence of interest in the theater, one who didn't attend plays with any regularity, but who learned so quickly . . . well, it was astounding.

"You have an excellent memory, Stevie," she said, looking straight ahead.

"It has been a hobby with me, Di. I make a habit of learning a stanza or two of poetry each day—" He began reciting Byron's latest and soon had her chuckling at the histrionics he added to his unexpected performance. "—and so you see," he finished, cutting off in the middle of a line, "I have, er, learned to learn. Quickly, I mean."

"It is a knack, I think. But some find it easier than others. I must work quite hard to get my lines down as well as you have in so short a time. Roger," she finished, as they entered the theater, "will be impressed."

"Ah, yes," said Lord Cartwright, his voice suddenly dry as dust. "I was forgetting Brown, was I not?"

Diane, confused by the sudden change in him, stared as he stalked down the aisle toward the stage. "Now, what was that all about?" she asked nobody in particular.

"Jealousy?" suggested Sir Cyrall, his mouth pursed into the V shape.

She turned and found him sitting, slouched in his seat, his crossed legs resting on a chair he'd turned sideways for the purpose. "Nonsense. For what possible reason would his lordship feel jealousy?"

"I don't *know*—" Sir Cyrall's eyes got a hooded look. "—but I seem to recall a bit of gossip. *Old* gossip. My grandmother and my great-aunts talk. And talk and talk and talk . . ." He suddenly looked up at her, his eyes much more alert. "I wonder what young Steven would think if he knew . . . ?"

Diane swallowed hard and stared at Sir Cyrall. *Roger*, she recalled, *had predicted the baronet might be trouble.*

"Perhaps I should," he began, his eyes dancing.

"Perhaps nothing," interrupted Diane sternly. "You would not be so cruel."

"But would it be a cruelty?" murmured Cyrall, staring at a glint from a crystal on the unlit chandelier above them. "Papa does not appear to be particularly sensitive where the boy is concerned. Don't you fear he'll do or say something which will hurt the lad more than the youthful aches he already experiences?"

Diane frowned. "You are more perceptive than you wish people to know, are you not?" she asked, becoming more and more curious about the elfish Cyrall Jamison. "That you see young Steven is hurting, I mean."

"Am I? Surely not. Besides, the least attentive must see he is suffering his calf love."

*Or perhaps not quite so perceptive as I thought?* she mused. *Steven's problems are far more complicated than first love.*

"Why do you hide it," she asked, "when it is not a sin or a failing or something about which you should be ashamed?"

"Is it not? Then why, I wonder, have I suffered for my sensitivity?" With a sudden smooth movement, Cyrall rose to his feet and, without another word, left the theater.

Diane stared after him, only coming to attention when her name had been called for the third time and that last rather loudly. "Coming," she responded. But for another moment or two, she stared out into the bright sunshine and wondered just what she had discovered—and what, if anything, she should do about it.

Diane shrugged. Whatever she decided, it must be for later and after she had had time to think. If she ever did—have time to think, that is. As she passed down the aisle, George Allingham looked up at her and smiled. She pressed her hand on his shoulder and smiled back but hadn't a notion why.

Lord Cartwright, who had, without appearing to, watched her from a darkened corner of the stage, frowned. Did the woman have to be so blidy friendly with every man she saw? And then his lordship grimaced. *Blidy*. Di had used that expletive so often when he'd first known her that he'd adopted it as his own and never lost the habit. He'd forgotten, until just now, where he'd learned it.

"Does she still say it?" he murmured.

"Who?" asked Rafe, Lord Morningside. "Say what?"

"Hmm? Oh. Morningside. Didn't see you there."

"No, you were too interested in watching our professional actress." Rafe's eyes narrowed ever so slightly. "So, does she still say *what*?"

Lord Cartwright was too old to dissemble. "Does she use the word *blidy* when angry or upset?"

A slashing grin crossed Morningside's face, his narrowed eyes narrowing still more in humor. "Not that I've heard, but then I don't believe I've seen her either angry or upset. Her vocabulary and her accent don't, however, lead one to think she'd ever allow such a crudity to pass her lips. And," he continued, "since you are aware she *has* used it, then I wonder just when and where you knew her?"

"A very long time ago," said Cartwright and then, firmly, changed the subject. "Explain to me how Brown goes about teaching us what to do."

Rafe, never one to tread where he was not wanted—except with Eustacia—obliged. "So," he summarized a bit later, "you'll first learn where you are to stand and when to move and where you are to move to. Only when you've learned that, so other actors know where to find you when they must speak to you—don't frown. That's what *Brown* says. Anyway, only then will you learn expression and drama and all the rest. Or," he added in a much dryer tone, "as much of the rest as amateurs such as ourselves are capable of learning."

"You are the King of Carthage?" asked Cartwright.

"Hmm. And Euphrasia is my Queen."

Cartwright looked startled. "I thought her name was Eustacia."

Rafe grinned a quick grin. "To everyone but me it is." He looked up. "Ah. Brown is calling for attention."

Diane found she was exhausted when Roger finally allowed the actors to leave the theater. He had, to everyone's surprise but her own, insisted on going over and over a scene between Odysseus and his foster mother, one where the adopted son takes a private leave of the queen just before leaving Carthage. The problem had not been with Miss Fairchild. She had done quite well, actually. The problem was Steven. Diane set her mind to trying to understand why, since he hadn't had a similar problem with other scenes.

The solution came to her, and she turned back into the theater. "Roger . . ."

Roger looked up from where he was talking to Lord Cartwright. "Yes, Diane?"

"I think I know why Steven is having difficulty with that scene."

"Then tell me. The boy does surprisingly well for the most part, but, in that scene, he is stiff as a plank and just about as thick." Roger made no attempt to hide his irritation.

Diane ignored her old love, who stood with his head tipped, revealing his curiosity. But she couldn't worry about his lordship when she needed to explain young Steven to Roger. "You must remember that he lost his real mother not so long ago. He is very likely afraid to let himself show emotion when acting this stage-leaving, a pretend one, lest he show *too much*."

Roger frowned. "Hmmm."

"Good grief, Di," said Cartwright. "That was all of four years ago."

"His *mother*, Stevie." Diane turned and caught his lordship's gaze. "And at an age when it is difficult for a boy to lose a parent. Worse, he is just at the age where he is learning he is not to show his emotions too freely—and yet he feels so much that it becomes a deep, dark struggle for him to control himself."

Roger looked from one to the other. "You two know each other?" he asked, his voice bland and without stress.

"Years ago. Long before I met you," said Diane impatiently, her eyes never leaving Cartwright's. "Can you not see," she said, becoming more heated, "that you have not encouraged him to grieve properly? He has not known how, and *you* have given him no help. Do you ever talk to him about her? Do you ever allow him to reminisce about the things you all used to do together? Is he ever allowed the freedom to simply *remember*?"

Lord Cartwright frowned. "He hasn't been told he cannot."

Diane huffed, her shoulders rising and falling. "Impossible. Men are such insensitive brutes." She turned on her heel and left the theater for a second time . . . and stalked off across the lawn toward the orchard. It was time to change for dinner. More than time. But Diane could not bring herself to enter the house and go to her room simply to oblige some unspoken tonnish rule of behavior. She had not been trained to hide her emotions behind a bland exterior. She did not find it necessary to pretend all was well when it was not. Indeed, when she allowed herself to think of such things, her preference was to work through whatever emotion filled her, work it out—and be rid of it. That is what she wanted now.

The light was fading to a late afternoon glow as the sun shone in a more horizontal path between the rows of fruit trees. Each tree shadowed the one beyond it, but a long swath of bright light remained where one walked. Diane was making her second turn toward the house when another figure appeared at the far end.

He started toward her . . . and then stopped.

Diane slowed. Then she picked up her pace. "I'm sorry," she said. "I had no right. . . ."

"You had no right, but you had the right of it," said Lord Cartwright quietly. "Di, I felt mild affection for my wife, but the feeling did not go deep. I did not *think*. Of course Steven felt her loss to a far greater degree. His mother . . ." He sighed. "I even hesitated to have him brought home from school for the funeral. But I did—"

The light was still strong, and Di saw color fill his face.

"—and then I had him returned immediately to Eton. I didn't even go with the lad. How could I have been so uncomprehending, Di? So unfeeling?" He began walking, his hands behind his back and his head bowed. "So thoughtless and, I suppose, cruel?"

He turned a quick look her way, but she didn't try to soothe his guilt. He had been cruel.

Cartwright sighed. "A blidy fool."

She chuckled.

He grinned a quick grin. "Blidy? You taught me that, Di."

"I still say it sometimes. I try not to. It gives away who I used to be, and the audience likes it better if I appear to be something more than I am."

"You cannot be more than you are. What you are, Di, is so much better than anyone in your audience that surely you do not worry about how *they* feel about you."

"Should I not? Ah! Then I wonder why I *do*." She waved a dismissive hand. "But this is far away from what we need to discuss. Stevie, you really need to talk to the boy. Remember at luncheon when he said you wanted him to be perfect? You know you never felt that way, but he *believes* it. Worse, he believes he cannot possibly live up to your expectations, so he despairs. He needs to know how you really feel. Stevie . . ."

Cartwright ran his fingers through his carefully arranged hair, allowing a thick swath to fall down over his forehead in a way that would drive his valet to distraction when he saw it. "Speak with him," repeated his lordship slowly. "Talk to him. . . . Di, I haven't a clue how a man goes about talking to his son. And that is an admission I would make to no one but you," he added, turning and putting his hands on her shoulders.

He stared down at her as she looked up at him. The odd light gave a sense of isolation. In that false solitude, each looked deeply into the other's eyes. Questions passed between them—silent, unspoken, but real. Real—but unanswered and perhaps, just yet, unanswerable.

Still, there was something. . . .

Slowly he bent his head. Slowly she rose to meet his lips with her own. Gently, carefully, they kissed. A brief kiss. A hello kiss. A kiss full of hidden meanings into which neither was ready to delve.

And then he broke away. "I'm sorry," he said.

Diane frowned. "Sorry."

"I've no right. . . ."

Had she heard just the hint of a question in that? She was uncertain, couldn't guess what it might have been if it was there, and sighed. "It is late, Stevie. I have yet to change for dinner." Promptly he offered his arm, and, side by side, they returned to the house.

As they approached, aware of no one but each other, young Steven hurried away from the terrace railing. He disappeared into the house and did not come down to dinner. Neither did he appear later to join in the charades, an entertainment he had always adored.

Her tongue had been firmly in cheek when Francine Witherspoon organized charades for her father's guests' evening entertainment. She had assumed that, after spending all day working on a real play, playing at charades would be a bit much. Francine, wishing them all to Jericho, was disappointed to find her father's guests loved it.

Steven, too, would have enjoyed it, but he was too self-conscious to go down, too afraid of what he might say or do. On the other hand, he would have been chagrined if he'd known how little he was missed.

Diane noticed his absence. But Diane was fretting about herself, worried she'd be an inadequate teammate thanks to her lack of formal education. She hadn't the energy to also wonder why the boy was missing.

Lord Cartwright noticed, but he assumed his son was sulking for one reason or another—the boy seemed to spend a great deal of his time that way. So he too ignored it.

The knowledge that the two people Steven wished to affect missed him for even a moment, might have soothed the young man. Very likely he'd not have been upset that no one else realized he was absent.

Except, of course, *one* other did. Sir Cyrall noted his absence. But then, it was the sort of thing the baronet *would* notice.

# CHAPTER
# SIX

Steven, with nothing else to do, had gone to bed early. He also woke early and was downstairs before the servants finished their morning chores of cleaning the public areas and setting out a breakfast. After flustering two maids by appearing in rooms in which they were removing ashes from grates, and another who was sweeping up damp tea leaves spread to catch up the carpet dust, Steven removed to the terrace, where he stared at the spot in which his father and Mrs. Runyard had stood. Had kissed.

Burning resentment and green jealousy swept through him all over again, and it was some time later when he came to himself with a start and hurried inside, fearing he'd have missed Mrs. Runyard, who almost always ate early. He rushed to the breakfast room but found it empty of everyone but the Witherspoon butler, who busied himself with a last check that all was properly ready for guests.

"Er . . . good morning," said Steven.

"Good morning, young sir." The butler beamed at him, a genial man very unlike the staid and proper personage one found acting the butler in most houses.

Steven was at the age that made few allowances for anything out of the ordinary. He felt insulted—both by the word "young" and by a smile-wreathed countenance when servants were supposed to be impassive, emotionless.

"You are down early, are you not, Mr. Cartwright?"

"Quite." Steven turned his back on the amiable servant, going to the sideboard. It was heavily laden with steaming hot dishes and platters, so he reached for a plate—and found the butler at his elbow, holding one and, silently, querying what was wanted.

Steven sighed. *Why won't anybody leave me alone*? he wondered crossly. The door opened, and he looked around, hopeful. He sighed again when it was someone other than the one person he'd *not* have wished elsewhere.

"Well, well," said Lord Witherspoon, rubbing his plump hands together. "Our young star! You are early this morning. Couldn't sleep, hmm? Worried about how you'll do? Hmm? Needn't worry, I think," he continued, already picking up a plate and shoveling onto it goodly portions of his favorite foods—after an aside to the effect of, "No, no, I'll do it myself," at which the butler smiled and nodded. "Not eating?" asked Witherspoon, pausing, when he noticed there was nothing on the plate held by the footman to whom his butler had passed it. "Can't tempt you? Dear, dear, that will not do. What is missing? What else might we find for a lad your age?"

"There is nothing wrong with the food." Steven did his best not to sound snide, but, despite his good intentions, there was just a touch of emphasis on the last word.

Witherspoon's mouth formed an *O* of surprise.

Steven felt himself turn red. He took the plate from the footman's hand and served himself—and, as usual, found he'd given himself too much of just about everything. He sat at his usual place and then wished he'd thought to wait for his goddess out in the hall. That way he could have entered the breakfast room behind her, might have chosen his breakfast as she did hers, and, most important of all, might have then, without embarrassment, quite naturally, have seated himself beside her.

And, having thought all that, he felt younger and less sure of himself than ever, so it was not surprising that, when Sir Cyrall entered the room a little after Witherspoon bustled out, the boy was still seated, one elbow on the table, the tines of his fork pushing cold eggs around and around his plate. He looked as if he had lost his very best friend in the entire world.

Or that he had no friends.

Cyrall's mouth tightened. He hated it when anything reminded him of how *he'd* felt at that age. How inadequate. How ignorant. How lacking in poise. In other words, how terribly *green* he'd been. Cyrall had worked hard to lose both ignorance and awkwardness. He'd succeeded but had, in the process, developed a thick shell of cynicism and adopted a variety of verbal weapons, sarcasm one of his sharpest.

Cyrall saw in Steven the boy he'd once been, and found, again, he could not put really sharp pins into that fragile, mostly undeveloped, personality. He sighed.

"Not feeling well, Mr. Cartwright?" asked Cyrall, putting his plate at a place not far from Steven's. "Noticed you weren't at dinner last night. Wondered if all was well with you," he added, signaling to a footman that he wanted coffee and, equally silently, asking that the preserves be moved nearer.

For a moment Steven didn't respond. Then he sighed. "Not sick. I guess."

"Just unhappy," said Cyrall.

The comment was made in such an offhand manner that, for another moment, Steven didn't realize exactly what had been said to him. "Why should I be unhappy?" asked Steven, belligerently.

"I can think of a lot of reasons," said Cyrall in a musing tone. The hand that stirred a lump of sugar into his coffee stilled. "There is your age to begin with. One tends to feel rather morose much of the time. One is no longer a boy and not yet quite a man, a difficult age." Cyrall resumed stirring, making slow circles in the dark brew. "That is normal for all of us, and enough of a reason right there. Then there is Mrs. Runyard. You really should not have aimed your sights in that particular direction, my lad. Really. Believe me. It will not do."

"She is an angel," blustered Steven. "You will not suggest she is not."

"As actresses go, she is, yes, an angel. Quite untouchable, assuming the gossip I've heard over the years is really true. And some of it," he added in a thoughtful tone, "has come directly from the mouths of horses that usually have no difficulty making the running."

Steven had to figure that one out, and, when he did, he stiffened. "Surely no one has insulted her by . . . by . . ."

"By attempting to mount her as their mistress?" asked Cyrall bluntly. "As you were hoping to do?"

The younger man's face burned with embarrassment. "That was before I knew her. Before I realized how good, how perfect, what an angel she is."

"Let old Uncle Cyrall give you a trifling bit of advice, halfling," the baronet said, the cynicism returning full force. "There is no woman on earth who is fully and freely an angel. Nor any man. There are better and there are worse, but there are no angels. Attempting to make of a human being, male or female, something perfect, is a huge mistake. No one can live up to such expectations. Such a one is certain to fall off the pedestal—and when she does, the person who puts her up on it is more hurt than if he had realized at the very beginning that pedestals are exceedingly uncomfortable places. Don't idealize Mrs. Runyard. She is a woman. Merely a woman."

Steven opened his mouth . . . and then shut it.

"But," continued Sir Cyrall, this time with a touch of humor, "that doesn't mean she isn't a good woman. I'd get *that* notion out of your head."

Steven turned to look at Sir Cyrall. "You can't have any idea at all of what is in my head."

Cyrall laughed. He was still chuckling when the door opened again and Mrs. Runyard entered—followed by Lord Cartwright.

"Oh, yes. I can know," said Cyrall so softly only Steven heard him. "I know very well what you had in mind almost from the instant you learned who, or should I say *what*, she is. Nor do I blame you for hoping. But believe me, young Steven, you would do far better looking toward the dairy-maid for the sort of education you desire at this point in your life than toward the untouchable Mrs. Runyard. If I remember ancient history, and I usually do, then there has only ever been one man in that lady's heart, and, I suspect, there only ever will be." Sir Cyrall rose to his feet, greeted the new-comers, and, his hand on Steven's shoulder, practically lifted the boy from his chair, very nearly marching him from the room. "And that," he said once the hall door was shut behind them, "is the man. You'll be a fool if you interfere."

Sir Cyrall turned on his heel, walking away from the stunned Steven, who was engulfed by any number of emotions—jealousy, inadequacy, lust-which-he-thought-was-love, anger, and he wasn't certain what else. . . .

Except that he also felt hungry.

Before Cyrall imparted his wisdom, if that was what it was, Steven had managed only a few bites of his food. He'd been unable to eat while Cyrall sermonized. Since he'd also had no supper, he was starved, but returning to the breakfast room after he'd been forcibly—there was no other word—removed from it was something he could not make himself do.

So embarrassing.

In fact, it seemed to Steven that there were more things in

the world that led to embarrassment than the other kind. Disconsolate, hands in his pockets and shoulders hunched, he wandered off to the theater—where he discovered Roger Brown, early as it was, talking to workmen hired to manage things such as building the sets and painting scenery.

"Ah. Steven," called a surprisingly genial Roger. "I don't suppose you have traveled to Greece?" He spoke half humorously and half hopefully. "I cannot decide what is best for the scene where Oedipus meets Laius on the road."

"It is an intense scene," said Steven, frowning. "Perhaps the setting should be simple so as not to detract. A painted hillside with a hint of a temple in the distance. Perhaps a broken pillar lying on the stage near the road."

Roger turned fully and stared at Steven. "Now, that is an excellent notion. I mean that the scene should be simple. However, I still don't know what the Greek countryside looks like, and I very much wish I did."

"Shall I go to the library and see if there is a sketchbook from some Witherspoon's journey there or an illustrated travel book?"

Roger blinked. "If you would only be so kind! I don't know why I didn't think of that, except perhaps that I am used to working in theaters where a library is not available." Roger shuffled some papers he'd clutched in one hand, found the one he wanted, and frowned at it. "According to today's schedule, you are unneeded until eleven or so. If you could be certain—" Roger looked up from the page to cast a stern look at Steven. "—to be back by eleven . . . ?"

"It shouldn't take anything like that long. I will find Miss Francine and see if she can point me to the proper shelves." Steven loped back up the aisle, his mood considerably lightened by the fact he had voiced an idea worthy of praise and, further, had been asked to help. He even forgot for all of half an hour—the time it took to find his hostess—that he was suffering from unrequited love. And then he put his worries behind him all over again when Francine showed him where, in the library, he might find the sort of drawings he needed.

"You appear to have had a great number of travelers in your family," he said, surprised at the low shelf stuffed with sketchbooks and journals.

"Yes. Some appear to have done nothing else. My father's uncle, for example." Miss Francine pulled out a large pile of different-sized pads and journals that had been tied together with a black ribbon. "I believe the old gentleman is in Canada now. Or perhaps he has moved south into the rebel colonies. He wrote at Christmas of the countryside in which he found himself. I fear he is greatly prone to exaggeration so cannot say if his sketches will help you. Perhaps his drawings tell fibs as well, and it makes no difference whether his exaggerations come in words or in the lines he draws."

"What sort of fibs, Miss Francine?" asked Steven, curious.

"His letters told of snowdrifts higher than the houses. That *must* be untrue. And of ancient forests that go on forever. And, in summer, exceedingly tiny insects that are so thick in the air one cannot breathe without inhaling them, and . . . Oh, I don't remember the rest of his nonsense." She shrugged.

"You are not fond of nonsense?" asked Steven, who firmly believed that almost anything was better than the reality in which he must live. Perhaps he could become an explorer like Miss Witherspoon's relative. . . .

"I am not one who . . ."

For a moment she looked so angry that Steven backed away a step before he stopped himself.

More calmly, she began again. "No. I do not find the world of the imagination of interest. I cannot comprehend what anyone sees in it. My father, for instance, *lives* for the theater." Something of the anger she'd pushed away crept back into her voice. "I have always suspected that, if his birth did not make it impossible, he would join a theater troupe. *Especially*, he would have done so when *your* age. I think he'd actually have *enjoyed* living a harsh, uncertain life among a roving band of players. It is incomprehensible, his obsession with such nonsense." She bit her lip, shrugged away her emotion, and added, "If you will excuse me—there are duties . . ."

*Or perhaps I should become an actor*? thought Steven as he watched her leave the room, her skirts swishing around her. It occurred to him that people he knew might discover him on stage and sneer, which would be unbearable no matter how much he enjoyed the work. He pushed that ambition aside and reconsidered exploring, in lands far from anyone he knew. It was by far the better notion. Finding what he needed took time, but, carrying two of the sketchbooks with him, Steven returned to the theater shortly before he was scheduled to rehearse the scene where he took private leave of his adoptive mother, the queen of Carthage.

"Ah. At last. Our young Oedipus," said Roger, who was ready earlier than expected and irritated the boy had not arrived, even if it was not yet time. He glanced at the sketchbooks handed him and set them aside.

"There are two sketches," began Steven, excited that he'd found exactly what he thought was wanted.

"Later. I want to talk to you about this scene."

Roger drew Steven to the side, away from where the others were congregated in small, babbling groups. Then, his hand on Steven's arm as if to prevent the lad's escape, he looked around, located Eustacia Fairchild, and motioned for her to join him.

"Now," he said when they were both there, "here is what I want of the two of you. Since showing *enough* emotion seems to be the problem with this scene, what I want you to do is think about what you would be feeling and then show much *more*. Exaggerate. Make a buffoonery of what is really a tragedy." Roger looked from one to the other. "Do you understand what I mean?"

"Emote," said Eustacia, nodding.

"Emote . . . ?" asked Steven, hesitantly.

"You feel sad. Cry and wail, scream, curse the Fates . . . and anything else you can think of," suggested Eustacia. "Just for instance."

"You feel anger. Perhaps you would curse and stomp around and shake your fists at the heavens," suggested Roger.

"Apollo's oracle's prediction," said Steven and looked from one to the other. "I thought I felt guilt that I was supposed to be the cause of my father's death. Perhaps *fear* that I'd be unable to avoid it."

"Fear, yes. Guilt? That too, perhaps, but"—Eustacia frowned, turned questioningly toward Roger—"I haven't a notion how one exaggerates guilt."

"Fall to one's knees. Beg forgiveness, perhaps?" asked Steven.

"You've got the idea," said Roger. "You will show every emotion to as extreme a degree as you can manage."

Steven frowned. "But the words. The play's lines . . ."

"For this particular exercise, don't worry about anything but the sense of what the scene is supposed to convey," said Roger, sternly. "Play it, as I've said, to the extreme. Then, once all those emotions are out in the open, we can turn them back into the tragic form we need for the play and make them work with the playwright's lines."

Steven bit his lip as he looked off into the distance.

"You are leaving the woman you believe is your mother. Leaving her forever," said Roger softly. "It puts very strong feelings into your heart. Into your very soul. . . ." Roger hoped very much that Diane had been correct that fears of showing those emotions were what kept the lad from acting them out.

Steven brought himself back from wherever it was he had gone to in his mind. He nodded. Silently he turned toward the stairs. Treading heavily, he made his way onto the stage, where, again, he seemed to withdraw into himself.

"Is he all right?" asked Eustacia, startled.

"I think he is looking inward to discover the emotions he needs," said Roger blandly, hoping it was so. "Go along now." Roger looked around. "And I think I will clear the house of everyone else, so he need not feel embarrassed. . . ."

While Eustacia made her way to the stage, Roger ejected everyone else from the theater. He turned back. Steven and Eustacia stood there, not far from each other but ignoring each other. Steven was still—thinking? Eustacia had her script open and appeared to be studying her lines. Roger sighed.

*It will*, he thought, *be a harassing time for all three of us.*

"Why did he send us away?" asked a young lady who played a maid to Corinth's queen. "I'm supposed to be in that scene."

"Yes, you are," said Diane soothingly, "but you don't say anything. Not until after Oedipus departs. Roger wants to work with those two." She smiled. "If they are alone, he can rant and rave and scold and cajole and do things he probably would not feel free to do if anyone else is there listening."

"Are we to wait here? Will he want us back soon?"

Diane pursed her lips. Roger had not said anything about the rest of the morning's schedule. "Let us pretend he dismissed us for good," she said lightly. "We will return for the afternoon practice as scheduled."

"Will we never begin at the beginning and go on to the end?" asked an irritated gentleman who had a minor role. "It is taking so long this way. I thought we'd just . . . do it."

"You will be surprised at how *well* you do it once all the pieces are put together," soothed Diane. "If we tried to do it from the beginning right on through to the end and we hadn't a notion where we were to stand or what emotions we should project . . . well, it would be very slow and awkward. Besides, everyone would have to be in the theater at all times, whereas this way, if you are not needed for any of the scenes to be rehearsed, you are free to enjoy yourself. And—" Diane looked around. "—it would be a shame to have no free time to enjoy all this."

She gestured, and, as if agreeing with her, the sun, which had been behind a bit of cloud, shone forth, brightening flower beds, sparkling off fountains, and, generally, showing approval for all it shone upon.

The guests broke into groups and wandered off in various directions. Lord Cartwright watched them go and then looked back down at Diane. "You do that very well," he said.

"Do what?" she asked, tipping her head to one side.

"Soothe ruffled feathers."

She nodded. "It seems to be a particular talent of mine. Roger is not the most tactful of men. Especially when he is having trouble with an actor or actress. When someone doesn't manage to understand what is wanted," she added in explanation. "So, when tempers are roused, I pour on the oil. Or perhaps I am able to explain the situation in some new way, so it *is* understood."

"You are a team, then. You work together often?"

"We've worked together for some years now." She nodded and began walking toward a particularly nice show of delphiniums.

He fell into step beside her. "Work together and . . . ?"

Diane frowned at the suggestive tone. Suddenly she understood what he was asking and stopped. She looked up at him, glaring. Without a word, she turned and stalked off. When he came after her, she turned, held up her hand, tilted her chin in the air, and then again stalked off.

Lord Cartwright stared after her, confused, unhappy, and just a touch irritated. "Now, why did she do that?"

"You'll have to ask when she comes down out of the boughs," said a voice off to the side.

Cartwright turned toward it. "You."

"I was here first," said Sir Cyrall. It was merely a statement, with neither belligerence nor the sound of an explanation in the tone.

"So you were." Cartwright moved toward the bench on which Cyrall sprawled very like a cat with the sun warming him. "You do seem to have a knack for being where you can do the most . . ." He paused. "I was going to say damage, but of course, you rarely do damage. Do you?"

"Do I not?" The baronet widened his exceedingly expressive eyes. "You will admit to a dig here or a dent there, perhaps?" He batted his long lashes. "It is such *fun*, you know, to ruffle feathers."

"Ah, but almost always, you do so in order to . . . to teach a lesson."

"Nonsense. I do so in order to amuse myself."

Cartwright eyed the younger man, who, under that steady look, twisted his mouth into that weird V shape it acquired at times. When the younger man batted his long lashes again, Cartwright nodded as if something were proven to him. "So, when you walked my son out of the breakfast room this morning, that was for your amusement?"

Cyrall felt his ears heating. "No, that was to prevent the boy from instigating an idiocy. He's in love with Mrs. Runyard. An exceedingly amusing happenstance, of course. You should congratulate him on his good taste, should you not?" He cast Cartwright a sly look from under those exceedingly long lashes.

"I don't think I understand," said Cartwright cautiously.

"Of course you do." Cyrall grinned a wryly twisted grin. "My grandmother," he added—and batted those absurd lashes still again, but this time with no reaction from his quarry. "My great-aunts too, come to that," he added. "They *talk*," he continued in a suggestive tone. His eyes widened when *that* produced a faint reddening in Cartwright's ears. "A lot," he added for good measure.

"And you are a good grandson and nephew? You listen?"

Cyrall nodded, the V of a smile reappearing.

"And, at some point, the old gossips gossiped about what is indeed old news?"

Cyrall ignored the question. "Watching the progress of a boy's first love is exceedingly tiresome, I suppose, assuming you've no taste for such things. But if you think, you will recall how it was."

Cartwright nodded, a thoughtful look in his eyes. "Yes. I would have to agree. Tiresomely intense . . ."

"But," said Cyrall, wheedling, those eyes again in action, "you *will* remember to congratulate the boy for his good taste?"

Cartwright's eyes narrowed, suddenly alert. "And if I do not?"

"Someone must, I think," said Cyrall in his most irritatingly insouciant manner.

"*You* will inform my son that, *before I knew his mother*, I was very much in love with Mrs. Runyard?"

"I might." Cyrall nodded.

"I think not."

"Not?"

"Not."

Cyrall got that mischievous look again, his eyes sparkling with something that might have been a touch of malice. "And if it is too late? If the cat is already out of the bag?"

Cartwright felt something inside him tighten. Anger? Fear for his son, fear *of* his son's reaction? Fear that his own feelings for Diane would become known to all, would, once again, become food for the gossip mill? He didn't want that. Not for himself and not for Di. "What did you do?"

Cyrall studied his fingernails. "If I recall correctly, I simply told him there had been only one love in the lady's life, and that love was you."

"*One*?" Cartwright swore silently at himself for giving away the fact that that revelation was important to him.

"It is the *on dit* that there is an actress who has remained true, for decades, to the only man she ever loved." Cyrall shrugged. Surreptitiously he watched Cartwright's impassive face—his *nearly* unrevealing features. Cyrall was good at reading emotions from the slightest of hints, and now he read something that might be labeled hope in the glint in his lordship's eye, noting it just before the man turned away from him and walked off toward the house.

Cyrall nodded and then, closing his eyes, turned his face back up to the sun. A sun-darkened skin was not much admired in tonnish circles, but Cyrall was lucky in that respect. He could bask in the sun as much as he pleased and never acquire that ruddy look but merely a faintly golden tone he'd been told was attractive. Besides, he *liked* the sun.

Oh, yes. Very much like a cat. . . .

# CHAPTER
# SEVEN

Rafe, Lord Morningside, found Sir Cyrall where Lord Cartwright left him. "You look comfortable," he said, taking for himself the little space unoccupied by Cyrall.

Cyrall moved, but not much. "Very comfortable."

"Why do you look so like the cat who got into the cream?"

Cyrall's odd little smile appeared.

"Or should I ask just who it is who will be out for your blood at any moment, providing us with melodrama as well as drama?"

"No, no. Pure drama all around." Cyrall chuckled as he turned a twinkling glance toward his friend. "Are you not aware of the very *real* drama in our midst? One very like that being staged?"

Rafe frowned. "Explain yourself to this poor, dense idiot."

"Now why do *you* sound a trifle worried?" Cyrall cast a sideways glance toward Rafe. His mouth tightened and his shoulders shook ever so slightly. "Surely you do not think I refer to *you*?"

Rafe bit his lip then shrugged. "With you, Cyrall, it is always best to be suspicious. I don't know, do I? I fear you have noted what I've tried hard to hide. You do that. If you have . . . Well, then I've reason to feel suspicious, do I not?"

"Oh, that. The prickly Miss Fairchild. But, Rafe, *your* situation resembles a comedy. One of the ridiculous sort in which each actor runs about mistaking the motives of every other character." His brows snapped together and he was suddenly serious. "The real drama to which I refer could become a *tragedy*. It is a tragedy that we stage, is it not?"

Raft turned slightly so that he could stare at Cyrall. "Why do you do it?"

"Do . . . it?"

"Make a mystery of everything."

Muscles in Cyrall's shoulders and thighs tensed ever so slightly. "Do I do that?"

"You know you do."

The baronet's smile returned as he forced himself to relax. "I suppose I do. But why ask why? The answer is obvious, is it not?" When Rafe merely shrugged, he added, "How else can someone so insignificant as myself manage to be the center of attention except by rousing curiosity in those around me?"

Rafe pounced. "*Insignificant*. You?"

The smile faded, and, with infinitesimal changes in body and tone, Cyrall appeared something far less substantial. "Always have been. Always will be."

Rafe frowned thoughtfully. "Your brother . . . ?"

Cyrall glanced at his friend. "You would say it is idiotic to feel jealous of Primus?"

"I suspect anyone, let alone a brother, could feel some jealousy for the ton's Golden Adonis. Even when you know that idiot for the tyrant he is. On the other hand, you've your own value among those who count. People, even when most irritated, find themselves amused by you. Many admit, privately, that you have been exceedingly helpful at one time or another." Rafe broke off and, after a moment, added, "I don't suppose—" He stared off at nothing in particular. "—you might feel moved to be a trifle helpful where *I* am concerned?" Another silence followed, and he brought his gaze to meet Cyrall's. "Or would you?"

"Because your *Euphrasia* will not come to hand?"

A muscle jumped in Rafe's jaw. "Depending on what you mean by that, yes. If you are suggesting what you *might* be suggesting, I will thank you to keep out of it instead of hoping for help." Again he turned a look of curiosity toward the baronet.

At the same time, Cyrall straightened and turned sideways to stare at Rafe. Rafe felt his skin heat and returned his gaze to the toes of his boots, which, in emulation of Cyrall, he had stretched out before him.

"You are in love with her," said Cyrall, surprised.

Rafe's brows arched. "Ha! For once I managed to surprise you. Instead of you surprising me, I mean," he said, a touch of acid in his tone.

"I guess you did."

They were silent for some time. Then Rafe sighed. He knew his friend of old and realized Cyrall had withdrawn within himself and that he'd get no more from him. He rose. "I must study my part," he said as he wandered off, only a trifle worried about what, exactly, Cyrall might decide to do. As he'd indicated, Cyrall *usually* helped rather than the other thing.

Rafe found George Allingham in the library. "Just the man I need," he said, and the two settled into a corner, where, without once looking at the script Rafe handed him, George prompted Rafe through his scenes.

Rafe, concentrating, didn't realize George had learned all the parts until the gong rang softly through the house, informing those who wished to eat a luncheon that food was available. Only then did Rafe glance up at George. When he realized the script lay unopened in his old friend's lap, he asked, "*You've learned the whole thing?*" His amazement was obvious.

"E-e-easy. I've a g-g-good me—" George drew in a deep breath and finished the word carefully. "—mory."

"I wish I found it so easy," said Rafe a bit ruefully. He stood. "Will you join me for a bite of lunch?" he asked.

George grinned. "*She'll* be eating, won't she?" he asked, not a stammer in sight.

"She will." Rafe grinned back. He didn't mind that *George* guessed at his hopes with regard to Eustacia. George wasn't a gossip—for obvious reasons.

Diane felt someone nearby and looked up, knowing before she did so that Lord Cartwright had approached. "Hello," she said softly.

"Hello, yourself," he answered.

They stared at each other. Once again it felt to Diane as if they had communicated. Ruefully, she wished she knew the language, since she hadn't a clue to what was said. She cleared her throat. His ears turned pink. She looked down and fingered the script that lay in her lap.

Cartwright seated himself in the chair one down from hers in the back of the theater. "You've been studying your part?"

She nodded.

"I'd have thought you'd know it. I thought you players learned parts in mere minutes."

She smiled. "Perhaps some do in a few *hours*, but that is a knack I don't have. I must work to memorize a new role. This is harder because it is tragedy. I've done almost none of that. No major roles, at least."

"I've watched you, how you help those on stage with you, how you seem to know exactly where everyone is—at least, is *supposed* to be. And you project your voice so that, even if

I sit in back, I can hear you clearly. You have grown into your work amazingly, have you not?"

She chuckled. "Two decades, Stevie. I should have learned *something*."

He wished Sir Cyrall was correct about Di having been true to him, however selfish the desire might be. But the baronet was *not* correct. Cartwright's mind returned to a certain journey north. . . .

His gaze lifted to the chandelier. "I saw you in York one summer," he said a trifle musingly, hiding how important it was to him.

She glanced at him, saw that he stared blankly, and wondered at his expression. "You should have come backstage and said hello." She quickly added, "For old times' sake. . . ."

"I did." She started to respond, but he added, "I was too late. You were leaving for . . . an appointment."

She frowned. "York?" It was obvious to the watching man that she searched her mind for a season in which she'd have been busy after the play. "What sort of appointment would I have had in York?" she muttered. "At night? After the play?" She shook her head as she looked at him. "You must be mistaken. Surely no one said any such thing to you."

"I saw you," he said quietly.

"*Saw* me." She turned in her chair, startled, and stared at him.

"You got into a carriage."

"So?" Her frown deepened.

He cast an irritated look her way. The irritation also showed in his tone. "An actress does not, on her wages, afford unnecessary trips in a carriage."

"Not from wages, of course, but . . ."

He straightened in his chair and turned from the waist to glare. "*Exactly.* Unless someone has her in keeping. Please don't think I am being derogatory, Di. Jealous, perhaps—" He grinned a rueful grin. "—but whatever my feelings, I had no claim on you. You had every right to find someone who could add to your comfort."

She rose slowly to her feet. "I . . ." Bewildered, she shook her head. "Stevie . . ." Again she paused. Finally, when he frowned, she drew in a deep breath. "I have had," she said quietly, "no protector since you, Steven. Not a one."

With that she turned and, glad there was trouble on stage, walked down the aisle to where Roger stood shouting at the actors rehearsing the scene in which Oedipus faced the Sphinx.

"No! Nonono." Roger put his head in his hands and groaned.

"What seems to be the problem, Roger?" asked Diane, keeping her voice steady with effort. Inside, where it could not show, she was in turmoil. Why did Stevie assume she had a protector when he must know of the exceedingly generous annuity she received each quarter? Why?

Even as part of her stewed and fretted, she listened to Roger's explanation of what it was he wanted from the actors in this scene. When he was done, she nodded, and, gracefully, climbed the stairs. She took the place of the priestess facing young Steven. Steven, for some reason, seemed unable to concentrate.

*Is it,* she wondered, *that he witnessed that scene just now between his father and me?*

Doing as she'd done so often, following Roger's instructions, she showed the amateur actress what he meant, what he wanted of her. But even when that problem was fixed, the scene did not go well. Their Oedipus did not seem to have the whole of his mind on his work, and, finally, Roger called for a break. An impatient jerk of his head told Diane she was to find out what bothered the boy. And fix it.

She sighed. She did not need this complication in her life.

"Come along, Steven," she said. "Let us get a little air. It is very close in here, is it not?" She led him toward a side door in order to avoid Lord Cartwright, who sat, slouched, in a chair toward the back of the theater, glaring at her.

"Never before have you asked me to join you. You are beginning to like me. Maybe you . . . ?"

Hearing the pleasure, the anticipation, in the lad's voice, Diane interrupted him. "Of course I like you, Steven, but you misunderstand. What I *am* is *worried* about you. In the past you've done very well with this scene. Tell me, please, why it is that today you cannot seem to put your heart into it?"

Steven's mouth formed that pouty look. He glowered at the path ahead. Then he stopped, turned, and grasped her shoulders. "When you suggested coming out, I thought . . ."

"No," she said, again interrupting him. "You didn't *think*. You *hoped*, but you didn't think." She smiled gently to soften the reprimand. "Now," she encouraged, "tell me what is wrong so we can get it behind us and you can, once again, do the excellent work you've been doing."

His shoulders slumped, and he looked over her shoulder. "Father . . ."

"Yes?"

"He was . . . not nice to you. He was telling you to leave me alone, was he not? Trying to make you . . . make you stay away from me."

Diane spoke evenly. "You refer to the little scene between us? In the back of the theater?" *As I guessed,* she told herself. "Actually, Steven, we neither of us mentioned you. We discussed my past, my work in the theater."

"But he was . . . angry."

"Angry?" Diane thought about it. "No. I don't know what you think you saw, but he was not *angry*."

"Yes, he was. He scowled. He drove you away from him. He was angry."

Diane sighed. "Steven . . . Your father and I knew each other a long time ago. *Before* he married your mother," she added, looking up at him, worried about how he would take that. "We were very young. Very nearly as young as *you* are now. It was a long time ago," she repeated.

A muscle in his jaw rolled over, and a pained look filled the gaze he turned on her. "You . . . He . . . ?"

She nodded.

"You . . . *Damn* you!" He stalked off down the path.

"Blidy hell," Diane said on a breath of air. "Blidy *damn* hell."

"What," asked Lord Cartwright, who had followed them but remained just out of hearing, "was that all about?"

"I was trying to . . . to make him understand. Oh blidy hell," she repeated. "I really messed it up, Stevie. I hurt him. Badly." She turned to face him. "Go after him. Make him understand."

"Understand what?" he asked, a certain bitterness in his tone. "Understand that we were once lovers? That we were forced to part? That, according to you—" Once again that scowl appeared. "—you remained true to that love?"

She stared, her eyes widening. Her mouth slowly dropped open. Then, forcing each word, she said, "*You do not believe me.*"

"I saw you get into that carriage," he retorted. "Explain *that.*"

"Blidy, blidy hell," she said, staring. Then anger steamed. "Damn you," she said, just as Steven had done, and, exactly as he had done, she stalked off—only to remember that the youth had gone that way. Not wishing to catch the lad up, she turned down a side path. She didn't want to see Steven.

Nor *anyone.*

She had never been so angry in her life. *How dare he disbelieve me? How dare he think me so changed that I would lie to him? How dare he . . .*

Diane's thoughts raged on, and, when she saw Lord Morningside and Miss Fairchild walking together, speaking of something that had both of them using their hands for emphasis, she turned into still another path, one that led more deeply into the Witherspoon gardens.

Diane could not bear the thought of attempting the polite nothings she would be forced to utter if she came near one other soul. She had to be alone. So when she practically walked into Sir Cyrall, she swore still again.

This time she managed to do it silently.

Sir Cyrall, his thoughts going in circles in an unusual attempt to straighten out an emotional tangle of his own, was not as perceptive as usual. When he looked up from where he prodded the moist, loamy soil with his toe, scraping dead leaves to one side with the sole of his shoe and generally making a mess of his boot, he scowled.

Diane's frown deepened. "Don't bother explaining you wish to be alone, because that is exactly how I feel," she said bitterly. "I'll go elsewhere."

Her tone and words cut through Cyrall's disquiet, and, with something else about which he could think, it fell away from him. "No. Please." He always found distraction in trying to understand another's foibles. "Don't go. Tell me what bothers you."

Diane's lips compressed, and she glowered.

He laughed a bitter little laugh. "The men in your life giving you grief? 'Twas to be expected, I suppose, although you've been handling them so delicately up to now, I had begun to think there would be no resolution of *any* sort. What has happened to change that?"

For a moment Diane didn't move—barely breathed—and then relaxed. "Why not? You appear to be aware of every tension, every little spat or momentary pleasure, among those around you. Why not ask your advice?"

He turned on the woodland path and offered his arm. "Shall we walk while we talk?"

"Hmm." They strolled for some time before he cleared

his throat. She glanced at him. "Hmm. I said something about asking advice, did I not?"

"You did. I will do my modest best to help, although I doubt very much I will do any good."

"But you *do* help. Often. In your sly and cynical fashion." She looked up, suddenly curious about what or who had ruffled *his* feathers, why *he* had been frowning when they'd met.

She opened her mouth to ask, but before she could speak he shook his head. "No, don't," he said, that insightfulness she'd mentioned telling him what she meant to do. "I detest it when I must be mendacious, and I would be sure to lie if you were to probe into *my* weaknesses." That odd smile formed his mouth into a V shape and then disappeared almost immediately. "I am, you see, far better at dealing with everyone's problems *but* my own. So do tell what has happened. I cannot help when I am missing large parts of the whole."

She grimaced but faced forward and explained the sequence of events that led to her stalking off in high dudgeon.

"One problem is easily solved," he said thoughtfully. "How *did* you afford a carriage while in York if someone did not have you in keeping?"

"But he *knows*." Diane's eyes widened. "But it *must* have been him. . . ."

"Knows what? About what?"

"Soon after coming into his title, he arranged that I have an annuity. It is quite generous. I don't often spend it as frivolously as I did in York, but the town was unsettled just then, the machine-breakers very active in the area. I did not like to walk to my room alone so late at night."

"You are certain he arranged it?"

"Who else could or would have done so?" she asked, looking up at him.

Sir Cyrall frowned, his head slightly bent. He stopped, the sole of his boot receiving still more damage as he scuffed it lightly against a large, moss-covered stone set near the path. "Who else might want to help you, you would ask?" He glanced at her. "Then it is true you've had no other lovers?"

She very nearly growled, but then it registered that he actually knew that fact, and she wondered how. "I never met anyone else who measured up to what I'd seen in the man I loved."

"I see. Very well." He walked on a few more paces. "Soon after his father's death you say?"

"Yes. A month or two after the previous baron died, a supercilious little rat of a man, who I assume was a solicitor's clerk, came to me. He handed me the first quarter's allowance and told me, when I asked, that it was none of my business whence it came but that it would be available quarterly. He explained how I was to receive it."

She looked at Sir Cyrall and thought, *And that, my laddy, is more than I ever told anyone. So why you*? Diane found it rather disconcerting to find herself *giving* confidences rather than *receiving* them.

"A month or so. . . ." Cyrall's voice trailed off. "Miss— *Mrs*. Runyard, this is something you really must ask Lord Cartwright to explain. If he did *not* arrange the allowance, then someone else did. He can discover for you who it is—" and, almost silently, added, "—or *was*."

She ignored that last bit. "Find out for me? So that I may *thank* him?" asked Diane, her tone suggestive of how she might be expected to show her appreciation.

"Lord Cartwright has held his title for years. If no one has yet asked for that sort of *thanks*, then I doubt they expect it. But I think you should know who it is. And I am certain *Lord Cartwright* will wish to know," he added, a touch of humor in that. "He'll not like the notion someone else is supporting you, even if you are not asked to provide the, hmmm, sort of *comfort* usually required in such cases."

Diane, returned by their discussion to her normally logical state of mind, nodded. "Yes. I see that. And if it was not he who arranged it all, then I see why he cannot believe me when I tell him I have had no other lovers. And I also see that *that* problem can be easily resolved. That leaves Steven, poor boy. How that lad misses his mother. I doubt anyone can solve *that* problem."

Sir Cyrall frowned a quick frown. "I had not thought him such a mama-boy."

"Not *that* sort of relationship. I think perhaps," she continued slowly, "that it is more that he never had the opportunity to grow away from her in a natural fashion as do most young boys in the years after they are sent off to school. He cannot manage it on his own. Only Stevie can help him, but Stevie . . ."

When it became clear she'd not finish, Cyrall said, "You would say that Lord Cartwright is a normal man, who did grow up naturally, and that he does not understand the problem. You call me sensitive, but, frankly, *I* don't see it."

"Hmm. And I cannot seem to find the words to explain what I mean."

Diane sighed and told herself it was something on which she must cogitate. Then, half a moment later, her stomach growled. She blushed slightly, glanced at Sir Cyrall to see if he noticed—and discovered he had. He dropped her arm, made a smart about-turn, and offered his other arm. He grinned down at her, but it was a smile without cruelty, more the humor of laughing *with* one than *at* one.

"I admit I like my meals at decent intervals," she said before he could comment. "It must be later than I thought. If I don't hurry, I'll not have time to rest after eating and before we reconvene for the afternoon rehearsal. Roger will tear his hair if his cast has gone off in different directions to indulge in private emotions when he thinks they should experience nothing beyond what is called for in the role they play."

"*He* is so lacking in sensitivity? But how can he be such

an excellent actor and such a good director if he cannot see the necessary emotions?"

"I did not say he doesn't see private emotions. He merely thinks none important unless played out on stage."

Sir Cyrall frowned. "Surely not. The man is forever indulging himself in one or another situation that rouses all sorts of—" His brows arched suggestively. "—*private emotions*. Emotions that have nothing to do with the stage."

Diane chuckled. "Roger occasionally finds himself in situations that result in shouting matches at a minimum. At the extreme, shooting matches." She shook her head. "But he is not of the peerage, so a duel would never do. Horsewhipping perhaps? I believe one husband threatened exactly that when his wife insisted she was as surprised as he to find herself in bed with Roger. She insisted she couldn't imagine how she got there." Diane shrugged. "I don't know how Roger got himself out of that one, but to his mind, such excesses of emotion are absurd and unnecessary—unless required by the part he currently plays."

"Nothing of the sort will happen this summer," said Cyrall, not really thinking about it.

"How can you know?" she asked.

He turned a look her way, recalled what they'd been discussing, and explained. "It is simple. There are no husbands involved this time."

She frowned.

"*Very* simple," he added. "A widow has him in hand."

Diane's eyes widened, and she wondered that she had not noticed. But she'd been preoccupied, so perhaps it was not so surprising after all.

The two walked along in silence for a bit, and then Sir Cyrall said, "That is young Steven, is it not? He looks lost and very young. Why do you not go that way—" He pointed. "—and I will intercept him."

Diane looked up, saw that Steven had not noticed them,

and set off alongside a hedge that hid her until she could safely turn toward the house. Steven was alone. Had his father not come up with him? Or would there be further problems because he *had*? Diane wished she had a bit more of Roger's attitude toward emotion so that she would not feel so confused, so very worried. . . .

Sir Cyrall watched Diane disappear before picking up his pace a trifle and catching up with the morose young man.

"The world is not always a pleasant place, is it?" he asked gently as he reached Steven.

Steven glanced up and then back to the path.

"The worst of it is that we make such plans, have such wonderful expectations," continued Cyrall in a musing tone. "When we discover our life heading in a direction other than that we envisaged, it is very easy to assume everything has gone wrong and will never again be right."

Again Steven glanced around. This time, when Cyrall did not continue, he sighed. "Nothing is like it should be," he said.

"What particular nothing?" asked the baronet.

Steven sent a sidewise glance, this one full of chagrin and something that might have been suspicion.

"I am not asking in order to pry," said Cyrall softly, "but to see if there is some way I might help."

"No one can help."

There was so much bitterness in that that Cyrall had difficulty restraining a laugh. *The young,* he thought, *are so very predictable.*

"My father . . ."

"Your father was once as young as you are now," said Cyrall gently when Steven didn't continue.

Steven's head came up. His mouth dropped open.

"Never thought of that, did you?" asked Cyrall with a touch of humor.

"Young . . . and . . . ?"

"Young, insecure, worried he might not measure up? All of that. We all feel that way except for a very few lucky ones who seem to have been born old." *My perfect brother* . . . "My friend Rafe, for instance. I don't think," mused Cyrall, sternly repressing all thoughts of his elder brother, "that he ever in his life wondered what, exactly, he should do next."

Steven sighed. "I never seem to know what to do about anything."

"You will—and don't ask when. It will be sooner than you expect." Inwardly, where it didn't show, Cyrall sent a small prayer skyward that what he had said was true and that the boy would mature quickly. They walked on a bit more, and then Cyrall said, "It is lunchtime, young Steven. Come fill one of the holes inside you."

He took the youth's arm and turned him down a path that led to the house.

"Amazing how much worse everything seems when one is hungry." That, at least, was true.

# CHAPTER EIGHT

When Diane entered the dining room soon after leaving the baronet, Lord Cartwright pushed back from the table and came to her.

"I apologize," he said softly, but not so softly he drew no eyes.

Diane felt heat in her neck and face. "Unnecessary." Then she recalled that she did think it necessary. "At least—there is something . . . but not now. We must talk. Later?"

He nodded and returned to his place, where, smoothly, he rejoined the conversation he'd interrupted to come to Diane.

Diane picked up a plate and served herself what she wanted and took it to the chair beside Lord Cartwright. Nothing but a tankard of homebrew stood at his place, revealing that he made no pretence but that he was there for the purpose of intercepting her. When she was seated, he broke off his conversation again and, speaking, urgently, repeated himself. "Di, I *must* apologize. I had no right . . ."

"Shh. We'll discuss it later. I think I see the problem, why you do not believe me, and we can resolve it." She looked across the table when Miss Fairchild called for her attention. "Yes, Miss Fairchild?"

"I have just been given a letter which requires an immediate response. In fact, the groom who brought it awaits my answer. Will you please inform Mr. Brown I'll be unavailable for rehearsal this afternoon, or at least the early part of it?" As she spoke, she rose to her feet.

"Problems, Euphrasia?" asked Lord Morningside.

"None with which you need concern yourself," she replied, her voice icy. She turned on her heel and swiftly, angrily, left the room.

"Why," asked Lord Cartwright, "do you call her that when she so obviously dislikes it so?"

"She does, does she not?" Rafe's eyes narrowed and a lopsided grin twisted his mouth. Reluctantly, he added, "It is the name she *should* have been given." He nodded toward Diane as he too rose and left the room.

"The name she *should* have?" repeated Diane, curious.

Cartwright frowned, his thoughts turned inward. "Blidy hell," he muttered. "It was so long ago when I last . . . Ah. Steven," he said as the lad and Sir Cyrall entered. "Perhaps you can help."

His son, who had tensed upon seeing that his father was not only present but, worse, that he and Mrs. Runyard were seated side by side, revealed his surprise at the request. "Help? *Me*?"

"You. I have forgotten my Greek. Tell me, do you know the Greek word from which the name Euphrasia is derived? For that matter, the derivation of Eustacia?"

Steven looked back into the hall. Just now they had passed an obviously angry Miss Fairchild. "Miss Fairchild's names?"

"She only has one of them," said Lord Cartwright with a touch of humor. "Lord Morningside teases her with the other. I want to know what they mean. Particularly Euphrasia."

After a quick, longing glance at the buffet, Steven spoke. "I shall go see if I can find out. The library—"

"Not now," interrupted his father. "You've come to eat. No sense in going off for something so unimportant."

*But*, wondered Diane, *is it unimportant*?

Quite obviously Miss Fairchild felt it *very* important. . . . Diane put the thought aside and set her mind to tactfully encouraging the communication that had begun between father and son.

"That," said Richard Coxwald to his valet as he handed over a leather pouch that clinked softly, "should be sufficient to cover any expenses on the road. Father ordered a carriage from home for you that should arrive soon. You need not hire a post chaise. Depart just as soon as you've packed." The valet moved off, and Richard looked around. "Now, I wonder . . ."

But before he could ask the hovering butler the whereabouts of his hostess and her father, he heard their raised voices drifting from a nearby room. There was a worried note in Francine's tone. "Father, really, you must . . ."

"Francine, I have told you and told you, *you* must manage such things and leave me in peace." Her father continued on a harsh note. "Go away. I cannot be bothered when we've so much going on and still another difficulty has arisen. Run along now. *You* decide." And, added on a mutter, "Whatever it may be."

Lord Witherspoon's eyes widened as he came into the hall. "Ah! Just the person for whom I was searching," he said, rubbing his hands and beaming at the sight of Richard, his irritation gone as if it had never existed.

Francine followed him into the hall. "Father, believe me, you *must*—"

"*No*." He turned, waving his hands in a shooing motion.

"You do it—whatever it is." He scowled at the girl before he turned, again smiling, toward Richard. "Now, Richard, we need you. At once. There is a problem with the scene where Oedipus meets his father on the road. Changes must be made. Do come, quickly." He started down the hall, only to stop when he realized Richard was not with him. "Come, lad," he said, beckoning. "We've work to do."

"I'm sorry, sir, but I cannot accompany you. I must leave for Bath at once. I have had a message—"

"Leave?" Witherspoon rushed back, his eyes almost starting from his head. "You mean *go away*? *Now*? Leave the *party*? Boy, you cannot leave. You are *needed*. Did I not just say—"

Very unlike his normally polite self, Richard actually interrupted. "I *must* leave. Francie—" A pained look crossed his features as he turned and held out his hands. "—it is Grandmother. Mother sent a groom over to tell me I must go quickly. At once."

"*You cannot go.*" Lord Witherspoon very nearly shouted the words. "What are you *thinking*? The *play* . . ."

Richard turned, still holding one of Francine's hands, which she'd offered the moment he revealed his pain. "Sir, my grandmother is ill and I have no time to argue with you. You will do very well with Mrs. Runyard, who can make any needed changes. Very likely, she will do it better than I. Francie," he said, turning back.

"Shh," she said, blushing rosily. "You must hurry. Richard," she added, rushing her words, "I was *wrong*. I'm sorry. When you return . . ."

"Wrong?" he asked but looked toward the open door, where a groom trotted up leading four horses harnessed to his curricle.

"I thought you had grown to be like Father," she said, her voice strained, low with tension.

Richard suddenly recalled that his love and her father had

been arguing. His hands tightened around hers. "What has happened? What is it that your father needs to do?"

"I'll manage," she said. "You . . ."

Richard, still holding Francine's hand, turned once again to his fuming host, who had not stopped muttering. "My lord, if Francie says there is something to which you must attend," he said sternly, "then you had best *listen* to her. The theater is all very well, but *real* life is far more important."

Lord Witherspoon actually began to gobble, he was so stunned at the notion the theater should take second place to *anything*.

Richard squeezed Francie's hand. "I really must be off. I'll write you . . . *your father*, that is," he said, remembering the proprieties, "and he can tell you how Grandmother goes on."

"Please do," she said. "And thank you." She watched him go.

"What is the world coming to, that a whippersnapper like that tries to tell *me*—"

"It is the Ambleside estate," said Francine in a rush, nerving herself to say what had to be said even if they were not alone. The hovering butler cocked an interested ear even when she scowled at him. "Your steward ran off with the strongbox, leaving no funds for the harvest. The haying requires the hiring of extra help *right now*." She had spoken in a rush to get it all out and then, a trifle more restrainedly, added, "Mr. Grainer is here." She started for the door but stopped when her father spoke, coldly, behind her.

"Grainer is supposed to be at Eastwark."

She didn't turn, again speaking quickly and, this time, still more bitterly. "So he *would* be if you had bothered to read even one of the missives from Ambleside. Or, for that matter, those from him written from Eastwark. They lie in a great jumble on your desk. A pile of correspondence you've not bothered to open. Mr. Grainer awaits you in your office."

Having said her piece, she rushed out the door and into the drive. Through a cloud of dust, she could barely see Richard's back. Driving his team to an inch, he was rapidly disappearing.

"Wrong," she said and moaned softly. "I was so very wrong." But then it hit her, and her mood lightened. "I was *wrong*. He *isn't* like Father." Very slowly a smile spread across her face. "He isn't so wrapped up with all that nonsense that he does not know what is important!"

She returned to the house and asked the butler if her father had gone to meet with Mr. Grainer or if he had returned to playing games with his guests.

"He seemed very angry, but he sent a footman to the theater with a message and he himself went off to his office."

"Thank goodness. I feared he would . . ."

Francine realized she was about to confide in a servant and closed her mouth—and then blushed when the irrepressible fellow actually winked at her. Her lips thinned as she turned away. The man would *never* learn his place.

Once, in an expansive mood, Lord Witherspoon told her that, in his youth, the butler had been an actor, that the two had known each other before her father married. When this estate came to his lordship as part of Francine's mother's dowry, Witherspoon hired his old friend as butler. Jenkins, she was told, sotto voce, had never been a very good actor.

He wasn't, Francine thought bitterly, a very good butler either.

The message Lord Witherspoon sent to the theater resulted in a demand from Roger for Diane's immediate presence there. Diane excused herself from the table. She wondered at the imperious wording of Roger's message, which the footman had quoted with great care to say nothing of badly suppressed relish.

"What is it?" she asked upon arriving in the theater, where Roger sat at a makeshift desk set to the side of the stage.

"We lost our playwright," fumed Roger. He explained that Richard Coxwald had had to go to an ailing relative's bedside. "The scene on the road to Thebes, Di. It needs work. With such a young Oedipus, Coxwald's conception will not do."

Diane mentally ran through the scene. "Oedipus is—or is thought to be—a prince of Corinth, is he not? He'd be an arrogant youngster, very likely in that stage of life where he cannot conceive anything bad happening to himself—why not the argument and challenges as Richard wrote them?"

Roger stared at nothing for a long moment, thinking. Then he shook his head. "It doesn't work for me. And I doubt Steven capable of playing it that way. He must be a polite young man, educated, and unhappy at leaving his home. He must be goaded into anger."

"So what is Laius's motivation for goading him?"

"Pure bloody-mindedness?" asked Roger with a sudden grin, his eyes lighting up. He sobered. "Laius doesn't need too much of a motive. Have Oedipus say just one thing to upset him and, despot that he is, that would be sufficient, would it not?" He frowned. "While you do that, I must find someone who fences, someone who can help me plan out the moves in the fight. . . ."

"I can do that," said Sir Cyrall. He had entered in his silent, cat-footed fashion and listened as Diane and Roger talked. "I think you are correct that our Oedipus is incapable of the sort of arrogance and stubbornness our playwright assigned to both men. The elder, yes. Our prince . . . I think not."

Diane sighed. "Very well. I will work on it."

"Be back for the afternoon rehearsal," ordered Roger while he weighed Cyrall's offer of help against what he knew of

the man's nature. *But is there*, he wondered, *anyone else?*
"Sir Cyrall and I will work out the moves for the fight."

Diane, muttering that he asked the impossible of her and
knowing she'd be distracted if she remained in the theater,
took a copy of the play to her room, got out paper, pen, and
ink, and, groaning at the necessity, set to work. She always
hated rewriting another's work. Now, when the author was
unavailable to consult and eventually agree with the result,
she was still more reluctant.


Steven finished eating and went to the library, where,
after some endeavor, he discovered the meanings for which
his father had asked. He asked three guests and two servants
if they'd seen Lord Cartwright before locating his father in
the music room, where his lordship was seated at the piano-
forte, playing softly. Steven's brows arched. He'd been unaware his father played so well. He waited until the piece
came to an end and then stepped forward, clearing his throat.

His lordship looked up, frowning. Music had become, for
him, a way of soothing emotion, working through a problem,
or easing stress. He was not happy to be interrupted before
he'd once again found his equilibrium. "Yes?" he asked
brusquely.

"You . . . you wanted those meanings?" asked Steven,
hesitantly. He'd been proud to have found them, happy to
have managed to complete the task his father set him—but
now felt as if it was all so unimportant he might not have
bothered.

"Meanings? Oh." His lordship's brows arched. "Well?"
he asked with a touch of arrogance that would have appalled
him if he'd recognized it in himself.

The boy and he had never managed to be at ease with
each other. It occurred to Cartwright to wonder why, and,

quick as lightning, a series of pictures flashed through his mind. In each of them his wife and his son had their heads together, laughing, singing, playing . . . together, with he himself excluded in some subtle fashion he had never understood.

"I did ask for them, did I not?" he added, speaking in a more normal tone. He swung around on the piano bench. "Well?" he asked again but in a different tone.

Steven relaxed a trifle. "The names. Eustacia means *to cause to stand,* and Euphrasia means *to delight the heart or mind.* Is that what you wanted?"

"To cause to stand? What does that mean?" mused Lord Cartwright.

"I think it referred to stands of grain," said his son diffidently. "That sort of thing."

"Ridiculous. No," he added quickly, "not you, but that a name means such a thing. I can understand why Lord Morningside prefers the other." He smiled a smile that asked his son to smile with him, but Steven was far too much in awe of his father to think of joining him in even such a mild jest. Cartwright sobered and sighed softly. "Thank you, Steven."

The lad nodded and turned away.

"Steven . . ."

He turned back, a wary look in his eyes.

"Steven, I am sorry you are unhappy. Is there anything I can do?"

Steven was not particularly aware of his deeper problems, only the immediate. He scowled. "Do? You can go away. You can leave me a fair field. She is so wonderful. . . . I don't suppose she'll ever look my way seriously, but with *you* here, spoiling everything, it is *impossible* that she do so. . . ." The boy's lips compressed; tension narrowed his eyes and creased his forehead. With something near a sob, he turned and ran from the room before his father could say a word.

Lord Cartwright stared after his son, a rueful look in his

eyes. Finally, he turned back to the piano, where the crashing notes of one of Herr Beethoven's newest works relieved a great deal of the emotions pouring through him.

But not all.

He was still in some turmoil when the footman he'd asked to warn him of the passing time came to him to tell him it was time to go to the theater for afternoon rehearsals.

Steven, who was also to attend them, forgot. He was miles away, using up a great deal of energy. Not only his raging emotions but the fast pace he set himself wore at him, tiring him. . . .

Roger was not pleased that their young star had absented himself until Diane pointed out that it would be easier to teach each of his actors, one at a time, the carefully plotted-out moves of the fight.

Sir Cyrall, playing the part of Oedipus, fought opposite Lord Cartwright, and, before the afternoon ended, his lordship, an adequate if out-of-practice duelist, had his part learned.

That evening, for the first time, Francine joined her father's guests in the salon. She joined in the charades she had once again arranged and recalled how she and Richard had once loved to plan out and play the roles demanded of them.

*Was it thus he learned to love play-acting and the writing of plays*? she wondered at one point, but then Sir Cyrall's clowning brought a laugh to everyone's lips and she forgot her question in the enjoyment of true amusement.

# CHAPTER
# NINE

Diane woke to the new day feeling as if something were wrong. She lay there, staring at the ceiling, and searched her mind for what it could be. A soft tap at the door heralded the entrance of a maid with her morning tea, for which she thanked the girl, thanking her again when the lass placed extra pillows at her back so she could sit comfortably in bed sipping the good, hot brew.

*I'll be terribly spoiled before this summer is over*, thought Diane, ruefully acknowledging that she *liked* being roused with a stimulating drink that she had not had to prepare for herself.

While the drapes were pulled back and the water in the ewer tested for warmth, she put thoughts of the future from her mind and returned to fretting about why she had wakened experiencing worry rather than the anticipation with which, each previous morning, she'd opened her eyes to the lovely room and much appreciated maid service.

*What? Whatwhatwhat . . . ?*

She had completed the necessary revisions as Sir Cyrall

and Roger worked out the sequence of moves that would result in Oedipus "killing" his father, so that wasn't it.

*It has, in fact, nothing to do with the play, so what . . . ?*

An image of Stevie exploded into her mind, a confused mixture of the young man he'd been and the man he'd become. Her hands shook, and she very nearly spilled her tea. Very carefully she set it on the table beside the bed and, folding her hands tightly, recalled they'd not resolved their misunderstanding.

Everything had conspired to make it impossible for them to have that talk she'd told him, while at luncheon, that they needed. Twice after that they had come together, but on both occasions someone had approached before they could do more than begin a word or two—he attempting further apologies and she trying to begin her explanation.

Diane compressed her lips, half laughing at the situation and half worrying herself to death. It was imperative that she explain, that she soothe his mind, allow him to understand . . . although that might be difficult since she didn't understand herself. Not if it was someone other than his lordship who had arranged for her to receive an annuity.

The maid left and Diane threw back the covers. *I will dress. I will find Stevie even if I must go to his room. I will explain*, she told herself as she headed for the basin—another luxury to which she was rapidly growing addicted, that of washing each morning before dressing. *How horrified Mama would be to know of it*, she told herself and chuckled. *I can hear her telling me I'll do myself a mischief, allowing so much contact with water.*

The moment of mild humor lightened her mood and she finished dressing in a more relaxed state of mind. She would explain, Stevie would understand, and all would be well.

*Except*, she thought, holding half-tied ribbons, *exactly what do I mean by that*?

What exactly *did* she expect? What did she want? Did she hope he would come back to her now he was free to do so? But his wife had been dead for years and he had not so much as come to see her onstage, let alone attempt to discover if she'd be willing to . . .

The corner of her lip found its way between her teeth as she finished tying the bow and began buttoning the row of tiny buttons holding the sleeves tight against her forearm.

*What is it that I want?*

It was a question she couldn't answer. His lordship was not the same man she'd once known. For that matter, she wasn't the same woman. They had both matured, changed beyond the simple souls they were when first they met. Even if it occurred to Stevie to renew their relationship, even if it were something he wanted . . . did she? Yes, her heart beat faster whenever she saw him, and she yearned to be held close in his arms. . . .

"But I want more than that," she murmured, unable to lie to herself about something so important. "The question," she continued, working at the buttons on her other arm, "is *why*. I know I still love the man he *was*—" She frowned thoughtfully and then nodded. "—but do I love the man he *is*? Do I even know the man he has become?"

Diane checked the mirror, discovered the frilly excuse for a cap she had adopted many years previously was slightly askew, fixed it, brushed back a strand of hair her fiddling allowed to escape, and then, quickly, before she could find another way to procrastinate, left her room.

"I must find Stevie," she muttered. Explanations concerning the annuity must be made before any other problem could be resolved.

Francine approached, singing softly, an old and joyful ballad, one with a lilt that might even be called rollicking.

"You seem particularly happy this morning," said Diane

in greeting and recalled how happy the girl had seemed while playing charades the previous evening.

Francine smiled broadly. "It is a beautiful day, is it not?"

Since Diane had noted the approach of a dark bank of clouds when looking out her window, she wondered how to reply to that but found it was unnecessary.

"I feel wonderful," continued her hostess. "It is amazing how wonderful I feel."

"I would have thought—" Diane hesitated to mention the situation, but her curiosity drove her on. "—that with Mr. Coxwald gone, you would feel quite the reverse."

Francine giggled. She covered her mouth with her hands, but her eyes sparkled. "Yes," she managed and then laughed again. "One would think I'd be quite downcast, would one not? Are you going down to breakfast? Will you walk down with me?"

Diane admitted to herself that not only would she be forced to join her hostess but that, if she did *not* want to go with her, it would be very hard to get rid of the woman. On the other hand, her curiosity was in full flow and she did wish to accompany Miss Francine. They linked arms, another surprise, since Francine had barely tolerated any of the guests and had tended to ignore the hired professionals altogether.

"You see," confided Francine as they walked down the hall toward the stairs, "I have discovered that what I feared, what I *believed*, is untrue. My Richard has *not* succumbed to the false glamour, the cheap glitter, the *lure* of the theater. That happened to my father, you see, and I believed Richard was another victim. I could not bear it, being second-best with him too. But it is *not* true. He knows what is important. He merely enjoys the theater in a purely normal fashion. Oh, it is so *freeing* to understand!"

Diane couldn't decide what to say to her hostess's confession. Buried in it was an insult to her profession in one way but truth in another. "The theater is nothing more than entertainment, of course. But in order to make it entertaining for our audience, we work very hard to do the very best we can."

"I have never objected to those who make it their life's work," said Francine, waving her free hand to indicate how unimportant that was to her. "It is people like my father, who become so caught up in it all that they will not or cannot remember that everyday real life and our responsibilities to our family and dependents are more important."

"Of course they are."

"My father," said Francine with more than a touch of her old bitterness, "does *not* think so. He resents everything and anything that interferes with his . . . his *obsession*."

"I see why it worried you that Mr. Coxwald might have succumbed to a like passion," said Diane soothingly.

Immediately, Francine began to glow. She actually took a skipping hop as a result of the excess of happiness filling her again. "Oh, it is such a beautiful day! And here we are." She nodded to the footman who opened the door to the breakfast room for them. She walked in, casting morning greetings toward the handful of people already eating.

Diane saw that Lord Cartwright was not down yet or—horrible thought—had eaten and gone on somewhere else. As the footman served her from the choices to which she pointed on the sideboard, she asked him.

"No, missus. His lordship has not yet appeared."

With her fear she'd missed him soothed, the pendulum of her emotions swung again. Diane could not decide whether it was a good thing he'd soon appear or if she'd have preferred, once again, to miss her opportunity for the talk they must have.

Eustacia Fairchild entered the room just then. Her frowning mien was a great contrast to Francine Witherspoon's radiant looks. She shook her head at the footman, seated herself, and, absently, requested a pot of tea and toast.

"What's the matter, Euphrasia?" asked Lord Morningside gently.

Eustacia was so preoccupied, she didn't react to his use of the hated name. "Nothing with which you need be concerned."

"I cannot help but be concerned. We have been friends for a very long time, my dear, and it is part and parcel of friendship that one be concerned for the other."

She compressed her lips tightly and then, suddenly, gave in. "My companion . . . Leticia."

"She is ill?" His brows snapped together. "Would you like that I arrange for a carriage to return you to Town?" he asked, his warm hand covering her clenched fist where it lay on the table beside her teacup.

"If only it were so simple!"

Rafe blinked. "She isn't *dead*."

Eustacia cast him a startled look. "No, no. Nothing like that." She dug into her reticule and pulled out a folded missive. "You can read for yourself. Or you can *try*. It took me quite half an hour to decipher the half of it. There are many phrases of which I can make not the least sense."

Having shared her trouble with another seemed to have eased her. She had picked at her dinner the evening before and ignored the supper Francine offered before bedtime. Now she discovered she was hungry. She rose to her feet and went to the sideboard, returning with a hearty breakfast of which she ate more than half before Rafe finished perusing the letter.

"You see?" she said. "Quite ridiculously hysterical."

"She has *eloped*?" he asked, deciding that was the most important single word among those of which he was uncertain.

"How missish of her," said Eustacia, half fondly and half in irritation. "She was afraid to tell me she and that visiting missionary were wishful to wed. As if I would not have done all I could to help. If you take the time to study out the meaning, you will find she feels guilty for deserting me, grateful to me because it was through me she met the gentleman, as low as a snake for lacking the courage to tell me earlier, and quite a hundred other equally dramatic effusions."

"Quite gothic," he said and added, "You must find another companion, must you not?"

Eustacia sighed. "That, in part, is why I am so preoccupied. I will write letters to a handful of the ladies I've met in the last few months, asking if they can introduce me to widows or spinsters I may interview for the position, but I am not hopeful. Leticia, despite her overly dramatic method of expressing herself, suited me. . . ."

Diane, sitting across the table, pretended she was not listening. It was just the sort of conversation on which she loved to eavesdrop—a weakness she could not make herself cease indulging. Her excuse was that it was by listening to others that she learned more of the art of portraying different characters on stage, but she knew in her heart it was more than that. She listened mostly for the simple reason that she had a great curiosity about people.

Miss Fairchild continued. "The groom my housekeeper sent with Leticia's letter and a second missive from herself has returned to town with orders for that good woman to carry on as she has done—but that, with both Leticia and me away, perhaps she might reduce the housemaids by one and the kitchen staff by at least one and . . ."

The door opened. Lord Cartwright entered. Diane instantly lost all interest in the low-voiced conversation across the table from her. She nodded when he smiled at her and gestured at the empty space to her right. He brought his breakfast and seated himself there.

"When you've finished, I will be in the orchard," she said, keeping her voice pitched so only he would hear.

"The conservatory," he suggested equally softly. "I don't like the looks of the weather."

She nodded, rose to her feet, and departed, making her

way there. The seating area on the far side from the door was, as usual at this time of year, unoccupied, and she chose a chaise longue, wondering how long she must wait amid the exotic greenery before Stevie came to her. . . .

Steven saw his father enter the breakfast room. Almost he turned away, thinking he might wait until later to break his fast . . . and then he saw Mrs. Runyard exit. He started to speak but noticed she seemed particularly preoccupied, so, instead, he followed her and watched her enter the conservatory.

Again he hesitated. It appeared to the lad that his idol wanted to be alone. He couldn't quite bring himself to interrupt the reverie into which she'd sunk. Not, he realized, because he didn't wish to interrupt her but that he feared she'd be angry if he did—and he did fear her anger. He didn't want her irritated with him. He wanted to give her everything. Wanted to make her always happy, with nary a worry to bring that little frown he'd seen marring her perfect forehead.

"I know. I will give her time for her cogitations, and then I will go to her and offer my assistance," he said to the portrait of a stern-faced Witherspoon ancestress hanging on the hall wall. He went into the room beside the conservatory and exited onto the terrace by way of a low-silled window. Once outside he found a spot shaded by a large potted plant, and, leaning against the rail just there, half hidden among the greenery, he crossed his arms, crossed one ankle over the other and, feeling quite good about himself, settled in to wait patiently for his goddess to show some sign she'd be ready to receive him.

Not ten minutes later, his goddess looked up, smiling, and held out her hand. Steven pulled away from the railing, straightening.

"*No!*" he said on a breath of air. "Not my father. Anyone but my *father*."

But it was Lord Cartwright who pushed aside the fronds of a tree fern and went to one knee beside the chaise, both his hands reaching for Mrs. Runyard's. The windows to the conservatory were tightly shut and Steven could not hear what was said. But he saw his father bend his head and place a kiss on the long, slender fingers he held so closely.

Steven didn't wait to see more but ran down the length of the terrace to the stairs at the far end. He strode off down the path, mumbling and muttering, angry with his father, angry with himself—but not, of course, at all angry with the poor deluded woman who was allowing herself to be beguiled and besmirched by the man Steven was beginning to hold in utter disgust.

The lad was passing the theater when the door opened. Roger, seeing him, called out. "You are late. We were scheduled for nine, and it is almost nine-twenty." He didn't glance at the watch he held in his hand, obviously having already consulted it. "Come along now. We must practice. That fight on the road to Thebes is an exceedingly difficult scene, as you will discover. Every movement must be just so or it will *look* staged, and it must not or it will spoil the tension, the horror we wish to rouse in the audience's minds. Oedipus, after all, is about to fulfill the prophecy—although *he* does not know it." Roger paused, his irritation growing. "What is the matter with you? Have you heard one word I've said? Now do come in and get to work."

Roger had not only had to wait for Steven, but Cyrall had only just arrived. It was outrageous that no one took the work seriously. They had only a long week—well, almost two—in which to pull the play together before dress rehearsals, and there was still a great deal to do. Roger fumed all the way down the aisle once he was assured that Steven, pouting, followed along behind.

\* \* \*

Back in the conservatory, Lord Cartwright seated himself on the edge of the chaise. He retained his hold of Diane's hand, but now he absently played with her fingers as he listened to her explain about the annuity and her belief he'd arranged it for her.

". . . but if you did *not*, Stevie, then who in the world could have done so?"

He had frowned at her first mention of an annuity. The frown deepened. "But surely you have some notion?"

"None whatsoever." Her fingers tightened around his. "I know you did not believe me when I told you I've had no other lovers, but I have *not*. I can think of no other reason why someone would arrange such a thing for me."

His hand clasped hers in a firm hold. He pursed his lips slightly, thinking. "My dear?"

"Yes?"

"When I first arrived, you mentioned that I had grown to look just like my father. *How do you know*?"

She smiled. "He never told you?"

"Told me what?"

She sighed softly. "He came to the theater." She looked up at him. "A month or so after you were called home to meet your betrothed."

He nodded. "If it was a month later, then we were wed by then."

"He offered me a . . . well, money." Her eyes twinkled. "I rather startled him when I threw it back at him and told him what we had had together could not be bought." She chuckled. "How very young and idealistic I must have been," she said. "I recall stalking off and slamming the door in a highly dramatic fashion, fuming that he should do such a thing, should taint our love that way."

"And when the annuity came?"

She sighed for real this time. "It was a bad time in my life, Stevie. I'd been out of work. A lot of us were out of work just then, the theaters in a bad way for one reason or another. Bad management, I suppose, combined with other problems, but whatever it was, I needed the money. I accepted—but in part because I thought *you* had arranged it." She bit her lip, looking at him a bit anxiously. "So soon after your father died, you see? I need to apologize to you about that. I was angry that you would do such a thing but not come to me to explain. That in fact you insisted it was unnecessary for me to know from whence the money came."

"Yes, I can see why you might find that a trifle insulting." He spoke absently, his free hand pulling gently at his pursed lips as he thought. Finally he straightened and, those lips tightly compressed, nodded. Speaking briskly, he said, "I will write my solicitor, Di. I will ask him to discover for us who has been so generous. You need to know and—" Suddenly his face was lit by a quick, self-deriding grin. "—so do I."

"I am so glad all that is behind us," she said, relaxing now she was certain he believed her.

"So am I."

Their eyes met. Once again that connection tightened between them. This time Diane was almost certain she did understand what he was trying to say—and found she had no answer for him. She was drawn to him. She wanted him as she had always wanted to be close to him, but she was no longer an innocent. Her body did not rule her.

"Stevie . . ."

He nodded. "I understand. You need to be cautious, need to be sure. . . ."

"So do you." She rushed on, once again wanting him to understand. "We are not the same people. We have changed. The both of us. You cannot know if you will even like me as I am now. And . . ."

And she could not say that she had to be certain she still

liked him as well as loved him. His lack of understanding of his son bothered her a great deal, his lack of sympathy and inability to relate to the boy. She sighed, her hand tightening again around his fingers.

Neither spoke for a long time, each lost in thoughts they were not ready to share—and that too gave Diane pause. Before, when first together, they had been able to say anything to each other, whatever came into their heads. Now she, at least, was far more cautious, far less willing to reveal concerns and definitely unwilling to fall into bed with him until she was certain she understood exactly what was between them.

Lord Cartwright squeezed her hand. "The hour grows late, Di. I believe I am scheduled at the theater to practice with Cyrall for the stage fight between Laius and Oedipus. I must go change into something that will allow me more freedom than this coat." He grinned suddenly. "Di, you remember Franklin, do you not?"

Diane wrinkled her nose. *That was his valet's name*, she thought. "Supercilious monkey."

Cartwright chuckled. "Now you say it, I see how you might feel that way. He discovered the other day that *you* are here. He's been watching me like a hawk ever since."

Diane frowned. "I sometimes wondered if he were not reporting to your father. I know it is a terrible thing to suggest, but he was so *very* pleased when you were called home."

Cartwright considered. "It is, I suppose, possible. Father found him for me before I went off on a rather attenuated grand tour right after I came down from my college and before I met you. I suppose he, as well as the bear leader chosen to guide my steps, was charged with seeing I did nothing foolish while on my travels. Perhaps he continued in that role even after we came home."

"And now?"

He chuckled. "You think he may still be keeping his eye

on me for my father's sake? Unlikely. My father has been in the family crypt for a dozen years."

"Old habits die hard, and he never liked me."

"Nonsense. What business did he have liking or not liking you? He's my valet, not my nanny."

Diane didn't persist, but she didn't change her mind either. "If you are due at the theater, Stevie, you had better go. Roger is at that stage where he is beginning to worry that the play will never come together. Not too many days now and it will be time for the dress rehearsals."

"Rehearsals? Plural?"

"We have found with amateurs it is necessary. The first will be for the cast. The second, a performance for Lord Witherspoon's servants and tenants, will not be called a rehearsal, of course. The third performance will be the real one. The whole of the countryside will undoubtedly arrive that night for a gala party and what Lord Witherspoon will consider the first-ever performance in his brand-new theater. It is rumored that his neighbors have invited houseguests who will swell the audience. Lord Witherspoon's mood will be exulted, will it not?"

His lordship's eyes widened, and then he grimaced. "I wonder why I agreed to take a part. I admit I had not, previous to this moment, thought of the actual *performance*."

"You will do very well." She frowned. "Oh, dear. I wonder if your son has thought of it."

Cartwright tipped his head a trifle to one side. "You are worried he'll be unable to go on? Be too frightened?"

She nodded. "Poor Steven. He is at that particularly odd age when one is neither a child nor an adult and life is so very difficult."

Cartwright frowned. "It is strange."

When he didn't continue but frowned down at where his foot rested on the rim of an oversized potted plant, she asked what he meant.

Her words drew his inward-turned attention back to her. "When I think about it, I see I never had an opportunity to get to know the boy."

Diane's gaze sharpened. "What can you mean?"

Cartwright shrugged, resettling a coat that seemed suddenly overly tight. "I was not allowed to, really. My wife . . . she . . ." He frowned. "Well, once the boy was born . . . umm, she seemed to think he was hers alone. Or something of the sort," he finished rather inadequately.

Diane studied him, her gaze steady and serious.

"What is it?" he asked.

"Stevie," she said slowly, "when you first met her, when the two of you agreed to wed, you didn't . . . you surely weren't so cruel . . ."

He released her hand and straightened. His mouth tightened. "That I mentioned you? No, of course not. On the other hand, we had never before met. We could make no pretense of being in love. And we didn't."

"She didn't fall in love with you? After the wedding?" asked Diane, thinking that it had been a very easy thing for her to do.

He frowned. "I shouldn't think so. . . ."

"A woman needs love," said Diane quietly.

"You would suggest she found that love in our son and, selfishly, kept it for herself alone?"

"Selfish? Perhaps. Or perhaps just very needy."

"Di, I was banished from her room once she found she was enceinte. I was not invited back and never found the courage to return to it." With that blunt confession, he turned away and didn't see the hand she held out to him in sympathy.

*Never found the courage . . . which means, I suppose, that his wife had not previously welcomed his attentions.* Diane shook her head. *Life is,* she thought, *so very complicated— and occasionally exceedingly uncomfortable.*

# CHAPTER
# TEN

Cyrall dropped the point of his sword and grinned at Lord Cartwright, who wore a sheen of sweat. The two had removed their coats before beginning their practice and now turned, as one, to look at Roger. Roger's lips were pursed and a faint frown creased his brow.

"Well?" asked Lord Cartwright. To his mind, the practice had gone very well and he couldn't understand their director's expression.

"Well done indeed," said Cyrall in a congratulatory tone. "You are a swordsman, my lord. I am glad of the exercise."

"Yes. Very well done," said Roger, slowly. "And just as we planned. Each move just as it should be—except for one thing. You, Sir Cyrall, were forgetting that you are not so practiced as his lordship. Or I should say that Oedipus is not so well practiced as Laius. You needed a touch of awkwardness, a bit of hesitation, and I did not see it.

"In other words, openings that Laius would have used to rid himself of such an impertinent upstart?" asked Cyrall with such a pretense of innocence that Lord Cartwright snorted.

Roger smiled a quickly disappearing smile. "Hmmm," he

mused, and rubbed his chin, thinking. He nodded. "I see the problem. I wonder if perhaps Laius limps." He looked toward Lord Cartwright. "Could you maintain a proper limp for the length of your appearances on stage?"

"I'd not need it in the earliest scene when the child is sent away. . . ."

"To the contrary. You must then as well, because if you did not, its appearance in this scene would surprise the audience. It must be from the beginning."

"Then Laius never was a great fighter?"

"Very likely not. Nevertheless, Laius would have had a great deal more experience than Oedipus and would have fought life-and-death battles in the past, whereas Oedipus is unlikely to have done more than fought mock-battles against his trainer."

Cyrall listened to each and then nodded. "I doubt that Steven has ever before held a blade. From what I saw, training him, the boy has no sense of the duello but did say he enjoyed it. I suggested, that when he goes to London, he arrange for lessons. There are still one or two reasonably good teachers of swordsmanship there." He glanced at Lord Cartwright. "*Now* I wonder if *you* might not teach him. You are out of practice, my lord, but it is obvious that, at one time, you were excellent."

Cartwright felt his ears heat. "It has been a long time since I last held a blade. As to teaching Steven—" His mouth compressed as he regretted their awkward relationship. "—we shall have to see."

Diane, coming down the aisle just then, heard the last part of the exchange and realized both her Stevie's reluctance *and* what an excellent notion it would be. But he was also correct in his unspoken belief that other problems had priority and must be solved before such a thing was attempted.

"Miss Fairchild asked to be excused from this afternoon's practice. I will take her place."

Roger grumbled, but, as Diane promptly reminded him, Eustacia was pretty much letter perfect in her part and therefore didn't really need the practice. Roger objected that other actors in those scenes were *not* and reminded *her* that actors did better when working with the person who should be opposite them.

He sighed, a scowl deepening the lines already marring his forehead.

Diane touched his arm. "You must keep in mind that this is an *amateur* group," she scolded. "You cannot expect nor can you demand the dedication required of professionals."

He sighed again, the lines not lessening a jot.

"Don't worry so much," she said. "They will do surprisingly well when it comes to it. Miss Fairchild had another request, one that surprised me very much. Roger, do we know what the next play will be?"

He cast her a look of bewilderment. "Sheridan's *School for Scandal* has been suggested, or perhaps one of Shakespeare's comedies."

She chuckled at his expression. "You cannot think why I wish to know. George Allingham would like a part."

All three men gaped at her.

"I am told that when he plays a part, he does not stutter, and he would enjoy that freedom from his disability. I want you to decide on a part for him and tell him, so he can begin learning it in advance and not have to stutter his way through a trial, reading it cold."

Roger blinked. Then he waved the problem away. "I cannot even begin to think of that now. Oh, go away. All of you. I must consult with the women sewing costumes." He stalked off toward the side door from where he could easily reach the building Lord Witherspoon had had erected for the construction and storage of sets, including as well a large, airy, well-lit room for the use of the wardrobe mistress and her sewing girls.

Sir Cyrall jumped from the stage and, grabbing his coat from where he had laid it earlier, disappeared out the front door while Lord Cartwright, more staidly, came down the stairs and approached Diane.

"I need to cool down after all that. The sky cleared, so we needn't fear it will rain. Do you care for a stroll in the orchard?"

As he spoke, he struggled into his own coat—one not quite so tight as that he'd worn earlier but still not easily donned. Diane helped and smoothed the wrinkles from the back. He looked over his shoulder and their gazes met. He smiled. Tentatively, she smiled back. Then she nodded. She shouldn't. She knew she shouldn't, but she wanted so badly to be with him, to learn more of who he had become, to discover whether the love she felt for him was for *him* or only for the young man he'd once been.

"If only Steven were not . . ."

He laughed lightly when she didn't continue. "If he were not complicating something which is already complicated enough?" he asked softly.

"Something of the sort. He is so very unhappy, Stevie. I wish . . ."

"You wish you could wave a magic wand and solve all the problems a youth faces when leaving behind the artificial world of his childhood and education and entering the real world where he must make a place for himself."

"You *do* understand." She cast him a grateful glance as they left the theater and was startled when he shook his head. "You do not?" she asked.

He glanced at her, a puzzled frown indicating confusion.

"You shook your head. You do not understand what he is feeling?"

He relaxed. "I understand, I think. What I do not know is what, if anything, should be done about it."

"Could you at least discuss his mother with him?" she

asked, speaking rather hesitantly after a moment's silence. She stared at the gate to the orchard.

He pushed it open. "If he could be at all rational, had enough maturity to understand there are other ways of feeling about things . . ." He glanced at her and saw that she was frowning. "Di, I fear that any attempt I made to discuss his mother with him would only result in further harm. I would have to tell him that I had felt excluded by her from ever getting to know him, for instance. Can you see him accepting that it was her fault he and I were never alone together? Never together much at all—even with her hovering nearby?"

"You lie!" Young Steven jumped down off the branch where they had not seen him sitting. "You *lie*. You never had time for me. You were always so busy. You—"

"Is that what she told you?" asked Cartwright.

"It is the truth. *She* would not lie to me."

Cartwright tipped his head slightly. "Steven, do you recall a summer day when I wanted to take you fishing but your mother insisted you could not possibly leave your studies? I think you and she had been making daisy chains at the time. I also recall a day after you had begun to ride really well when I wanted to take you around the home farms, introduce you to our tenants. She insisted it would be far too tiring for you to do any such thing—and then took you off for a round of visits with her friends."

Steven's eyes widened. He bit his lip. "No . . . she *wouldn't*. She *loved* me." He turned and raced away.

"Do you see?" asked his lordship, staring sadly after his son.

"What I see is that you have made him think. He will not like it, but it is necessary for him to come to a more realistic notion of his growing-up years than that he now embraces." She grasped his arm and squeezed it. "You did not handle that badly. None of this will be *easy*, Stevie, but I think it must be done."

He nodded, still staring toward where his son had disappeared. Then he looked down at Diane and gestured onward. She nodded and they walked on. Silently.

"Something has you pretty well twisted into a bow knot, has it not?" said Sir Cyrall in a dry but not unsympathetic tone as Steven crashed through a hedge and into the formerly silent bower in which Cyrall, once again enjoying the sun, lolled.

Steven looked about wildly.

"Oh, do relax. Come seat yourself here where it is warm and allow all that heat within you be gentled by that from the sun."

"You don't understand."

"And I won't if you will not explain," said Cyrall, feeling as if they had had this conversation more than once.

"He said my mother . . . He said she . . ."

"What did he say?"

"She *didn't* lie. She *loved* me. She wouldn't lie. Not to *me*." Steven cast a pleading look toward Cyrall.

"I doubt very much that your father suggested your mother lied to you."

Steven blinked. "He did. He said he wasn't too busy for me. He said he did want to do things with me. He said—"

"He is your father. I doubt very much that he did not wish to have you at his side—at least occasionally. Not every day and not every minute but often enough you might have grown to be friends."

"No. She said . . ." Steven's voice faded and then returned more strongly. "She *loved* me. I know she did."

"And always wanted you at her side?"

"Of course."

"Always?"

Steven blinked. "Well, not when I was with my tutor. Or when I was preparing for bed. Or—"

"Or when *she* was preparing to go out to a party, or when she went off to London and left you in the nursery, or—"

Steven threw his palms up over his ears. "I won't listen. She loved me."

"*Yes*. She loved you." Before Steven could relax, Cyrall continued. "She *loved* you, but love takes many forms, Steven. Sometimes it is selfish." Cyrall rose to his feet and looked at the youth facing him. The lad's features were wreathed in confusion. Cyrall sighed, wondered if there was something else he might say, decided there was not, and added, "Come along now. One must feed the inner man as well as the emotions, so let us go ask for a tray."

"I'm not hungry!"

Once again Steven ran off, racing away, trying very hard to run from the chaotic emotions inside him and not yet old enough to know that one carried them with one. His nervously erratic rambling brought him to the stable.

"Champion," he muttered. "I have not checked on Champion since I arrived. *Not once.*"

His favorite hunter, and he had forgotten to check on the gelding's welfare. Feeling guilty—which was bad, but better than the other emotions he'd been experiencing—Steven entered the dim, cool building and found the stall in which his horse was stabled.

"Goo'day, young sir," said a gruff voice. "Needin' a horse, are you?"

"What?" Steven turned from where he was fondling Champion's nose. "Ah. You are the head groom, are you not?"

"'Enry Farmer. At your service, young sir."

Steven had had quite enough of being called young but managed to ignore it. Instead, he asked, "Has Champ been exercised today?"

"Ah. 'Tis *your* horse, then? Now then, *'course* I remember," said the groom, nodding his head. "Champ," he repeated. "Had him out early this morning. We give all the horses a bit of a run early on, you know. While it is cool. Don't think he was ridden, though." The man frowned and lifted his cap to scratch his head. "Think we had your Champion on a lead this morning."

"I'll take him out," said Steven, impulsively.

"Very well, young sir." The groom motioned to a lad, who ran to the tack room. "Now, let's have the brute out," said the older man, opening the stall. "There you be, you great beast, you. Now, now," he said tolerantly, as Champion tossed his head, "you be wanting a good run, don't you, you fine, big boy, you." The man jumped to reach the halter as Champion rose onto his hind feet. "Come along now," crooned the groom. "You just come along now, you old softie. None of this nonsense. . . ."

Steven grinned. "*Champion*. Behave yourself."

The horse instantly settled and walked out into the alley, the groom still holding onto the halter. The horse nuzzled Steven's shoulder, whoofed, then nuzzled where a pocket would be hidden in the lad's trousers.

Steven shook his head. "Don't have anything for you, Champ. I would have, but I didn't think about coming out here today. Sorry." Steven rubbed the animal, scratching up around the ears the way Champ liked, and the horse obligingly lowered his neck. Steven laughed, delighted, and the groom nodded his approbation. "Oh, yes," crowed Steven, "you surely are a champion."

"You raced 'im?" asked the stable boy, a lad very little younger than Steven. He was laden with saddle, bridle, and blanket.

"Only against friends. You know."

The two talked about Champion while the head groom tacked him up. Mounting, Steven allowed a bit of cavorting, showing off really, before settling his mount and leaving the stable yard.

It was all of half an hour later before he recalled how very unhappy he was, how confused, and, pulling Champion to a walk, he wandered on, morose, paying no attention to his whereabouts . . . and eventually felt more than a trifle hungry since he'd missed his breakfast and it was a long time past lunch.

He glanced around, wondering where he was. Projecting up over the next hill was a church spire. Where there was a church, very likely there'd be an inn. He could get himself something—but then he recalled he'd left his purse on his dressing table. He hadn't any money. He looked at the ring on his finger, a small seal with an initial that his mother had given him.

*Mother. Was her love a selfish love as Sir Cyrall said?*

A dozen different scenes raced through his head, times when his father had approached them, and his mother, one way or another, turned him away. Revulsion filled him, and he wrenched off the ring. He was about to throw it away when his stomach growled. He glanced at the spire.

Satisfaction filled him. He did have the means of a meal!

He was all the way back to the Witherspoon estate before he realized he'd given away his mother's gift. With a touch of panic, he left Champion with the groom, hurried into the house, retrieved his purse, and returned to the stable, where, after a word with the head groom, he hunted up the stable lad. Obligingly, the boy tacked up an elderly horse, accepted some coins and the note Steven hastily scribbled, and rode off to retrieve the ring.

Steven hoped very much the woman who had fed him would make the exchange. He sighed, wondering why he had been so foolish. Then he recalled the reason he'd been so upset, so angry, so irrational.

Surely his mother had loved him. Had she not told him

often that she did? Had she not spent the whole of her life assuring his was full of joy and interest? Offering new books, taking him places, watching while he learned to read, to ride, to do all sorts of things—praising him for his successes, commiserating when things went wrong?

She had done all of that. But was it not possible she had also made it difficult, perhaps impossible, for his father to do any of those things?

That evening, at dinner, Steven cast the occasional curious glance toward his father. For once, neither of them was seated anywhere near Mrs. Runyard, so Steven's jealousy did not come in the way of his observations. He saw those around his sire laugh at something said to them. Since they all glanced toward Sir Cyrall, Steven did not instantly fear they had laughed at him. He could see that others enjoyed his father's company . . . so why had his mother avoided it?

And she had, had she not?

He remembered times when, suddenly, for no particular reason, she had interrupted what they were doing and gone elsewhere with him in tow. He recalled that, once or twice, he'd seen his father approaching.

Steven frowned at his plate, stirring the new peas into the dark gravy, dividing them into sections, pushing them together . . . until a servant cleared his throat and he realized the man wanted to take away the messy plate. Steven felt his ears heat, looked around, and breathed again when it appeared no one noticed his distraction.

It would be the last straw if someone were to inquire why he had no appetite. It might not be so awful if he could tell even himself exactly what it was that upset him so, but he could not. He sighed.

Diane, across the table and down a bit, watched Steven from under her lashes, her attention seemingly on Lord Benningcorn's rambling monologue. It wasn't difficult to keep an eye on the lad and still keep track of what his lordship said. She wondered what Steven was thinking, why he was so preoccupied that, given his normal healthy appetite, he seemed unable to eat.

Sir Cyrall, down the table from Diane, also managed to note Steven's preoccupation. He sighed softly, fearing his comments that afternoon had done damage rather than helped, and decided that once supper was over he had better corner Lord Cartwright and tell him what had happened. Once again Sir Cyrall swore, silently, that he would avoid sticking his nose into other people's problems.

And once again Cyrall laughed at himself. He knew very well he was fated to wander unthinkingly into places angels feared to go. It was part of his character that he was forever seeing a situation, a misunderstanding, a dish of emotional pottage that called out for a thoughtful hand to season it properly and bring it to perfection. And, as usual, whenever he noticed such a situation, he would stir the pot, add the salt, put in an herb here, a spice there, and do his best to come up with a recipe that would solve whatever problem he perceived.

He finished his beetroot—which needed just a touch more cider vinegar—and nodded when the footman offered another portion of the pork roast. He also agreed to a small serving of the applesauce and discovered the Witherspoon chef had no more of a hand for that than he'd had for the beetroot. Sir Cyrall suppressed a desire to sigh. He did like good food. It was the one area where he was not only expert but found nothing but pleasure in the indulgence of his palate.

Sir Cyrall intercepted another of those quick glances that Steven threw toward his father. This one, unlike earlier occasions, seemed to be of curiosity rather than animosity. *Poor lad*, Cyrall commiserated silently. *You are just discovering what hell it is for most of us to grow up.*

Cyrall renewed his vow to have a little talk with the boy's sire.

* * *

As soon as Lord Witherspoon released the men to join the women in the salon, Lord Morningside approached Miss Fairchild. "I have had a thought, Euphrasia"—he frowned and grasped her arm—"and just this once you will listen without walking off in a huff."

She glared at him, at his hand on her arm, and back up at him. "Release me."

"I will release you if you promise to hear me out." When she appeared to be pondering this, his hand tightened nearly imperceptibly, but a smile played around his lips. "So difficult to decide, my dear?"

She smiled ruefully. "You know I hate it when you call me that. It is *not* my name."

"I have told you before, it is the name you should have been given. I merely correct your father's misjudgment. I have thought of a possible new companion," he added quickly, before she could make the scathing comment he could see hovering on her tongue.

That startled Eustacia from her irritation. "Who?"

"Do you remember my aunt Cilly?"

"Silly Cilly?"

"That name came from my mother's dislike of her sister-in-law. Cilly is not at all silly, as I recently discovered. I went to straighten out her affairs after my unspeakable uncle died. It seems that, from the first, she perceived he was a wastrel. She feared he would go through his considerable fortune long before he died, leaving her destitute, which he might have done if he'd been a gambler as well as a spendthrift. As it was, he came near enough to it. Anyway, since spending money hand over fist was something of a compulsion, she convinced him she loved jewelry, and he gifted her with a great deal of it. Also, in a truly miserly fashion, she collected all coins that came her way. Over the years his gifts and her coins have added up to a fair amount. So, although my uncle managed to bring a nice fortune pretty much to nothing, she has saved enough that she will live comfortably but with little in the way of elegance. If you were to hire her as your companion, she could also have the elegance—your home in which to live, for instance."

"But . . ."

He nodded. "Yes, of course, you should meet first, but I think you would like each other. My mother thought her frivolous—her love of jewelry and bibelots, you see. But that seeming frivolity was because of her fear of eventual poverty and her rather ingenious solution for averting it. Shall I arrange a meeting when we leave here? She is living in a village not far north of Cambridge on the London road."

"I will think about it." Then Eustacia cast her old friend and sometimes enemy a thoughtful glance. "Did you know how truly difficult life would be for me after my cousin died?"

"I guessed," he responded quietly. "But you were so determined. . . ."

"Determined to find a life of my own, a life that had not been organized by someone else into a form into which I did not fit."

The lines at the corners of his eyes deepened. "Or perhaps the old life was only a trifle uncomfortable, and then only off and on?"

She sighed. "I suppose I must have imbibed more of my cousin's interests than I knew, more of his dilettantish attitudes, his curiosity about this and that and the other. And his impatience with tonnish shibboleths, to say nothing of his lack of interest in the proprieties! A spinster is considered exceedingly odd if she has interests beyond gossip or the latest fashion or is not properly modest and retiring, is she not?"

"Poor puss. Is it so very bad?"

Eustacia tipped her head. "Not altogether," she said but didn't explain. Instead, she pointed out that Lord Cartwright was glaring daggers at Sir Cyrall, who looked determined if embarrassed. "What is going on between those two?"

Rafe thought of demanding further explanation but knew his Euphrasia. She was done with confiding and very likely ruing that she had said so much. He cast a glance toward the two men, who had retreated to a deep bay window for a bit of privacy. "I cannot think what it could be."

Rafe turned back to Eustacia. He knew she would now look for a way of abandoning him, of running away from further talk, since she feared his ability to tease her into saying more than she wished. He decided that, for once, it would be he who cut short their communication.

"I think," said Rafe, musingly, "that I will just go make certain that doesn't escalate into an argument. Excuse me." He cast her a grin filled with irony. "And thank you for pointing out the situation."

It then occurred to him that she had done so in order to get him away from her, that she had expected him to do just as he did—go to Sir Cyrall's rescue. In other words, she had, once again, managed to terminate their conversation just when it was getting interesting. Rafe decided that, at some point, he had to make it impossible for her to escape him. It was more than time that something was settled between them.

She'd had her months of freedom. She had discovered life as a spinster was far more complicated than she'd ever dreamed, more restricted than she found bearable. Surely the time had come to offer for her hand.

But that was for later.

Right now it was necessary to discover exactly what was going on between his old friend and Lord Cartwright.

". . . so I apologize," said Sir Cyrall, speaking hurriedly and before his lordship could actually explode. "I fear what I

meant to be a help, bringing the boy to think seriously of
what *was,* rather than what he *thought* was, might help him
to see you as something other than a villain."

"Villain."

Lord Cartwright spoke the word with such a chill in his
tone that Rafe was glad he'd arrived when he did. He immediately drew his lordship's fire. "Is that not how your son
sees you? I suppose because of the way your wife felt about
you and passed on to him?"

Cartwright struggled with roiling emotions that he hoped
were well hidden. "I have no notion what you think you
know or what you think was the case between my wife and
myself. She had no reason to fear me. She could not possibly
have thought me a *villain* or have said as much to our son."

"She would not have had to, would she?" asked Sir
Cyrall, again speaking in that rapid, get-it-all-out style. "All
she need do is make him think you wanted nothing to do
with either of them, make it impossible for you to have anything to do with either of them, and then never explain a
thing to him."

The need to explode within Cartwright grew. That there
was a great deal of truth in Sir Cyrall's comment made it no
easier to swallow. That he had allowed his wife to separate
him from his son was something he had only recently come
to realize—and to rue. It was intolerable that anyone touched
that wound before it had time to form a scar. Cartwright
looked across the room to where his son stood looking rather
disconsolate. His lips compressed.

*What the devil am I to do about the boy?*

He considered that for a moment but realized Lord
Morningside was speaking. He brought his attention back to
the two men confronting him.

"He is a nice lad, but he needs direction. I wonder if you
have thought to bring him into the management of your es-

tates now he has left school? He is at that point in his life where it will be very easy for him to fall in with bad companions—"

Cartwright remembered old gossip concerning Morningside.

"—as happened to me at that age," finished Rafe, confirming Cartwright's memory. "It is something that becomes very difficult to live down when one comes to one's senses, assuming one survives to the point one comes to one's senses. Before disaster strikes, I mean."

"What brought you to your senses?" asked Cartwright bluntly.

"The help of a good man. One who saw where I was headed and turned me around a corner," said Rafe promptly. "Miss Fairchild's cousin, actually."

Cartwright's eyes widened and a snort of disbelief escaped him. Miss Fairchild's late cousin had been a well-known eccentric, an oddity in the ton, and not someone one thought of as a guide, going to the aid of a youth whose steps had wandered off the straight and narrow path.

Rafe's most sardonic look appeared. "You find that difficult to believe, do you not?" One brow arched queryingly. "It started when I made a rather wild comment in his hearing, one that led him to assume I knew more than I did. His assumption, and his treatment of me as someone worth speaking to, made me want him to continue to believe it. That, of course, led to a great deal of time away from my old companions—studying, you know—and threw me in with a number of new ones cut from a far different bolt of cloth."

"I see," said Cartwright. He glanced again at his son. "Or perhaps I see."

"It is possible," said Rafe, gently, "that the boy's experience on stage this summer will lead to just such an epiphany and put his steps on the road to maturity."

Cartwright cast a rather appalled glance toward their host. "I do not like to think of Steven wishing to emulate Witherspoon."

Both Cyrall and Rafe chuckled, and Cartwright added a wry smile. The three relaxed when, thinking it was time to ease things, Rafe asked how the fight scene was shaping. Cartwright was glad of the change of subject to one about which he could feel some enthusiasm. Talk drifted from the play to politics and back to the play—where it ended as the supper trays were brought in and another day was about to end.

# CHAPTER
# ELEVEN

Diane rose feeling ambivalent about the watery light coming in the windows the maid uncovered. She leaned forward for the pillows, accepted the tea, but never stopped staring at the drops collecting and running down the panes. She wondered what was in her wardrobe that would not be ruined by the wet as she went back and forth to the theater.

*How foolish to leave behind all my workaday gowns, wanting to look only my best.*

The old saw about pride going before a fall ran through her mind, and she smiled a rather wry smile.

"Tea no good?" asked the maid hesitantly. "Should I get you hot chocolate?"

Diane looked down and realized she held the cup and saucer without really being aware of it. "No, no, this is fine. I was just trying to decide what to wear that I wouldn't mind getting wet."

"Mr. Jenkins dug out a whole big pile of waxed parasols. The footmen are to walk you women back and forth. You won't get wet."

"But the footmen? Won't they get wet?"

The maid grinned. "Broom, a particular friend of mine," she confided, "was complaining that his new uniform would be ruined. He was told to wear his old one, which didn't please him at all 'cause he's growed and it don't fit right."

"But he won't ruin the good one, so he shouldn't worry. And I'll not worry either. Still—" Diane tipped her head and considered. "—the green, I think. The skirt is narrow and just a trifle shorter than the others."

The maid drew it from the armoire, held it up, and tut-tutted. "Creased, that is. I'll just go give it a bit of a press."

She was out the door before Diane could stop her, and now Diane had a new worry. From the beginning, the girl had been helpful, acting as if the actress were a guest the same as any of the tonnish guests. A rather large vail would be appropriate for the girl. But if she gave the girl what she deserved, then, traditionally, pourboires to the other servants should be in proportion, and frankly, Diane was not particularly interested in leaving anything at all for one supercilious footman who was forever looking down his nose at her or another who, she suspected, had actually given her misinformation concerning the location of the billiards room, sending her to get lost in the far wing. Worse, the butler and housekeeper would expect still more. . . .

Diane grinned to herself as a solution occurred to her. She wasn't of the ton. She needn't pretend she was. She simply wouldn't let anyone know she knew anything about proper tipping. The maid would get what she deserved. The rest would go begging. Diane, feeling much better, tossed back the covers and was washed and in a clean shift before the maid returned with her gown.

The morose feeling returned as she took a last look at the rain before she went down to the breakfast room. She was rather surprised to find no one there but herself and was about to ask if she were late when she noticed the food was barely touched. She was early.

*Now why*, she wondered, *did I wake so early*?

She wasn't allowed to think about it. Lord Witherspoon bustled in, rubbing his hands together, delighted to have found her there. "Good day, good day," he said, beaming. "Delightful. Never seem to have a moment with you, Mrs. Runyard." He seated himself, gestured to the footman to bring his breakfast and, still beaming delightedly, asked how his dear Mrs. Runyard thought the rehearsals were coming along.

"And do be frank," he finished earnestly. "I truly wish to know. You see, I can always send messages, postponing our opening if you think it necessary." His round, rosy features, to the degree they could, grew rather glum. "Mr. Brown seems to feel—"

"Mr. Brown," interrupted Diane, "is convinced that the play cannot possibly be ready in time, that it is the most awful play he has ever put on, that the actors are terrible and the scenery worse, and the wardrobe lady hasn't a single proper notion for costumes and doesn't understand at all what is needed." Her brows arched. "Am I correct so far?"

Partway through her string of disasters, Lord Witherspoon's eyes had begun to bulge. At her final question, he relaxed, grinning. "You would say," he asked, just to be certain he understood her, "that he always feels this way at this point in a production?"

"Always. Total disaster. Nothing works. It is all wrong." She smiled. "And then in a few days, suddenly all is well. You will see."

"Then I need not postpone . . . ?"

"I wouldn't. I have never known a play that didn't fall together at the last moment—usually just when Roger has nearly convinced himself he should jump off Tower Bridge and be done with it."

Lord Cartwright arriving just then, chuckled. "I suppose it is good to know that his ranting brings results."

"Has he been ranting?"

"He had several of us off in a corner last night after the ladies went to bed, scolding and cajoling and acting as if he thought the world about to end."

"*His* world. Do keep in mind that the theater *is* his whole world."

Lord Witherspoon finished eating and, with excuses, bustled off, leaving the two together.

"Is it your whole world, Di?" asked Cartwright once they were alone, the footman off getting his lordship a fresh pot of tea.

She looked up and found him staring at her so seriously she froze. "The theater? The whole of it?"

"Have you room in it for—"

The door opened, and the footman followed Miss Fairchild into the room.

"—another bowl of fruit, my dear?" he asked smoothly, changing from what, impulsively, he'd been about to ask of her.

Actually, when he realized what he'd about done, he was rather thankful he'd been stopped. He wasn't ready to suggest any sort of new relationship. They hadn't yet had time to come to terms with the changes each found in the other, and it was far too soon to be thinking of . . .

Cartwright's mouth dropped open at the word that slipped into his mind. He shook his head slightly. *What in Hades am I thinking?*

Diane was speaking to Miss Fairchild but glanced at his lordship when, suddenly, he pushed back from the table and, leaving his breakfast uneaten, departed without a word.

"Well, that was unusually rude of his lordship," said Miss Fairchild, casting a surprised glance at the door. "I had not thought him the moody sort who ignored polite conventions."

"I don't believe he is," said Diane slowly. "It appeared to

me that some thought crossed his mind that rather shocked him. I wonder what it could have been."

"Or perhaps he bit down on something that slid between his teeth," suggested Miss Fairchild. "I had that happen once. Most uncomfortable. I see by the schedule that I am not needed today. I do wish the weather would improve. I might ride into the village if it did. Do you ride, Mrs. Runyard?"

"I haven't had the opportunity to learn," said Diane politely.

"I enjoy it when in the country but dislike it in town, where there is such traffic and, in the park, the restrictions on what one may or may not do are so very irksome. But—" She cast another glance toward the window. "—I fear the rain will keep me home today. It looks very much as if it has settled in for hours of misery."

Diane didn't respond but finished her tea, shook her head at the footman who offered more, and rose to her feet. "I had best find one of the footmen ordered to hold umbrellas over us and get myself to the theater. Everyone is telling me that Mr. Brown is behaving in an impossible fashion, and I must be there to see that neither he nor one of our cast explodes." She nodded good-bye and left just as Steven arrived.

He tried to get her to return to the breakfast room, but she repeated what she had said to Miss Fairchild and continued on her way, so Steven was staring at his plate of food when his father returned.

Lord Cartwright hesitated and then entered. Choosing a second breakfast, one he meant to eat this time, he reseated himself. "Good morning, Steven," he said.

Steven looked up. "Good morning . . . , sir."

Cartwright smiled a wry smile. "I wonder. Have you ever in all your life called me 'Father'? I cannot recall it."

Steven colored. "Probably not. But then, you weren't much of one, were you?" The belligerency faded instantly. "I mean,"

he added hurriedly, "Mother very likely made it impossible
for you to . . . ?"

That last was more than half a question, and Cartwright
picked up his tea, holding the cup with both hands. "She
made it difficult, yes. But I am very much afraid I did not
persist as I should have done. I might, for instance, have
come to your nursery occasionally when she was not there
and asked to hear your lessons. I did not. I am sorry, Steven.
I should have insisted I had time with you." He thought of
the temper tantrums whenever he'd tried to discuss the problem with his wife. Temper would turn to hysteria if he per-
sisted. He sighed. "I should have, but I did not."

"Oh. Well. That's all right." Steven looked terribly embarrassed and picked up a piece of toast. Gobbling it down, he
followed it with a gulp of tea.

"Water under the bridge, you would say?" asked his father dryly, eying his son's obvious embarrassment. "It wasn't
all right, Steven. It was failure on my part that I could not
bring myself to interfere in your mother's . . . decisions."

"You didn't love her, did you?" Again the belligerency
was apparent.

Cartwright sighed, glanced at the footman, at the door,
and sighed again. "If we are to discuss this, shall we go elsewhere?"

Once again he abandoned his breakfast. Steven, remembering that too often recently he had gone hungry, picked up
the rest of his toast and an apple and carried them along.
They found a small room looking out onto the terrace, and
Lord Cartwright gestured toward a chair. Steven took it—
and then rose to his feet when his father continued to stand.

"You asked if I loved your mother." Cartwright stared out
the window. "I am going to be honest with you, Steven. You
aren't going to like it, but please listen to what I have to say
before you become too angry to hear me."

Steven nodded, his lips compressed but a worried look in his eyes.

"I had never met your mother when I was introduced to her as my future bride. The banns were called immediately, and less than a month later we were married. We didn't know each other. Your mother had romantic notions of what a husband should be. I was too young to pretend to be that sort of man." Cartwright's lips compressed. "I was very likely at fault. I very likely handled her badly. But I could not pretend to love her when I didn't even know her."

"All she wanted was love."

"She wanted *all* my love and *all* my attention, every moment of it. She thought . . . I don't know what she thought, but I felt stifled, chained, all my freedom at an end."

"So why did you agree to the wedding?" asked Steven.

"I didn't know I had a choice." Cartwright thought about that. "I don't think I did, actually. Our fathers had signed contracts. They made plans. We were expected to fall into them and live happily ever after, I suppose."

Steven looked rather appalled. "You mean *you* could make *me* marry someone . . . just anyone . . . whenever you decide to?"

Cartwright threw a sardonic look toward his son. "After my own experience? I think not. I would—I *will* do my best to see you do not make a misalliance, but I would never force you to wed against your inclinations."

Steven relaxed. "She loved me."

"Yes. She loved you. In her way, she was an excellent mother. And despite her unhappiness when you left for school, she did not argue that you should not go. Boys, after all, go to school, so you must as well. She did not turn you into a child utterly dependent on his mother, as she might have done, even though I think it was not easy for her to allow you to learn dangerous things, such as riding and jumping, or, another instance, going out with a gun and learning to hunt."

As unperceptive as he was in the self-centeredness of youth, Steven heard and understood the regret in that. "You wish you could have taught me to ride? To hunt?"

Cartwright nodded. "As I had wished to teach you to fish. You *do* remember that day when she forbade us to go fishing?"

Steven sighed. He looked at the toast in his hand, felt revulsion at the thought of food, and threw it into the grate. "I don't understand. None of it. I wish you hadn't hated each other."

"I cannot tell you how your mother felt, but I didn't hate her. I respected her ability to manage our homes. I admired her for letting you grow up as a man, even if she would not allow me a role in that. I even felt some affection for her." Steven looked up, eagerly. "But not love. Not as I think of love."

Steven slumped. "You loved Mrs. Runyard." He cast a quick glance at his father.

"We were very much in love, Steven," said his father quietly. "The message came that I was to return home to meet my future bride—and it about killed me."

"So you kept her as your mistress." A pugnacious look took up residence on Steven's young features.

"No. I couldn't. I was too idealistic. Even if I could have, she would not have allowed it. She too was idealistic."

Steven's eyes widened. "But she is an *actress*."

"You think an actress can only live an immoral existence? She was and *is* a woman, Steven, before anything else," said his father, speaking in an even tone that brooked no argument. "She is a good woman."

Steven looked a trifle shocked. "You still love her?" he asked after a moment.

"I still love the woman she was. That young love has always had a small, private corner of my heart and always will. What I do not know is exactly what I feel for her now. Or—"

Cartwright swallowed. "—what she feels for me. We have changed. The both of us. As is normal with the passing of time."

Steven sighed. "Why is it all so difficult? Why can't things be easy?"

"I don't know *why*, my son," said Cartwright softly, "but it never is."

Once again Steven looked startled. Then he looked pleased. Then he frowned.

"What is it?"

Embarrassed, Steven dug his toe into the rug. "Don't know," he mumbled after a moment.

"I suspect you do, but there is no reason why you must confide in me. Believe that I wish to be your friend, Steven, as well as your father. If you need me, I will be there for you, but now we are late for rehearsal. Mr. Brown will not be happy with us. Shall we go?"

Steven sighed. "I suppose. I wish I hadn't wanted to play a part."

"You do?" asked his father, surprised. "But you are doing so very well. I have been surprised at how well." Steven bridled at the implication his father had thought him incapable. "Not that there is any reason," Cartwright added hurriedly, "that you should *not*, but I'd no idea the theater *interested* you." He glanced sideways and relaxed when he saw that Steven appeared to have accepted his smoothing over of what had been a rather infelicitous phrasing.

They hurried through the rain, not speaking, and reached the theater to find Diane huddled with one of the minor characters, a young lady who was in tears. Diane looked harassed and irritated and—her hair loosened and her cheeks rosy—particularly attractive. Steven, seeing her, was struck all over again by a deep, hurting longing. As if in a dream, the youth approached her. His father watched him, his eyes narrowed.

"Ah, Steven," said Diane, glancing up. Then she saw the hot look in his eyes and very nearly groaned. "You know Miss Overwold, do you not?" She spoke hurriedly, wanting to nip in the bud the scene she feared the young man was about to instigate. "Miss Overwold—"

The girl hurriedly, if surreptitiously, wiped her eyes.

"—has been having difficulties this morning understanding exactly what Mr. Brown requires in this scene with Jocasta, but I think perhaps I have explained it satisfactorily." She arched her brows, and the chit nodded, her shy gaze lifting to look admiringly at Steven and then quickly dropping back to her twisting fingers. "Do you think you and she might go over in that corner and, speaking softly, work on it?"

"I would very much appreciate your help," said the girl softly. "You are so very good, are you not? You will know exactly *how* I should say the lines." She again lifted her gaze to briefly search his face. "It is the emotion I was doing all wrong, I guess." She sighed.

"It would be a great help, Steven," said Diane softly.

The young woman's praise reached Steven as nothing else could have done, but it was Diane's wishes that had him nodding. "Very well," he said a trifle shortly, pretending to ignore the girl's flattering remarks. "Since *you* ask it of me, Mrs. Runyard." He turned to the chit and seemed to notice for the first time how lovely she was. He drew in a breath and offered his arm. "Shall we go across to the costume room? The women will be working there, so you will not be unchaperoned," he added quickly, "and it might be easier to concentrate there than here, where they will be speaking from the stage." He turned back to Diane, silently asking if he had done the proper thing.

"Thank you, Steven." Diane smiled at him. "Not only will you find it easier, but your voices need not be softened to the point it is difficult to express the emotions." She went with them to find a large umbrella and sent them off by way of the side door only to hear her name called as Roger, again, required her immediate assistance with still another problem. She passed Lord Cartwright on her way.

His lordship grasped her hand, halting her. "Di . . ."

"Not now," she said, her eyes on Roger, who appeared to be trying to tear large hanks of hair from his head. "I—"

"I just wanted to say thank you for how you just handled Steven." He released her.

She cast him a quick look but, when her name was called again, expelled an exasperated huff of air and called, "I'm coming. I'm *coming*, Roger." She hurried off.

The morning passed without Lord Cartwright and Steven called to practice the fight scene. His lordship was glad. He and Steven had parted on far easier terms than ever before, but there had still been a lack of real emotional understanding. Cartwright didn't think that Roger Brown's current level of frustration would lead to anything good if the two of them didn't handle the scene well, so, when the morning's work ended, he approached the actor.

"I wondered," said his lordship politely when he had most of Roger's attention, "whether it might not be better if Sir Cyrall worked on the fight scene between my son and myself. Cyrall is very good, and I think he knows what you want of us." He put a touch of humor into his tone. "He could smooth out most of the rough spots and then, when we finally come to the stage, perhaps you won't have quite so many difficulties sorting out the rest."

Roger, who had reached that point of worry where it was easy to believe that *nothing* would ever go right, that everyone needed a lot more rehearsal time, and that there wasn't enough time in the world to do all that had to be done, stared at Lord Cartwright. "Why," he asked, "did I not think of that?" He turned in a circle. "But where will you work?"

"If nothing else," said his lordship, who had already thought of that problem, "the footmen may clear the entrance hall, moving the furnishings out of the way so that we can work there. Or—is there a ballroom? I have not asked."

"If there is," said Diane, approaching in time to hear the question, "it is very likely being cleaned or painted or decorated for the ball that Miss Francine told me will be held after the performance. She would not appreciate your interference. The hall is a better notion."

"Where," said Cartwright, the humor more evident, "we may make a May-game of ourselves for the entertainment of anyone wandering by. So be it. I will find Sir Cyrall and ask if he is free to help us."

Cartwright nodded to Roger, smiled at Diane—a smile containing more warmth than he'd previously allowed himself to reveal in public—and then moved back up the aisle toward the door, wondering where he would find the baronet.

*Sir Cyrall? Baronet?* Cartwright frowned. *Is there not an older brother? Yes! The Golden Adonis.* His lordship grimaced at the thought of a young man he disliked heartily. *Unusual that Cyrall has a courtesy title as well—but not impossible, of course.* He was still frowning as he chose an umbrella and turned to the door. "Ah. Morningside. I don't suppose you know where I might find Sir Cyrall, do you?"

"Cyrall? He said he'd retire to the library, something about reading being the only possible way to pass the time in weather meant only for ducks."

Cartwright nodded. "There is another thing with which you might help me," he said, speaking slowly, thoughtfully. "I have been searching my mind and am confused. His older brother has a courtesy title, of course, but, from what I remember, I had thought there was no further title available for Sir Cyrall's use?"

"You are correct. He is a baronet in his own right. The Golden Adonis and he were rowing off the south coast when they happened to see two of the princesses in difficulties. Their royal highnesses had eluded their ladies to go boating by themselves and lost their oars, you see. Primus and Cyrall approached, but the cliff and rocks were too near and waves too rough to actually reach the other boat without endangering both of them. Cyrall dove in, retrieved the oars, swam to the boat, and rowed it to the pier. His brother took the princesses home while Cyrall went immediately to change from his soaking garments."

Rafe did not go on to describe the actual scene in which the king, thanking the wrong brother, was corrected by his younger daughter, who, or so the story went, glared at Primus Jamison for blandly taking credit for what Cyrall had done. King George was not amused, dismissed Primus, and sent for Cyrall.

Cyrall was knighted on the spot and his brother refused admission to the king's presence ever since. It was a story that had not made the rounds. Few had even noticed Primus was banished from royalty's presence since many younger men avoided the royal levees when at all possible. Cyrall had reluctantly told Rafe the truth when Rafe questioned him.

Cartwright's eyelids lowered as he guessed at much of what was left unsaid. "I have never liked Primus."

Rafe's eyes narrowed with amusement. "I believe you are in good company. Among others, of course, our good Farmer George dislikes him." And with that further clue to the truth of Cyrall's baronetcy, he nodded and continued down the aisle to where Eustacia sat, not yet quite ready to face the elements in order to return to the house.

Cartwright found Cyrall right where he'd been told to look. "I've a request and an impertinent question."

Cyrall's brows arched. "Shall we take the request first? I might be reluctant to grant it if I find the question too impertinent."

Cartwright grinned. "Will you coach my son and myself

in our fight scene? Today. Perhaps in the front hall, unless you've a better suggestion."

"The music room," said Cyrall promptly. "Far more private. Privacy is unlikely to be a problem for you but will be for your son."

Cartwright nodded. "Excellent notion. Now the question. What is the true story about you acquiring your baronetcy?" He grinned again when Cyrall immediately colored a furious red. "Come now. It cannot be that bad if it led to such honor."

"An honor for *me*."

"And your brother does not like that."

Cyrall noticed that was *not* a question. "There has been a ridiculous sort of rivalry between us since the death of Secondus. You'll recall our middle brother?" He looked up and met Cartwright's eyes. Cartwright nodded. "I presume Rafe told the first part?"

"To where your brother returned the princesses to their summer abode."

Cyrall almost hid his bitterness when he said, "Primus jumped at the opportunity."

"Of course he did," said Cartwright smoothly.

Cyrall's gaze drifted to the far corner of the room. "Can we not leave it at that?"

"I think not."

"Why not?" Cyrall caught and held Cartwright's gaze.

"Because," said Cartwright promptly, "your brother has become entangled with the daughter of a friend of mine. I am worried about my goddaughter. It looks as if an engagement may result."

Cyrall's breath caught. "Miss Madeline Winthrop? It has gone so far? That the world knows?" Cartwright nodded. A bit of Cyrall's lip disappeared beneath his teeth. Finally, a decision made, he met Cartwright's gaze. "When the princesses reached their temporary home, the king began by thanking my brother, who blandly accepted it as if by right. One of them objected and told the tale. Primus has never again been allowed in the king's presence."

"And you were honored with a baronetcy. Why do you keep the story a secret?"

Cyrall hesitated.

"If *you* were banished, your brother would not be so reticent as to why."

Cyrall's lips compressed. Once again his gaze drifted away.

"Loyalty is all very well, but it is not always a blessing to protect another from his faults," said Cartwright softly. "Thank you for allowing me to know the truth. I will demand discretion from Winthrop when I tell him, but I will tell him. Madeline . . . She's too sweet, too soft, too young to deal with a man of your brother's stripe."

"She is so very beautiful." Cyrall revealed more emotion than he liked but then controlled himself. "I feel a traitor for denigrating Primus. My brother will demand beauty in his wife—to match his own, you know? There are few young women on the marriage market right now who come near to Miss Winthrop's perfection."

"They exist. Cold beauties who will not be hurt by his equally cold heart. Let him choose one of them."

"Cold . . . but *because* they are cold, they cannot equal Miss Winthrop's perfection," said Cyrall, recovering his usual sangfroid. "Still, I agree there are others, and that is why I was weak enough to tell the truth. Madeline—Miss Winthrop, that is—is far too much an angel for a devil like my brother."

"Devil. *A fallen angel.* I find it in me to pity him."

"Can you?" Cyrall nodded but not as if he agreed. "Pride was supposed to be the sin that resulted in Lucifer's fall from grace, was it not?"

"You suggest it is pride that has ruined your brother? I am of another mind. The answer appears to me something far less admirable. Nothing more or less than a bloody-minded and selfish insistence on having his own way, to say nothing of a greedy desire to have all the best for himself. When will you be prepared to work with Steven and myself?"

Cyrall, glad of the abrupt change of subject, took out his watch and flicked it open. He returned the watch to his fob pocket. "Shall we say half past two? It is about twenty past twelve at the moment. Lunch will be available soon, and, besides, I'll need to arrange to have the chairs in the music room moved to the side."

"Two-thirty. I will tell Steven."

"I will tell him. I think it will be better coming from me."

Cartwright barked a harsh laugh. "You are very likely correct." He turned on his heel and left the library—and then couldn't think what to do with himself until time to face his son across the blades.

# CHAPTER
# TWELVE

Steven and Miss Overwold joined Diane on the way to the house as everyone who wished to indulge in a bite to eat returned there. Steven, who had not had nearly enough breakfast, was determined that, this time, he would not leave the dining room until he had had all he wished. Nothing, he determined, would drive him away. Not this time.

"Did it go well?" asked Diane, smiling at Miss Overwold.

"Mr. Cartwright is truly an excellent tutor," said the girl in her shyest voice, admiration filling the gaze she turned on the young man. "He is so patient with me when I am stupid," she added.

"You are easy to be patient to," said Steven gallantly if a trifle absentmindedly. "Are you going in to lunch?" he asked Diane, all his admiration focused on the actress.

"Yes. Roger has asked that sandwiches be sent out for him and the people with whom he is working."

Steven actually chuckled. "What you mean is that you told him you would ask that sandwiches be sent out. I doubt very much Mr. Brown has a thought in his head but to browbeat us all into submission so that the play will be the tragedy it is supposed to be and not a tragic happening because we've turned it into a farce."

Diane laughed with genuine amusement, which pleased Steven. Then she stopped when she saw that Miss Overwold looked confused. "He means," she explained, "that Roger fears you will all do so badly the play will make the audience laugh instead of cry."

Miss Overwold's eyes widened. "Oh, dear," she said. "Do you think that will happen?"

"Not at all," said Diane promptly. She entered the house through the door held for her by a footman, said thank you softly, and continued, "It is merely that we've reached the last week before a play comes together, that time when nothing seems to quite be what one wants it to be. You will find that, very suddenly, it does come together and you will put on an excellent production."

"You mean *we* will," said Steven. "You are one of us, are you not?"

"Am I? Yes, I suppose I am. If you will excuse me, I must go up to my room for a moment." She smiled at the young lady and nodded toward Steven and went on toward the main staircase. Steven stared after her, longingly.

"She is very nice, is she not?" asked Miss Overwold. "I didn't think an actress could be so nice."

Steven turned a scowl toward the chit. "Why not? She is merely a woman, is she not?" he said, the belligerency in full force. "*Any* woman can be nice. Or *not*, as the case may be. I know a duchess who is not nice at all. To anyone."

Miss Overwold blinked. "Oh, but a duchess . . ."

"They have a right to be other than nice? I don't think so." Steven turned on his heel and stalked off, angry with the girl as he had not been before. *She had no business insulting Mrs. Runyard*, he fumed. *She's just a chit of a girl. More hair than sense*. A tiny thought reminded him that he'd thought

Miss Overwold quite lovely, but he pushed it away. "Insulting child!" he muttered. "Just a child . . . not like Mrs. Runyard."

He took the stairs two at a time, hurrying to his room, where he wished to wash up before going down to eat. He hurried. If he were before Mrs. Runyard and waited for her, he might find it possible to sit beside her.

Unfortunately, he did not manage it. Hungry, he sat off at a far corner of the crowded table, fuming that his father *had*. He wolfed down his food so he could leave the room as soon as possible, get away from the sight of them smiling at each other, talking quietly, even laughing occasionally.

Steven swore softly, angry once again at what he perceived as his father's interference.

*Why couldn't my father have stayed home where he belongs and not stuck his nose into what isn't his business?*

Steven looked at his empty plate, thought for a moment that perhaps he might get more, but looked up when Sir Cyrall stopped beside his chair. "Yes?" he asked, frowning.

"Take it easy, bantling," said Cyrall, smiling. "I merely wished to tell you that it has been suggested I direct you and your father in that fight scene. I have asked that the music room be cleared so that we can work there. Two-thirty?" he asked.

Steven glowered but nodded and looked again at his plate, thinking of the fact he must soon face his father, must reveal how very bad a swordsman he was, must, once again, look like a nothing when his father was so very good at everything he did. Steven's appetite disappeared, and, morosely, he took himself away, surprised when, at the door, Miss Overwold accosted him. He turned the glower on her and then felt like a total beast when she grew red in the face and looked as if she might cry.

He took her arm. "Come along," he said. "It isn't you I'm angry with. I apologize if I, er, startled you."

"I just wanted to thank you for your help," she said, her eyes wide open, shiny with unshed tears. "I'm sorry. I shouldn't have bothered you."

"No bother. It is just that I have to practice that scene where Oedipus fights his real father, and I know I'll do it all wrong. I've never learned to fight with swords, you see, and don't know at all what I'm doing."

"No one will expect you to know," she said, staring up at him. "Really. One isn't *born* knowing such things," she added with great earnestness.

Steven blinked. "No, of course not." He sighed. "I guess I just don't like playing the fool in front of my father."

"One always wants one's mother or father to think well of one," she said with great seriousness. "It is natural, is it not?" When he didn't reply, she added, "I know I become flustered and unhappy when I realize I've done something which makes my mother feel disappointed in me."

They had reached the front hall at this point. The wide front doors were flung open and a flurry of footmen carrying umbrellas rushed out. The two young people stopped to see what was happening. They watched a family enter, the mother a comfortably plump sort of gentlewoman but with a touch of superciliousness etching her features. Her hand was on the arm of her tall, stern-faced husband. Coming in behind was a young lady perhaps a year or two older than Miss Overwold. *Her* face was set in lines that could only denote stubborn determination.

Determination to do what or be what neither Steven nor Miss Overwold could guess. "Who are they?" asked the chit, speaking softly. "I don't believe I have ever met any of them?"

"Probably not. Lord Winthrop and his family spend very little time in London. This year they did. My father is the chit's godfather, so I saw quite a lot of them. When I left town, everyone was saying she'd marry the Golden Adonis. I wonder why they are here?"

"Golden Adonis?" asked Miss Overwold.

"Sir Cyrall's older brother. He looks like a Greek god."

"Oh." Her voice had a flat tone. "That one."

"You look as if you don't like him."

"He . . . isn't very nice," said Miss Overwold, speaking hesitantly. She put away whatever thoughts were upsetting her and excused herself. "I must go up to my room for a bit," she said shyly.

"And I'd better go to the music room. It is almost time for our practice." Steven sighed.

"Just remember," said Miss Overwold in a slightly scolding tone, "you are not expected to know anything about swords and fighting. Sir Cyrall will help you. He's nice. And I think your father would be nice too . . . if you'd let him."

With that last bit, she headed up the stairs, her back determinedly turned to him. Steven stared after her but looked around in time to make polite greetings to Lord Winthrop and his family and then moved on to the music room.

He tried to convince himself that Miss Overwold was correct, that no one expected him to know anything about swordplay, but the insecurities that riddled him could not be so easily smoothed over. He was standing near the harp, plucking one and then another string, when Sir Cyrall and his father entered the room. The two were laughing. Steven instantly knew it was at him they laughed and turned painfully red.

Sir Cyrall, in that way he had, read Steven's mind and beckoned. "Your father has just told me a joke. I wonder if you know it."

Steven hesitated. *Perhaps it is true*, he thought, but the notion his father ever told a joke was almost more than he could accept. "A jest?" he asked.

"Tell it again," said Cyrall, "while I take the swords from their case and check them."

Lord Cartwright did so, and Steven, nearly convinced, laughed. It was not difficult to laugh. It was an excellent jest. But . . . had his father told it to Sir Cyrall—or had he quickly thought of it as Cyrall hinted he should? Steven turned away and picked up one of the long, slender blades. He shook it, and the button-tipped end wavered up and down.

"Shall we begin?" asked Cyrall.


"How," asked Diane softly, "did it go?"

Lord Cartwright grimaced. "He cannot face me and re-member one thing of what he is supposed to do. Cyrall shows him, and he is perfect, knows every move. Then we try again . . . and disaster. Brown is not going to be pleased." His lips pulled in again, and there was a bleak look about his eyes. "What can I do, Di? He is such a *child*."

She nodded thoughtfully. "You mean his *reaction* to you is childish, which is not the same, is it? Did I hear Sir Cyrall say you were to work again once dinner was over?"

"Not instantly. We'd be too full. But later, yes. We'll try again."

"I don't suppose . . ." Diane shook her head. "No. My being there would only complicate his problem, not solve it. Ah. There goes the dinner bell." The good smells of well-prepared food drifted from the hall. Diane drew in a deep breath. "Oh, dear," she said, taking the arm Cartwright offered, "I will be so spoiled by the end of our visit. In the past when we've been hired to do this sort of thing, we've eaten with the upper servants rather than with the guests. I had not known there was such good food in the world!"

Cartwright smiled, the corners of his eyes crinkling. "You should talk to Sir Cyrall. He is convinced Witherspoon has the worst cook in Sussex."

Diane's eyes widened. "Then what can it possibly be like to enjoy what the *best* conjures up?"

Cartwright's smile turned to a chuckle. "Perhaps, once this is over, I will ask Sir Cyrall to invite us to one of his little dinners. He cannot afford the Frenchman he prefers as a full-time employee, but when the family that has him in their kitchen has no need of him, Cyrall hires him just for the evening for small groups of like-minded souls. Cyrall, you will discover, is something of an epicure when it comes to dining."

"I *will* discover?"

Cartwright hesitated. He realized he had made up his mind without ever thinking about it. He wanted Di for his wife, meant to ask her to wed him, but he was not certain she would agree, and he dared not broach the subject just yet. Certainly not immediately, just when they were about to enter the dining room in the midst of other guests. All that went through his mind in a fraction of a second but not so quickly Diane didn't notice.

"Stevie?"

"Another time, Di. We cannot talk about the future at the moment."

"No. Of course not."

But Diane's dinner partners discovered she was very poor company that evening, preoccupied, absentminded, and inattentive. The men seated to either side of her gave up after one or two attempts at conversation and allowed her to withdraw into herself entirely. Both men, unaware of anything beyond the play that might hold her interest to such a degree, wondered if things were going more badly than they had thought.

Before the meal ended, they too were somewhat thoughtful, and the instant the door closed behind the women, they pounced on Roger Brown, asking if there were serious problems.

Roger's comments did not soothe them, since he was, as was normal with him at this point, totally convinced the play would never come together.

And Steven, overhearing, was, of course, absolutely convinced it was *all his fault*.


Cyrall left the dining room with a handful of other men once the ladies were gone and went out onto the terrace for a breath of air. He found Rafe there, smoking a cigarillo, and wrinkled his nose. "Those things ruin your palate, you know," he chided.

"That is important to you, Cyr, but I was never so interested in my food as you are."

Cyrall smiled wryly. "I am in no danger, here, of becoming a glutton," he replied, but absently.

"She is quite lovely," said Rafe softly.

Cyrall nodded and then, suddenly, turned. "What do you know about it?" he asked with just a touch of belligerence.

"I know you showed more than a little interest in the young woman when she was introduced to the ton. I know that the Adonis didn't notice her at all—until you did. I know her mother is ambitious for her."

"You know too much," said Cyrall, and this time there was bitterness to be heard. "My brother—"

"Your brother is an ass, and you should not concern yourself with his feelings, as he doesn't concern himself with yours. Why did you back off when he began pursuing Miss Winthrop?"

"Why?" Cyrall grasped the terrace railing with a grip that turned his knuckles white. "I suppose because I have learned over the years that I cannot win when Primus is determined. And, about this, he is very determined, is he not?"

"But she is here . . . and he is not."

Cyrall nodded. He tipped a glance toward his old friend. "Have you heard any suggestions as to why?"

"The engagement has never been announced, has it?"

"Primus's intentions are known only to the families . . . and every fool who listens to the whispers." The bitterness was still harsher.

"But she is *here*. And there has been no announcement."

Cyrall straightened. "Are you suggesting . . . ?"

"That there is not, perhaps has never been, an engagement?" Rafe nodded.

"But . . ."

"Yes?"

"That means . . ."

"Yes?" asked Rafe more softly.

"Surely not . . ."

"Not?"

Cyrall drew in a deep breath, opened his mouth, closed it, stared at nothing at all—and then turned on Rafe. "Do something for me?"

"I will discover what I can. For you," said Rafe, grinning.

"A prince among men!" Cyrall clasped Rafe's shoulder, gave it a gentle shake, and then started for the house.

"Where are you going?"

"To the music room—with a far lighter heart than I expected to have." He turned, backing toward the house. "Discover for me what I want to hear, and I will be in your debt forever."

"She isn't wearing the Jamison betrothal ring."

Cyrall's eyes widened, and then he laughed, a lighthearted laugh Rafe had not heard for some time. "Thank you again. Now I must see if I can convince Steven Cartwright it is all right to remain his usual graceful self while facing his father over the swords."

\* \* \*

Steven, another who had left the dining room, looked up from the garden toward the terrace. He had not meant to eavesdrop but hadn't known how to tell the older men he was there, and he'd feared moving off lest they hear him and think he was sneaking away for all the wrong reasons. The conversation had startled him a great deal. It had never crossed his mind that someone as old as Cyrall Jamison might have problems. He always seemed so knowing, so secure, so able to deal with a world Steven found impossibly confusing.

And then there had been that last bit. Sir Cyrall thought him graceful. He thought him capable of doing well in that fight scene—unlike Mr. Brown, who didn't seem to think any of them could do anything right.

Steven sighed softly. *Why*, he wondered, *do I feel such a fool whenever I must face my father? What do I expect? Has he ever beaten me? Has he been nasty to me? No. He ignores me. And that is it, is it not?* he asked himself. *I want him to notice me. I want him to admire me. I want him to like me . . . and I can see no good reason why he should.*

Steven groaned softly, rose to his feet and, moving more like a nonagenarian than an eighteen-year-old, got himself to the music room for the scheduled practice.

Once there, he recalled that Cyrall had problems too. He watched the older man, curious as to how he managed to keep all that inside himself rather than allowing it to interfere with everything he did. No one would ever know that Cyrall had been courting the woman his older brother had decided to wed. No one would ever know it bothered him.

*How does he do it?*

For perhaps a minute, Steven decided Sir Cyrall's problems could not possibly mean half so much to him as Steven's did to himself. But then he recalled the intensity of feeling he'd heard in that overheard conversation and could not lie to himself. Sir Cyrall felt deeply, and felt a great deal—but somehow managed to hide it from those who need know nothing of it.

Steven decided it behooved him to try to do likewise. *I must pretend*, he told himself, *that it truly is Laius I am fighting. I will pretend I am the young Oedipus. I am well trained but have never before fought a real battle. I am fighting an experienced fighter—and if he limps, well, he is still very good and stronger than I, but I am young and agile and quick, and I will take advantage when he slips. . . .*

"I am Oedipus," he breathed, his eyes going slightly out of focus.

Laius appeared, took up his sword, and approached. Steven glanced around, saw his sword lying where he'd left it, and retrieved it. He turned, his back straight, his mind focused on the play, and found, much to his later surprise, that the practice went very well indeed.

# CHAPTER
# THIRTEEN

Lord Winthrop looked around the salon, a frown on his face. Near the fireplace, his arm along the mantel, stood Lord Morningside. Winthrop hesitated, and then, determination in his stride, he approached. "Evening," he said abruptly, ignoring the fact the sun still shone through the long, undraped windows. "Friend of Jamison's, are you not?"

"Which Jamison," asked Rafe, hiding the curiosity that swept through him.

"Sir *Cyrall* Jamison. Got a letter from an old friend. Want to know the ins and outs."

"The ins and outs of what?"

"Don't want to discuss your friend, hmm?" Winthrop looked irritated. "Need to know, and Sir Cyrall avoids me. Need to talk. You tell him."

Lord Winthrop turned on his heel and stalked from the room. Rafe studied the toe of his dress shoe, tipping it one way and then the other. A frown formed, disappeared. Eyes narrowed, widened, and narrowed again, along with a new frown.

Eustacia, who had been hiding in a window seat nearly

hidden by a drape, could stand it no longer. She rose and crossed the room to where he stood. "What is it? Why do you look that way?"

His head came up, and he stared at her. "Where did you come from?"

"Does it matter? What did Winthrop say to you that has you in such a dither?"

Rafe tipped his head ever so slightly. "Why would Winthrop want to talk to Cyr?"

"Sir Cyrall?" Eutacia frowned slightly. "Isn't his daughter about to announce her engagement to his brother?"

"I wonder . . ."

"Well?" asked Eustacia after a moment, when he didn't continue.

"Is it well? Perhaps it is. I don't suppose you've any notion where I might find Cyr?"

Eustacia sighed. "You are not going to tell me what bothers you, are you? Even though you always insist I tell you my every thought and worry. Is friendship only one way with you, Rafe?" His gaze swung to meet hers, and she held his stare steadily.

Rafe barked a laugh. "I had not noticed before. . . ."

"What?" she asked and caught herself before stamping her foot in irritation.

"You've grown up, have you not? You've become a woman without my noticing."

"Rafe, what are you talking about? I am very nearly twenty-eight years old. I should hope I have *grown up*."

He shook his head. "Years have nothing to do with it. Euphrasia, we must talk—" He reached out and grasped her wrist as she swung away. "—and do not run from me. Why," he asked, "have you never bothered to discover the *meaning* of that name? Never mind," he continued before she could respond. "I have to find Cyr, but sometime soon we really must talk."

He reached for her shoulders and set her aside, striding from the room without a backward glance.

Eustacia's frown deepened as she stared after him. "The meaning?" she muttered. "Do names have meanings?" She headed for the library, determined she'd not leave it until she had searched out the meaning behind the name Euphrasia. Perhaps she'd check on Eustacia too.

*And, while I am at it, what does Rafe's name mean? Raphael?*


Diane strolled along the path from the orchard and was halfway back to the house when a young woman, white faced and tear streaked, came running toward her.

Diane stopped her simply by standing in her way. "My dear, what is the matter? What has happened to upset you so?"

The young woman turned her head to the side, brushing away the tears, and Diane saw that it was Miss Winthrop, who, with her stern-looking father and plump mother, had arrived the evening before.

"Come, my dear. Let us walk among the apple trees. I have found it a very good place for thinking. Perhaps together we can think what to do to make you happy again."

Miss Winthrop really looked at Diane. She blinked and then stepped back a step. "But you are . . ." Her complexion grew pink.

"An actress?" asked Diane, guessing at the reason for her embarrassment. "Yes. I am an actress. But I am also a woman, and I see another woman in distress. Should I step aside and allow her to go on her sad way and offer no help at all?"

"The Good Samaritan," exclaimed Miss Winthrop, her tear-wet eyes shining. "Vicar spoke on the Samaritan's actions only last week in church."

"And?" Diane smiled a gentle smile.

Miss Winthrop drew in a deep breath. She let it out and seemed to collapse. The tears coursed down her cheeks once again. "No one can help me," she said despairingly. And then, well trained, she added, "But thank you very much for offering."

"Sometimes," said Diane, "it helps to merely talk about one's problems. Do let us stroll among the apples. Really, it is quite lovely there, and no one else is likely to come, so we would be quite private and—" She grinned a quick conspiratorial grin. "—if we stay near the fence at the far end, no one at the house can see us. I've checked."

Miss Winthrop smiled a weak smile and allowed herself to be drawn through the orchard. Diane seated herself on the wall, and, after a moment in which to check that the stones were dry and clean, Miss Winthrop did likewise.

"Now. Tell me all about it. I promise I'll not tell anyone you'd not like to hear the tale. And I suspect that means I shan't tell anyone, but we can discuss that once you've told me the problem."

"Mother."

"Your mother is the problem?" Diane recalled the disdainful looks the rosy-cheeked woman had cast toward Roger and herself once her ladyship discovered their occupation. She also recalled how firmly the woman had kept her daughter at her side, restrained her from talking to anyone at all, and, when Sir Cyrall had moved nearer, whisked the girl from the room as if he carried the plague.

"Has your mother been scolding you?" asked Diane when Miss Winthrop didn't go on.

The young woman sighed. "She insists I must marry Lord—" She cast a look at Diane and quickly away. "A certain man. I don't want to. He is horrible. Just horrible. She says that isn't important."

"Not important?" asked Diane, blinking. "What could be *more* important?"

"I'd be a countess someday. I'd be wealthy. I'd have everything I ever wanted. *She* says."

"Everything . . . but love?" Diane recalled the rumor that Miss Winthrop was to marry the Golden Adonis. She herself had had to deal with the Adonis once. She shuddered. If Roger hadn't appeared just when . . . but he had. Another woman had caught his lordship's eye, and he'd not repeated his demands. His exceedingly unwelcome, won't-take-no-for-an-answer demands . . .

"Mother says love isn't important," said Miss Winthrop, and the tears flowed faster. "Mother says . . ."

"What does your father say?" asked Diane, interrupting.

"Father?" Miss Winthrop blinked. "My father . . ." A wondering look came into her eye. "But he has never . . . She has always . . . Do you think . . . ?"

"I think you should tell him that you do not wish to wed the lord your mother thinks you should wed and would he please see that you do not have to do so."

"My *father* . . ."

Suddenly Miss Winthrop smiled a glorious smile, lighting her whole face, and Diane saw the animation that must have been hers before she'd become so fearful of the future.

"What about your father, Miss Winthrop?"

"Before we came to London—you know, when we were packing and planning and doing all those busy, *busy* things one must do before leaving one's home for months . . ."

"He said something to you? Something you forgot in all the rush and the excitement?"

Miss Winthrop nodded. "He said he wanted me to be happy. He said I was to come to him when I thought I wanted to marry a certain gentleman so he could find out about him, find out if he was worthy of me . . . and that he'd not allow me to wed where I'd be miserable." A sudden hardness made her eyes glitter. "And I would. I'd be terribly miserable with the Gold—" Again she cast a quick look at Diane, who pretended she'd not heard the name. "—that man," Miss Winthrop corrected herself. "I must find my father." She looked around rather blankly, as if he might be hiding behind one of the fruit-laden trees.

"Perhaps you would like to come with me to see the theater? It is possible that that is where your father has gone. He may have wished to see Lord Witherspoon's pride and joy."

"Thank you." Miss Winthrop turned a face expressing a great deal of surprise up toward Diane, who was considerably taller. "You are very kind, are you not?"

"I try," said Diane rather dryly. "The world is a happier place when we are kind to one another. Come along now. We shall see if your father has gone to the theater."

Fearing that Lady Winthrop might be looking for her errant daughter, Diane led the girl by paths that would keep them invisible from anyone looking out windows or off the terrace into the gardens. The hedges forming windbreaks here and there had not been planted with the need for secrecy in mind, but they were very useful when one wished to avoid some particular person who might be seeking one.

As it turned out, Lord Winthrop and Sir Cyrall, the latter with a frown on his face, were pacing back and forth outside the theater. Sir Cyrall looked up, saw Miss Winthrop, and his already pale skin lost all hint of color.

"Miss Winthrop," he said, interrupting the other man. He bowed.

Lord Winthrop broke off what he was saying and turned. "Ah. Maddy. There you are. Come along, my dear, I've a few things I must say to you."

Diane cleared her throat. "My lord."

"Eh? Eh?" He turned a surprised look on Mrs. Runyard.

"I believe," said Diane when she had his attention, "that your daughter has something to say to you, as well. She has recalled something you said to her before you all went up to

London for the Season, and she would like to ask you if you meant it . . . and then perhaps tell you something."

Diane smiled encouragingly at Miss Winthrop, who drew in a deep breath and turned to her father. "Yes, please, Father. If you have a moment?" she added rather diffidently. "I know you are a very busy man and I am not to bother you, but—" She bit her lip, her eyes suddenly glistening with, this time, unshed tears. "—this is important."

"My dear child," blustered Lord Winthrop, "wherever did you get the notion that I have no time for you? You are my much-beloved daughter. Of course I will listen. Come along, now. . . ." And he looked around, wondering where they might be private—somewhere where his wife, in particular, would not find them.

"There is a very nice orchard just back that way," said his daughter shyly. "We would be alone there, I think."

"Excellent notion," said the father, casting his daughter a knowing look that brought roses to the young lady's cheeks. "A truly excellent notion."

The father offered the daughter his arm, and they strolled off, returning along the route Diane used to keep Miss Winthrop from any eyes peering out from the house. Diane brushed the palm of one hand across the palm of the other and then did it the other way. She nodded.

Sir Cyrall tipped his head. "You've been up to mischief, have you not, Mrs. Runyard?"

"Mischief? No. Definitely not. Quite otherwise. I have done a very good day's work, and it cannot yet be ten of the clock!"

"Nearer ten-thirty," corrected Cyrall.

Diane's brows rose. "So late? Roger will be furious." She hurried up the steps and into the dim theater.

Cyrall didn't watch her go. Instead, a speculative look in his eye, he wondered just what was going on between Lord Winthrop and his daughter. Reluctantly, Cyrall had given brief answers to his lordship's bluntly phrased questions concerning his brother. His reticence had not pleased Lord Winthrop, but he had understood it. He'd told Cyrall it was quite right for him to be loyal, but that it made it damn difficult for a father to know what was best. His lordship had eyed Cyrall with a sapient eye and grinned. "But your demmed careful tongue is answer itself, is it not? I must conclude that your brother will not do for my girlie." He'd frowned. "Going to take a fistful of arguments to convince her mother . . ."

And at that point, Miss Winthrop herself had appeared . . . and they'd gone off, a very determined-looking young lady and a man more at peace with himself. Sir Cyrall was exceedingly interested in the results of that conversation. He hoped all would end as he wished, but he very much feared that Miss Winthrop was so in awe of her managing mother that what the chit wished to do was convince her father that Mother Knew Best.

In this case, Mother Did Not.

*Perhaps,* thought Cyrall, *there is no more difficult tyrant than one who believes that what they do for or to another is for the best!*

Cyrall suddenly wished he'd not been quite so careful, that he'd not kept his tongue so firmly between his teeth but had told his lordship exactly why his daughter had no business wedding Primus. Armed with more detail, perhaps Lord Winthrop could convince Miss Winthrop she did not wish to wed the title or the wealth, not when those things could not possibly compensate for being tied to Primus.

Sir Cyrall sighed softly. It was going to be very difficult to contain himself until he could discover the outcome of the discussion going on right now among the apples.

Lord Cartwright, released from rehearsal, went looking for Diane, who had left only minutes earlier. Steven, seeing his father wearing a determined expression, immediately guessed the reason for it and followed. Others who had had part in the morning's schedule also left as quickly as they could.

Roger, shaking his head at the lack of dedication of his cast, went to the long building alongside the theater and, after checking the state of the scenery, went to see how the costumes were coming along. He was not entirely pleased, but the seamstress in charge shook her head.

"Ye'll not get those ladies to wear the sort of thing you're asking fer," she said, and then, mincing no words, she looked over the top of the spectacles she pulled down her nose and added, "Besides, 'twouldn't be at all proper, now, would it?"

Roger, who might have lost his temper, suddenly saw the humor in that and chuckled. "Right you are, and I should never have suggested the baring of one shoulder—even if that is what is shown on old Greek vases and suchlike. You've done well adapting what is needed."

"And still quite daring. *Some* ladies will *like* that. But others'll be wearing fichus. You'll see." She cocked her head. "Hmm . . . I'd better design wraps with proper Greeklike decoration." She moved off, obviously thinking about this new thing that needed to be done and done quickly. "Just in case . . ."

Roger was returning to the theater when his rumbling stomach caught his attention. He pulled his watch from the fob pocket and opened it. "Cannot be that late," he muttered and then looked up at the sun. It was. No wonder everyone had hurried away from rehearsal. He turned toward the house and was nearly there when he heard voices just beyond the hedge through which an arch had been cut. He paused.

"No." Her voice was pitched just a trifle high. "I *won't.*"

*Diane?* thought Roger. *And just what won't she do*? He waited.

"I thought it an excellent plan. To what do you object?"

*Lord Cartwright,* thought Roger and grimaced. *I might have known.*

"You *know* why it will not do."

"No." His lordship sounded particularly stubborn. "I do *not* understand. Explain."

"Steven . . ."

"What of my son?"

"Arrogant," she muttered. "So blidy arrogant."

Roger heard Cartwright sigh. "Did I sound overly haughty? I'm sorry. I didn't mean to. On the other hand, I cannot see why Steven has anything to do with what is between us. We need time together, Di. We cannot sort this out here—"

The actor in Roger imagined a hand waving gracefully in a broad gesture.

"—where there is always someone to interfere. Someone listening. Someone . . ."

Roger cleared his throat, his sense of humor roused. Silence ensued, and, attempting to suppress a smile, Roger stepped through the arch. "Someone like myself, for instance?"

Lord Cartwright rolled his eyes.

"Carry on. I'm just on the way to the house for lunch. Now I think of it, I must have forgotten to eat breakfast." He took a few more steps and then turned, walking backward as he added, "I should tell you, perhaps, that this morning's rehearsal went surprisingly well. Now if only the fight scene goes smoothly when we stage it this afternoon!" He turned back and went along, whistling softly.

Lord Cartwright followed him with his gaze then turned back to Diane. "You see? Always it is someone. You know we must have time together to—"

"To seduce her all over again?" asked his son, coming around a pillar holding up a huge alabaster vase. "To debauch her? To soil her reputation? To make of her a byword when she has done her best to be a woman of honor and keep her reputation spotless?"

Steven stalked forward, his chin out and a gleam in his eye.

"You know nothing about it, Son," said his father on a sigh. "Nothing at all."

"I know Franklin thinks you will be made a fool of, but he is wrong." He turned toward Diane. "It is you *he* would make the fool, Mrs. Runyard!"

Diane bit her lip. "Steven, what did Mr. Franklin say to you, and why?"

"He is worried. He fears my father may do something foolish, but I know better." He glared. "It isn't *himself* who will be sorry. . . ."

Cartwright's lips firmed. "Steven . . ."

"No. Don't try to excuse yourself. You cannot do it. You cannot pretend you want anything—"

"Other," interrupted Diane, rudely, "than what you wanted when you first met me? I think your father is right. You have no understanding at all of what has been between us or what might be if we had a chance to discover it. Stevie," she said, turning back to Lord Cartwright, her patience with Steven gone and her anger forcing words from her she'd been determined she'd not speak, "once my work here is ended, I will happily tour the Lake District. With you." A startled look widened her eyes. "Oh blidy hell, what have I done? To the devil with the both of you! Oh, *go away*."

Not waiting to see what they would do, Diane herself went off in a huff. Angry at young Steven, angry at her old love, but, most of all, angry with herself, she stalked toward the orchard and the long, open alleyway between the rows of fruit trees. The worst of it was that when she finally managed to come to some sort of calm, she realized she'd missed her luncheon and that she was late for the afternoon rehearsal.

An exceedingly important rehearsal.

As Diane approached the theater, she heard raised voices, a feminine scream, the slam of feet against the stage floor, and the metallic clash of swords. She hurried in and stood blinking, unable to see. Coming from the bright sun into the dim light had blinded her.

Moments later her vision cleared, and she wished it hadn't. Steven was obviously doing his best to do serious damage to his father, and no one, it seemed, wanted to interfere. Shouting, Diane hurried down the aisle and up onto the stage.

Still the fight went on. She looked around, saw a shawl someone had dropped, and caught it up. She approached and, when given the opportunity, threw the shawl over the tips of the blades and pulled. Hard. The button-dulled points went through the thin cloth but were pulled to one side. Stevie, seeing her, instantly dropped his blade. Steven, red faced, panting, angry beyond control, pulled his blade back and the button fell off. He raised it.

Diane instantly stepped between the two men.

"Di. *No*."

Lord Cartwright reached for her shoulders to pull her away but was too late.

Steven saw her, but his arm was already thrusting, and he could only partially stop it.

Diane, shocked by sudden pain, looked down at her arm. Blood seeped from the wound where the unprotected point had sliced through her sleeve and stabbed her. She stared, stupidly. Then she raised her gaze to meet Steven's shocked and horrified gaze.

"Not your fault," she said . . . and fainted.

Somehow that broke the spell by which everyone else had frozen in place. Cyrall and Rafe rushed forward and Roger hopped onto the stage. Lord Cartwright was already kneeling at Diane's side, ripping the sleeve away from her arm.

"A handkerchief," he said, holding up a free hand for it,

not caring who handed it to him. "That should do," he said a moment later. Then he looked up at his son. White faced, frightened by what he'd done, he hadn't moved except to lower the point of the blade to the floor. "Satisfied?" asked Lord Cartwright

"She . . . I didn't . . . Father . . . ?" He begged silently for reassurance.

Cartwright struggled with his temper. The woman he loved lay there wounded, but his son was truly remorseful and afraid. He sighed. "As she said, Steven. Not your fault."

"But why doesn't she wake up? She won't . . . won't . . . ?"

"Die?" Cartwright shook his head. "No, of course not," he said and hoped the wound didn't go septic and make a liar out of him. "Merely a scratch. Very likely painful, but she'll be all right."

Very carefully, he picked Diane up. She was heavier than he expected, and, for a moment, he wondered if he could carry her. Then she stirred, looked up at him . . . and threw her good arm around his neck. He smiled down at her, nodded to those around them, and stalked toward the stairs . . . and then wondered if he should attempt them, burdened as he was.

"I can walk," she said, guessing at his concern.

"We'll manage," he retorted softly. "I like you just where you are."

But he only carried her from the theater to where a bench was set in a bower. There he seated himself with her still in his arms. "Damn it, Di, don't you ever do anything so stupid ever again. He might have . . ." His mouth snapped shut, and, suddenly, he pulled her up and kissed her. Hard.

Inside the theater, everyone looked at Steven. He stared at accusing or curious eyes. On a sob, he ran, leaving by the side door.

Swearing softly, Cyrall ran after him.

# CHAPTER FOURTEEN

Eustacia, feeling a deep-seated chagrin, approached where Rafe stood near the undraped windows. The sun was setting. Dinner would be announced soon. Surely there wouldn't be time for embarrassment to sink her utterly.

Rafe watched her blurred reflection in the panes of the window. When she neared, he turned. They stared at each other. She sighed. When he still said nothing but merely stared down at her, she stamped her foot lightly. "You'll not make this easy for me, will you?"

He grinned. "My dear, you have never liked things made easy for you. Why should I think this would be different?"

"You know what I would do?"

"I can guess. Cyrall admitted that he helped you."

"You are amused."

"Are you not?" he asked, his brows arching.

She sighed again. "Actually . . . no."

He sobered. "My dear . . ."

"I am *embarrassed*. Why did it never occur to me that there was good reason for you to tease me so?"

"Because I made it clear I was teasing, and you dislike

being teased?" he asked, the faintest of frowns drawing a line between his eyes.

"And, knowing my weakness, you cannot resist." There was a gleam in her eye. He nodded, and the frown faded as if it had never been. "Rafe—"

He interrupted. "Shall I promise never again to use Euphrasia when speaking to you?"

"*No*." She cast him a startled look. "That wasn't at all what I meant to say to you."

"*Say* to me?"

She stared out the window.

"Not *demand* of me?"

Her lips twisted slightly. "I suppose it would be more in character if I *demanded*, would it not?"

"Make your demands, Eustacia."

The twist tightened. "I suppose, now that I have decided I prefer Euphrasia, you will insist on calling me Eustacia."

His eyes narrowed. "Tell me."

"The meanings. I am not *a stand of grain*."

"No. You are *a delight to the heart and mind*. I have always told you it is the name you *should* have been given."

She cast him a shy smile. "You truly mean that? You find me . . ." She bit her lip, unable to finish.

"I have always found you delightful, my dear. From the first time I saw you, your hair coming out of its braid, your hem dragging, and a look in your eye of pure mischief. I never did discover what you'd been up to that day, but, in that instant, you entered into my heart and have never left it."

Her eyes widened.

He cast a quick look around, but no one was near enough to overhear. "Do I have to say the words?"

"Please?" Again she revealed that unexpected shyness.

"I love you, Euphrasia, delight of my heart."

Her breath came in quicker, shallower bursts. "Truly, Rafe?"

"Truly. You sound as if you cannot believe me."

"I . . . thought I was unlovable, I guess," she said, hanging her head. She looked up. "My cousin . . . perhaps he was incapable of love?"

"He was a cold man who lived in his mind, my dear. Forget him. In his way he was fond of you, but he'd have found the notion that he loved you quite humorous. I don't think he believed in love."

"I recall," she mused, "one dinner-table discussion about agape and eros, an argument as to the existence of pure love against the passions of desire. He used humor that night—defensively?"

"Very likely." He reached out and touched her mouth.

It was a soft touch, barely skimming her lips, and yet it was the most arousing touch Eustacia had ever felt. Her flesh heated.

"I like that. I like to see you rosy, your eyes heavy. Marry me, Euphrasia. *Soon*?"

Eustacia drew in a deep breath. Could she? Should she? Did she dare?

"You *will*," he said, certain of her—but also teasing her.

For a moment rebellion stiffened her spine, and he grinned down at her, his eyes narrowing and those lines she loved radiating from the corners. She relaxed. "Yes," she said, surprising him. "*How* soon?"

"That depends, does it not? Shall I buy a license and we slip away to wed or would you like a great, huge, fancy wedding in Hanover Square?"

She shuddered. "If only we could simply be married and need not even announce it." She looked wistful.

"Let the rest of the world go hang itself from the nearest bough?" He chuckled. "We cannot be quite so rude, but we can prevent the world from making it a circus. This play will be over soon. I'll go for a license and return for you. We'll find a vicar somewhere to do the deed." He touched her lightly once again, a touch of color highlighting his cheekbones. Almost absently he continued. "I'll send a notice to the papers on the day we leave England." At her expression, he chuckled. "*We*, my dear, will take an extended wedding journey, thereby avoiding all the usual nonsense. To Italy? Perhaps on to Greece? You would like that, Euphrasia."

She nodded. She *would* like that. "And in the meantime no one need know?"

"No one." A third time he touched her lips. "There is one problem," he said, his eyes smiling down at her in a way that warmed her from the very center of her. "Having revealed to you how I feel, it is going to be very difficult to keep my hands off you."

Her eyes narrowed. She cast him a sideways look. "It is a very large house, Rafe." It was half a statement and half a question.

"So it is."

He drew in a breath and let it out slowly. The look in his eyes wasn't merely warm. It was heated. Once again that odd sensation that her insides were turning liquid filled her.

"So it is," he repeated, the words heavy with meaning, and then laughed softly when she blushed again. "Ah, my dear, I will so enjoy—"

"Educating me?" she interrupted, looking around. "Rafe, don't tease. I'll embarrass myself dreadfully. But—" She grinned a quick, slightly raffish, grin. "—I suspect I'll enjoy learning what you have to teach me as much if not more than you'll enjoy the teaching. Now, behave. There is Lord Witherspoon's excuse for a butler, ready to announce dinner."

Dinner was very nearly over when Lord Winthrop rose to his feet, a glass in his hand. His usual stern expression faded, and he smiled across the table to where his daughter, Madeline, sat between men she didn't know very well. She smiled back at him. "I've an announcement I wish to make," said his lordship, speaking loudly to call attention to himself.

Those talking softly to their dinner partners stilled. Heads turned, eyes stared.

"I wish to announce an engagement."

Cyrall rose quietly to his feet and moved to stand behind Madeline's chair. She raised her hand to her shoulder, and he covered it with one of his own.

"My daughter Madeline and Sir Cyrall have this day plighted their troth. They will be married during the autumn Little Season."

Lady Winthrop rose to her feet so quickly her chair tipped and crashed to the floor behind her. "You are mistaken. She is to wed—"

"*Sir Cyrall*. Our *daughter*—" His lordship's tone brooked no argument. "—came to me this afternoon, and we spoke for some time. Then we sought out Sir Cyrall. He was of the same mind he was before his brother took notice of my little girl. *Madeline has made her choice*," he finished, his gaze holding his wife's, silently daring her to say more.

Her ladyship glared, first at her husband and then at her daughter and finally at Sir Cyrall. Then, head high, she shoved away the footman waiting to reseat her and rushed from the room.

"Papa . . . ?"

"*No*." His look was momentarily hard but then softened. "My dear, I've a toast to make," said his lordship, beaming at her, and, after that one stern look, ignored his wife's departure. He did it in such a way that everyone else was forced to do so as well. The footmen refilled everyone's glass, and then, raising his own slightly, Lord Winthrop beamed. "To my daughter's happiness with a man who loves her as much as I do."

Everyone drank. More toasts were proposed as others

managed to remember their manners and put off speculation to a later, more appropriate time.

Dinner would have given every guest fodder for many a tale in the years to come, but, later that evening, it was followed by still another and far more titivating scene.

When the men joined the ladies after dinner, Miss Witherspoon suggested that dancing was in order and offered to play the piano, which, just that day, she'd had moved into the ballroom.

"It is not really a proper announcement ball," she told Miss Winthrop later, when an older guest took over the playing, "but I wanted to do something more special than merely bringing up the few bottles of champagne resting in the cellar, and I thought—"

"Oh, no," interrupted Miss Winthrop. "Please. No champagne."

"No?"

"It is *French*," said Miss Winthrop in a tight voice. "I will have nothing to do with the French or anything French." Her mouth tightened.

"The war . . . ?"

Miss Winthrop nodded, and one tear ran down her cheek. "My middle brother and an uncle . . ."

"Oh, my dear . . ."

Miss Witherspoon looked around for help, and Sir Cyrall, who had awaited his chance to come forward for his betrothed, instantly appeared. A quick look took in the situation. "John?" he asked softly.

Miss Winthrop nodded. She turned to Cyrall, and he put his hand to her waist. "I am sorry to spoil . . ."

"Nonsense," he said, easing her onto the floor and into the slow waltz lilting from under the pianist's nimble fingers. It was daring, taking his bride-to-be onto the floor for a waltz, but she needed distraction. "I too mourn John. He was a dear friend, as you know, and I know he was a very special brother to you." He drew her a trifle nearer than propriety allowed. "Never be embarrassed that you miss him, my love."

Not long after, Miss Winthrop realized that what she was dancing was the scandalous waltz. She cast a questioning look up at Cyrall. He grinned down at her and eased his hold so that she could move a bit away from him. "You are a devil, Cyrall Jamison," she scolded, but her eyes smiled.

"Am I not?" he asked and pretended to preen. "But you must admit my ploy answered. Far more appropriate to rouse a mild scandal than allow . . ." There was a touch of ice in his tone. "—anyone to guess you mourn your brother."

Miss Winthrop smiled a bit sadly. "Do you know that that is just the sort of thing that first drew me to you, Cyrall?"

He blinked, his long lashes batting several times in a row. "My sarcasm?" he asked, after a moment's startled thought.

"Your clear-eyed view of tonnish matters—and your dislike of many of the hypocrisies people deem important."

He blinked once more. "I had not realized you knew me so well," he said slowly.

"Why would I love you, if I did not know you?" she asked, turning a wide-eyed, questioning look up toward him.

Rafe swung Eustacia past them just then and grinned at Cyrall.

Miss Fairchild smiled and nodded to Miss Winthrop. "Had you a clue," Eustacia asked Rafe as they moved away, "that Sir Cyrall and Miss Winthrop had . . . were . . . hmm . . . ?"

He grinned the narrow-eyed, sardonic grin that was so much a part of him. "How unlike you, Euphrasia. To be tongue-tied, I mean."

She drew in a breath and let it out. "True. I am usually frank to a fault. Were you," she continued, speaking more firmly, "aware of Sir Cyrall's feelings for Miss Winthrop and hers for him?"

Rafe nodded. "I knew."

Eustacia eyed the tight-mouthed grimness marring his features. "And?"

"The Golden Adonis cannot bear to see his brother happy. He instantly took a hand in the game and was supported by Lady Winthrop, who is a bit of a climber."

"A *bit?*" asked Eustacia, every bit as sardonically as Rafe had ever managed.

He laughed. "I was trying," he said with pretend innocence, "to be polite." He executed three fast turns in a row without bumping into anyone—something of a miracle since few of those attempting the daring dance in public for the first time knew what they were doing and were in each other's way more than not.

Lord Cartwright was one who did know. He swung Di around a couple carefully counting their steps and into a long glide toward the far end of the ballroom. Farther from the piano, fewer people cluttered the floor, and he revealed just how adept he was.

Diane caught her breath after a particularly daring move and then smiled at him. "I wonder," she said, crinkles forming at the corners of her sparkling eyes, "with whom you have practiced to become so good."

"It was the one thing my wife and I enjoyed together . . . once Steven was abed. A way of passing a long winter evening, for instance. My secretary played well and was willing to provide music for us. One needn't talk when one dances, you know. And that suited the both of us." He sighed.

Diane nodded. "I am sorry, Stevie."

"Don't be. If anyone is to blame, it is I for not having the courage to end the thing before it began. I could have. My father was not a monster. Nor was hers. They'd not have been happy about it, but they'd have arranged things so that we needn't have wed." He shook his head. "I don't know why . . ."

"You were very young, Stevie. You had been taught you'd a duty to your name and title. You believed you must fulfill that duty, and you did. You did it honorably, as I knew you would, not allowing her to know—"

Lord Cartwright gave fleeting thought to the generous woman from whom, for a price, he had reluctantly taken his comfort off and on, a woman who had died of a pleurisy only a year or two earlier. He sighed, wondering if he should tell Diane.

"—when you took your comfort secretly. You wouldn't embarrass your wife with that knowledge or with any other rudeness."

His eyes widened.

She chuckled. "You are a man, Stevie, and you had a wife you've admitted refused you her bed. I do not fault you for finding another, and I am glad you never hurt her ladyship."

"I sometimes wondered if it *would* hurt her. If she knew."

"Oh, yes. Even if she didn't want you herself, she'd have been jealous and hurt. Irrational—but very human, you will admit."

He swung her around again, and then, in the middle of a phrase, the music came to an abrupt halt. They stopped dancing and turned toward the door, where Cyrall's brother stood, a supercilious expression on his handsome face.

"I have come for my betrothed," he said, looking down his nose.

Lord Winthrop moved forward quickly, putting out a hand to stop Cyrall, who also stepped forward. "I will deal with your brother," he said, loudly enough that everyone near them overheard. "I will enjoy dealing with your brother," he added, his voice cold.

His lordship reached the doorway where Primus, Lord Elden, more commonly known as the Golden Adonis, waited. He looked from one face to another, his eyes blank of any feeling. He turned his gaze on Lord Winthrop. The Adonis bowed. Lord Winthrop nodded.

"We will talk in the library," he said and moved to exit the room.

"We'll do no such thing. I have come for my betrothed, and I will have her."

"She is not and has never been your betrothed," said Lord Winthrop, each word a drop of ice.

"Of course she is. Everyone knows I mean to ask her to wed me."

"Everyone knows you mean to ask, but does everyone know what she meant to answer?" retorted his lordship. He realized Elden had no intention of leaving without a scene. "It was to be a refusal, my lord," he said, still speaking in that cold way that made several ladies shiver and the men look from one to another, a question in their eyes. "A *refusal*," he repeated.

Lord Elden blinked. "Refuse? *Me?*" He laughed. "What nonsense. She knew what an honor it would be. She was quite ready to say yes. I know she was."

"You cannot know."

"Oh, but I can," said Lord Elden triumphantly. "Her mother told me so."

Lord Winthrop compressed his lips and shook his head. "Her mother, my lord, was mistaken. My daughter has no desire to wed you. We have discussed it. Now, if you would be kind enough to depart . . . ?"

"Before," said Rafe, sotto voce into Eustacia's ear, "he discovers Miss Winthrop is engaged to Cyrall."

"Leave?" Lord Elden looked startled. "But I just got here. Of course I'll not leave."

"Do you often decide to visit homes where you have not been invited?" asked Lord Winthrop. The pretense at curiosity very nearly hid the insult.

Lord Elden's eyes narrowed, but then he smiled. "How

can I court my future wife if I go away?" he asked as if that answered everything.

"As long as you realize that *my* daughter is *not* that woman, then I can say nothing, can I? But if you think to court a woman engaged to another man, then you'd better consider how that will look. My daughter, my lord, is engaged to wed your brother. The date has been set and the notice sent off to the papers. All is settled."

Lord Elden turned white. Then lividly red. He glared around the room, saw his brother, who had his arm around Miss Winthrop's waist, and sneered. Without a word, he turned on his heel and disappeared.

Gradually most everyone relaxed. Rafe, however, moved with Eustacia to Sir Cyrall's side. "Cyr?"

Sir Cyrall shook his head, casting a quick look at his trembling bride-to-be. He looked at Eustacia, an intent look that demanded aid.

Eustacia instantly responded. "My dear, that was exceedingly stressful, was it not? I think a cup of tea is in order. Sweetened tea. Do not you?" She took Miss Winthrop's arm, gently leading her away, talking all the time in a soothing manner.

As they neared the door, they were joined by Miss Witherspoon. She too was suffering from shock.

"My dear Miss Witherspoon," said Eustacia, "do you think you might order us a pot of tea? There is a comfortable little room just down the hall—a sewing room, I think? And you will join us, will you not? You look as if you too could make good use of time to consider what has occurred." Eustacia spoke the last with the merest hint of humor.

Miss Witherspoon nodded. With something to do, she felt more herself and, after accepting the invitation to join them, ordered a footman off for the tray. She looked around the ballroom, nodded at the woman at the piano, who, after casting a startled look at the keyboard, placed her hands above it and—after a moment's thought—began the quick-paced music of a well-loved reel.

Miss Witherspoon watched several pairs of guests line up facing each other and hoped that meant the scandalous scene was over. She went off to join Miss Winthrop and Miss Fairchild.

"You must not worry," Miss Fairchild was saying as Miss Witherspoon entered the room. "The men will take care of any problems. They will not allow harm to come to you."

"My mother is so angry." Miss Winthrop sighed. "She wanted me to marry Lord Elden, but I could not like him. I could not even admire him—except, of course, for his looks. He truly is an Adonis, is he not? But he is . . . he isn't . . . he isn't *nice*," she finished in a rush.

"Rafe—Lord Morningside, I mean—says he is spoiled. His looks gave him everything he wanted when he was young. He could cajole anyone into anything, you see—except Cyrall. Cyrall was just enough younger that Lord Elden ignored him, and Cyrall developed his own personality long before Primus noticed. And, becoming his own man as it were, Cyrall would not fall into his brother's plans and plots or run the Adonis's errands or any of those menial things Lord Elden expected everyone around him to do with and for him. Lord Elden did not like that."

Miss Winthrop nodded. "I think he hates Cyrall. Sir Cyrall, I should say," she corrected herself.

Eustacia grimaced. "Do you *think* of him as *Sir* Cyrall? Or is it like my thinking of Lord Morningside as Rafe? I detest the social necessity of overweening formality, and you, at least, have the excuse of your engagement. May we speak without pretense?" she asked a trifle wistfully. "Just for this little while?"

Miss Witherspoon, listening politely, looked a trifle shocked but said nothing. It was certainly true that she thought of Richard Coxwald as Richard even if it had never occurred to her to speak of him so with others. Her hand went to the pocket in which she'd placed the letter Richard had sent in care of her father. His grandmother was recovering nicely, and he had hopes that perhaps he could return for the first real performance of his play, but he wouldn't promise. How she wanted to see him.

The door cracked open just a bit. "May I join you?" asked Diane. She wore a worried look. "I fear I bring bad news."

"Bad . . ." Miss Winthrop rose to her feet, her eyes wide with horror. "*Cyrall?*"

"No. Nor your father," said Diane quickly, seeing that was Miss Winthrop's next question. "Miss Witherspoon," she added, turning to her hostess, "your father, unaware of the situation, met Lord Elden in the hall and invited him to stay. The idiot promptly *agreed*. I was there." Diane took in a deep breath, let it out, and then shook her head. "I do not understand the man. He looked complacent to a degree I'd not thought possible to express with nothing more than a look." She frowned. "I wonder how he did it." As she spoke, she moved toward a mirror and tried out several expressions but turned when Eustacia chuckled. "What is it?" Her eyes widened. "Oh. I apologize. It is the actress in me, you see. Learning to express emotion is important, and that was a new one."

Eustacia nodded. She looked at the door when a knock preceded the entrance of the footman with the tea tray. Only when she was certain no one followed along behind did she relax. Her eyes met Diane's. Their gazes meshed.

Diane had no trouble at all decoding this wordless conversation. Eustacia was worried. And, not without reason. . . .

# CHAPTER FIFTEEN

The next morning Diane searched until she found Lord Cartwright. "Your son has disappeared," she said without preamble. Then, at his shocked expression, she added, "I am sorry, Stevie. I should not have spoken so abruptly, but when he did not appear for rehearsal this morning, I went to find him. He had not broken his fast—which surprised me, since he was not at dinner yesterday evening. I remember noticing that, but I fear I didn't think too much of it, since he has done the same before, has he not?"

Cartwright touched the creases marring her forehead, running his finger gently along them. "Shush, my dear." Hiding his own concern, he did as best he could to soothe hers. "As you'll recall, there was a great deal else to think about, but surely you worry for nothing. Where have you looked?"

Diane drew in a breath at his touch but didn't relax. If anything, she grew more tense and found she had to concentrate to remember his question. "I sent a footman to his room. His bed was not slept in, so I sent him to the stables. Stevie, your son took out his horse *yesterday*, *late* in the afternoon. He did not return. What if he was thrown? What if he is lying hurt and unable to reach help . . . ?"

A finger across her lips hushed her, but he could no longer conceal his own concern. "He is a truly excellent horseman, Di. I doubt he has come off a horse since he was ten. *Then* he tried to jump a five-bar gate on a pony that could barely manage the low bars set up for jump practice." The humor he tried to put into that didn't sound as he wished it to, and he gave into his feelings. "But even the very best can come off a horse under difficult situations."

She watched him stalk off. "Where are you going?"

"To set in motion a search of the surrounding area." His voice drifted back to her as his pace increased. "I doubt very much anything of the sort has happened, but we must check. Blasted boy. I swear . . ."

But Diane heard no more. Since he was headed toward the stables, she turned in the other direction, going off to find Miss Witherspoon. From her hostess, Diane learned that Lord Witherspoon, hating every moment of it, was in his office. After the problem with the absconding overseer, his daughter had urged that his lordship hire the vicar's son as secretary. Lord Witherspoon had done so and was, reluctantly, reading letters the young man found impossible to answer without direction.

"One good result of that venal man running off with the strongbox," confided Miss Witherspoon as she walked with Diane toward the office, "is that my father is paying more attention to his responsibilities."

There was an unexpressed "and about time" tone to her voice, but Diane, preoccupied with Steven's absence, ignored it. Given permission to enter the small room set aside for business, she went up to the desk behind which Lord Witherspoon sat. He was frowning at a paper held as far from his face as he could reach, and Diane made a mental note to suggest to Miss Witherspoon that she buy her father a pair of spectacles—but instantly put the thought aside when he looked up at her from under lowered brows.

Before he could ask what the devil she wanted—although he'd very likely phrase it more politely—Diane told him the situation and that Lord Cartwright had gone to ask the head groom to organize a search. "I thought perhaps you would have suggestions as to where they should look and perhaps know of neighbors who could add their aid to the effort."

Lord Witherspoon was already on his feet. He cast the paper on the desk, speaking over his shoulder as he left the room. "I'll return tomorrow. Take care of the rest as I said. I'll think about that one . . ."

His voice faded as he walked on, although Di could hear that he still spoke. She looked at Miss Witherspoon. "It seems as if there is no end of your difficulties this summer, Miss Witherspoon. I hope you don't hate us all before it ends."

Miss Witherspoon shook her head. "Oh, no. Why should I?" she asked. "Or, perhaps one . . ."

Diane smiled when, abruptly, her hostess shut her mouth with a snap. The Adonis was already making his presence felt as a most awkward and unwanted guest, and, Di knew, Miss Witherspoon had been forced to deal with a number of complaints, to say nothing of a comely maid who, hysterical, had threatened to leave. Instantly.

"May I suggest," Diane asked diffidently, "that orders be given so that if Steven *is* brought home on a gate, your housekeeper will be prepared?" Miss Witherspoon's cheeks paled. "I do not believe it will happen. I think the lad went off to nurse his anger or, perhaps, to face up to it and try to understand it. I think he'll come home."

"Anger?" Miss Witherspoon blinked in confusion.

Diane shifted from that thought into an explanation.

"Evidently you have not heard what happened at yesterday's rehearsal. He was angry with his father, and, instead of practicing the movements they were to use for the pretend fight, he turned it into a real one. I think he frightened *himself* more than he did Lord Cartwright, who—" Unconsciously, Di placed one hand over the wound in her arm. "—is well able to defend himself. I truly think the boy will come back with his tail between his legs, hoping to be forgiven but fearing he went too far and will be sent to Coventry—or perhaps, since he is prone to exaggeration, nursing expectations that the local magistrate will arrest him. He is not a coward, however, and he will return." She bit her lip, visualizing a contorted and broken body lying beyond a hedge or gate. "If he can. . . ."

They entered the housekeeper's rooms. Word had already reached that comfortable woman that a young man had taken out a horse the preceding evening and not returned. "Very likely he'll ride in this afternoon," she said, "and not have a clue as to why everyone is upset with him. Boys do that, you know. When they reach his age. They are all grown up, or so they think, and so why has anyone any reason to run after them or worry about them since *they* believe they are able to take care of themselves, and, besides—" She cast the actress a knowing look. "—they want privacy for their doings at that age, don't they now?"

Miss Witherspoon pretended she didn't understand that last comment. Diane grinned, but it quickly faded. "I sincerely hope you have the right of it," she said. "But just in case, you will be prepared?"

"Oh, yes. I've given orders, never fear," she said, still in that comfortable, competent way that soothed ragged nerves and left her auditors with the feeling that there was one problem less about which they need concern themselves.

* * *

Elsewhere, Lord Elden sat with Lady Winthrop, who wrung a handkerchief so tightly the lace edging unraveled. "I cannot understand it," her ladyship moaned.

"Understand?" he asked.

"How she can prefer your brother to *you*." A tear ran down her ladyship's plump cheek. Naively, she continued. "You have *everything*. You have money and position and are handsome as the devil. Oh!" Shocked by her own words, her eyes widened. "Do pardon me. But you have *everything*. How can she possibly object to . . ." Her eyes widened, and she closed her mouth.

"To . . . ?" he asked. A rather dangerous note to that single word.

Lady Winthrop bit her lip. "Oh, it is *nothing*. Nothing at all. The chit is stupid and disobedient. A snake in the bosom. A cuckoo in the nest. A *changeling* . . ."

Elden changed tactics. "My dear Lady Winthrop, she must have thought she had reason. You *can* tell me, you know," he coaxed, and smiled the brilliant, practiced smile that always got him what he wanted. "How may I convince her she is wrong, that she must change her mind, if I do not know what it is to which she objects?"

Lady Winthrop eyed him. She had heard whispers that Lord Elden had a temper but, given all his assets, had discounted it. What if it were true? What if he . . .

He coaxed a bit more, complimenting her, and, as he knew she would, she sighed and told him. He stiffened. "Nonsense. Utter nonsense."

"That is what I told her," said Lady Winthrop.

"How can she think that I don't love her? Have I not told her I love her?"

"*She* says," explained Lady Winthrop, "that you love only yourself."

His mouth opened, and his eyes blinked rapidly. "That . . . that . . ." He could think of no term that would not insult the chit's mother to the point of alienating her, something he could not do so long as he needed her help. "Nonsense."

"Besides, you have great reason to think well of yourself. You are the Golden Adonis, after all," said Lady Winthrop. She felt much better for unburdening herself, and he had *not* become angry, so *that* was all right. Lady Winthrop was not particularly perceptive and did not notice how difficult it was for Elden to restrain himself. "Now perhaps you can make her see sense," she added, still hoping to find her daughter married to the heir to an earldom.

"Of course I can."

The Adonis went off to plot strategy and, for long moments, reveled in the anticipation of putting his brother's nose out of joint. He also plotted his revenge on the chit who was causing him such problems. The chit who didn't want him. The chit who thought him incapable of loving her.

*But I do love her. Of course I love her. And*, he gloated, *my brother will not have her.*

He was not pleased to run into an old friend of his father's when he went looking for his brother, with whom he hoped to pick a quarrel. He always won when they fought, and he needed that reaffirmation of his superiority. He nodded to the gentleman but immediately frowned and stalked on.

*It is*, he mused, *more and more difficult to rouse that . . . that . . . that . . .*

Once again he was at a loss for words—this time because he could think of nothing insulting enough to express his feelings for his brother.

Primus was so preoccupied, he didn't notice his father's friend send a thoughtful look after him. He couldn't know that the man went to his room, found his traveling writing desk, and wrote a letter to the earl. Nor could he know that the letter was sent off in the hands of the man's personal groom less than an hour later with orders he was not to spare his horse.

Lord Elden would have been exceedingly upset to discover any of that. Only a month earlier his father had given him still another long, unwanted, and obviously undeserved lecture concerning his behavior toward Cyrall. Why his father preferred Cyrall to himself, Primus had never understood. As Lady Winthrop had pointed out, *he* was the Golden Adonis. Not *Cyrall*.

Unfortunately for his temper, when he did run into his brother on those rare occasions when the men returned from searching for Steven, coming in for a quick sandwich or hunk of meat pie or a fresh horse, there were too many others around and about. What Primus intended required they be alone.

Primus never did get Cyrall alone. He'd have been surprised to learn that Rafe, along with other friends, made it certain he did not.

Cyrall would have laughed to know he was under their protection. He would also have been touched by their concern and would have thoroughly approved that the conspiracy extended to Miss Winthrop. She too was never, ever alone. If one or two of the women were not with her, then her father was.

Lord Elden had achieved neither of his goals, the fight with his brother or the wooing of Miss Winthrop away from Cyrall, when, very late that afternoon, Steven returned.

Diane was the first to see him. She had gone to the stables, hoping for some word, and was there when he rode in. He looked exhausted, rumpled, and very worried.

"Where," she asked, "have you been? We are all worried sick."

"*All*?" he asked, a look that contained both disbelief and hope in his eyes.

"*All*. Your father has ridden miles looking for your *body*."

Steven blanched. "I never thought of that. I didn't mean to frighten . . ." He looked defeated. "Something *else* I did wrong." He grimaced. "The devil. I can never do anything right."

"You did right to come back." Diane turned to the one lad remaining at the stables under orders to look after things and help anyone returning for a fresh horse. "Saddle up," ordered Diane, "and find someone among the searchers and then return to your duties here. Whoever you find will spread the word." She turned back to Steven.

Steven looked appalled. "Searchers?

"All the grooms, most of Witherspoon's male guests, a number of neighbors, and many of *their* servants . . . shall I go on?" she asked tartly, her concern expressed in a scold. She sighed. "I'm sorry, Steven. I should not have said that. At least not in that tone. You had reason to go away, but I do wish you'd left a note."

Steven groaned but followed her rapid footsteps as she headed back toward the house, meaning to reassure everyone there. "How will he ever forgive me?"

"Forgive yourself, Steven. That is the first thing."

"I can't. I wanted to hurt him. I knew I couldn't, but I wanted to." He caught up to her. "Why did I want to hurt him? How could I have even thought to try to—"

"Enough." She stopped, and, perforce, so did he. "You have been confused and hurt. You have been in that awful state of growing up that all must go through. Some have an easier time than others, so, in that respect, you are unlucky. Then too you have been under pressure because you have undertaken a role on stage that a *professional* would find daunting. Steven, you have reason for going to pieces, but now you must find your equilibrium and go on. You have responsibilities. You must apologize to your father, yes, but you needn't make a huge thing of it. He does understand. He isn't the most tactful soul in the world, so he may not make that clear to you, but he understands. But he may *not* if you try to avoid your responsibilities. Believe me."

"Responsibilities?" he asked, a tentative note to his voice.

She nodded. "It is a huge part of growing up, Steven, accepting that others are important, that duties must be fulfilled—*not* by wallowing in the emotions driving one or the distractions or the wish to be something one is not. You will find that doing what is necessary very often leads to becoming the person you want to be. Dreaming. Thinking about it. Wishing it were so. Those things do not help. Not at all."

The youth straightened. "I'll . . . try."

"Of course you will. You will mature and be as good a man as your father. I just hope that when the time comes when you truly fall in love, you find a woman who will help you and not become an impediment."

He sighed. "As was my mother?" A faintly belligerent expression slipped into that. "She *loved* me."

"Yes, of course she loved you. It is also true, unfortunately, that she *needed* you."

"Needed?" he asked, frowning.

"Hmm. Your father could not give her the sort of romantic love she wanted. I have come to think she was the sort who needed to feel as if she were the complete center of someone's existence. She made herself the center of yours. She loved you, Steven, and you are very lucky that she was not so selfish that she turned you into one of those boys who feels that every woman they meet should mother them. She allowed you to become the sort of man you should be."

"I wish I could be so certain of that."

But Diane saw that some of the tension had drained from him. She nodded. "Come along now. I must tell the others that you are found and in good health. . . . " She frowned. "Steven, have you eaten?"

He smiled. "Not since early this morning. I found a small

hostelry and stopped there. The host's wife was an excellent cook."

*This morning. Well, that explains why he was so rumpled and grubby! He was forced to sleep under a hedge or in a barn loft.* All she said, however, was, "Good." They approached the theater. "Let me tell Roger you are back."

". . . and about time. Cartwright, I want you here in half an hour. Diane, collect those in the scene with the Sphinx. We'll—" He scowled when she shook her head. "What do you mean, no? We must rehearse every scene this young fool—"

"I am sorry that I caused so much trouble," interrupted Steven. "I believe the reason Mrs. Runyard shakes her head is that I am still causing it. Evidently a great number of your actors are out looking for me."

Diane hid a smile at the touch of real arrogance she heard. If nothing else, Steven appeared to have attained another step or two on the rough road to adulthood.

"I will put in as many hours as you think necessary," added Steven, "but not until I've had a chance to apologize to my father and—" The boy in him reappeared. "—if I am very lucky, make him understand."

Roger rolled his eyes. "Everyone is against me. This play will be a disaster!" Steven looked worried. Roger sighed. "Oh, do not mind me. I am always an ogre at this stage of production. Ask Diane." He glowered at her when she laughed.

"So you are," she agreed cheerfully. "Come along, Steven. We still have to inform those at the house of your appearance back in our midst. Perhaps, Roger, we can have a short rehearsal this evening after dinner."

At that notion, Roger relaxed. He nodded. "I will not waste my time now but will go check the scenery. And the costumes. You might send Miss Fairchild and some of the other women out to try theirs on. I know you tried yours this morning, so that is all right. *You* return as well," he said to Steven. "The seamstress can see if *your* costumes fit." He was almost at the side door when he finished speaking. His hand on the doorknob, he turned. "Glad you're back, Cartwright. Worried about you." He disappeared.

Steven, his brows arched, looked at Diane. "Because of the play?"

She chuckled. "Only in part, Steven. Only in part."

Roger did work his cast late that evening, and everyone was exhausted when they finally got to bed. Cyrall and Miss Winthrop, chaperoned that evening by Lord Winthrop, were among those who went upstairs early and had already had several hours sleep when the rest crept up the stairs to their rooms.

Some time after that a door opened, and, on nearly silent feet, a man edged his way down the dark hall. Very lightly he ran his fingers along the wall ahead of him, avoiding a table here, a bench there, and, as he went, carefully counting doorways. Before one he paused. Then, unsure, he went on to the far end of the hall and started back, once again counting.

Nodding, he carefully cracked open the door and listened. A soft sigh. The rustle of bedclothes. He waited. And waited longer when there were more sounds of restlessness. Somewhere in the distance, he heard a door click shut. Quickly, he slipped inside the room and, his lip between his teeth, eased the door closed, releasing the handle slowly and carefully so he'd not do as someone else had done and make a noise that might alert others to his intent.

He straightened away from the door and, once again, listened. There was another sigh. Another disturbance of the bedding . . . and then the covers were thrown back. He stiffened. The occupant of the bed sat up and scuffled against the floor for slippers. Indecision held the intruder still, but irritation grew. Why did the chit move about at this time of night? Why was she not soundly asleep?

The room's legitimate occupant yawned, stood, moved toward the window, and stared out of it. Then she turned to the table next to it, and soft noises indicated a search for something. . . .

The worst happened. A skritching noise preceded the flicker of a spark. The glow of tinder. A candle held to it . . . and the flare of light.

Madeline Winthrop turned, once again yawning, opened her eyes . . . and screamed. Primus, growling, opened the door and ran lightly down the hall. Madeline screamed a second time as her father burst through the door connecting to his lordship's and Lady Winthrop's room.

"Maddy?" He glanced around, saw she stood alone near the window, saw the door open to the hall, heard voices and steps, and sighed. "Lord Elden?" he asked softly. His daughter nodded, biting her lip, her eyes wide and full of fright. "The man is mad," muttered Winthrop.

"With love," said his wife, cooingly. Her hands clasped. "My dear," she said to her daughter, "you must not blame the poor man. His head is turned by your beauty. He lost all control of himself and—"

"Be still, you foolish woman," interrupted her husband. "It isn't love that drives him but a bloody-minded determination to have his way whatever the cost to others."

"No, no . . ."

"*Yes*." He moved toward the door, where, after a tentative tap, Miss Witherspoon looked in. "Everything is quite all right," he said. "My daughter suffered one of her nasty nightmares. She apologizes for waking everyone, but she'll be fine now. No, we'll not be needing a pot of tea, thank you just the same. . . ."

And with more of the same he managed to soothe those standing in the hall, shut the door, and lean back against it.

His lordship stared at his wife. "This is your fault," he said, testy due to being wakened in such a way from a sound sleep.

"My . . . !"

"Yes. Yours. You encouraged a man of no character to think our daughter is so shallow she'd be happy with nothing more than status and wealth."

His wife blinked. "But . . ."

"Perhaps *you* think that is sufficient," he said softly, but with a dangerous edge to his voice. "For most of us it is not. Not for anyone who is at all sensitive. I am proud of our daughter, my lady. She has chosen a far better man than that you'd have foisted upon her."

"A second son! A sarcastic, bitter man who plays the fool more often than not! Better? How can you think him better? Half the looks! A tenth the wealth! A nobody!"

"You cannot call the son of an earl a nobody, even a second son," retorted her husband bitingly. "And you are wrong about everything but the wealth. He has enough, however, to keep our daughter in the elegancies of life, and, most important, he loves her sincerely and truly. If you even look as if you commiserated with that creature who just now attempted to ruin your daughter, I will—" He broke off, gnashed his teeth a few times, and tried again. "I will cut your allowance to the barest of bones and keep you at Windy Hill year in and year out."

His wife blanched. She hated the months they spent at the Winthrop's most northern estate, which was her husband's favorite. She hated the bleak moors, the distance between neighbors, the fact it was a major journey merely to go shopping for trifles in York.

"No London? No society?" she whispered.

"I have said it," said her husband wearily. "Now go to bed. I wish to talk to our daughter."

Through all this Miss Winthrop had stood like a statue, her horrified gaze on the door. Her father shut the connecting door with his wife on the far side and went to Maddy. He took the candle from her hand and set it firmly into the candlestick holder. Then he took her hands in his. "He is gone. He'll not be back. Believe me," said her father.

Her blank gaze cleared. Her gaze moved to meet the steady look in her father's eyes. She blinked. "He . . ."

"Yes, he acted like an animal, but luckily you screamed and frightened him away. *Nothing happened.*" Lord Winthrop was almost certain nothing had happened. There hadn't been time. "Nothing," he repeated.

"He . . ."

"*He will not come back.* First of all, I have locked the door. Secondly—" A smile formed lines at the corners of his eyes. "—I will remain here for the rest of the night. You will be perfectly safe, my dear."

"Remain here?" Her eyes had a hopeful look in them when she turned her face up to his. "Here? But, Father . . ."

"You think I'll be uncomfortable in that nicely padded chair?" he asked, tipping his chin toward the fireplace in front of which it stood. "There is, I see, a footstool as well. I will be comfortable enough, but I would stay even if I were forced to stand in a corner for the rest of the night. I'll not have you frightened like that ever again."

She bit her lip. "Tomorrow . . . ?"

"Tomorrow—we will see."

Maddy frowned. "You look grim, Papa. You won't . . ."

He didn't pretend to misunderstand. "You think me so foolish that I'd thrust a duel upon him? He is not worthy of it. A horsewhip," he added thoughtfully, "might be appropriate, but I doubt he'll stay to suffer such indignity."

A smile twitched her lips.

"That's better," he said, squeezing her hands. He moved his arm to her shoulders, turning her, and led her to her bed. "Now, in you go. I'll pull the covers up as I did when you were really little and tell the bedbugs they are not to bite your precious skin. Shall I? As I did when you where a child and still believed in such nonsense?" He smiled down at her as she settled herself and then, gently, smoothed her covers around her slim form.

She yawned.

"Sleep, child. No bedbugs tonight. . . ."

Her eyes closed, and, after a moment, her breathing slowed. He nodded to himself, moved to the chair, and settled himself for what remained of the night.

*Which will be*, he thought ruefully, *far less comfortable than I managed to convince dear little Maddy it would be. . . .*

He shifted, stretched his legs over the small stool, shifted again and, sighing, did his best to doze away the hours until dawn. Unfortunately, the angry thoughts rampaging through his mind allowed very little rest, and he was exceedingly glad when, finally, he saw a light patch of gray where Maddy had disturbed the drapery the night before.

# CHAPTER
# SIXTEEN

The next day Lord Cartwright, who had been strolling the terrace with his son, was informed his solicitor had arrived and awaited his convenience in the library. "My *solicitor*?"

"Something has gone awry?" asked Steven, sounding worried.

Cartwright's mind caught up with him, and he smiled. "No, nothing like that, Steven. I'd almost forgotten I wrote him about a certain matter, and I think he has come to confirm a suspicion. Why the blithering idiot didn't merely write me a letter I cannot understand, but he didn't. He's here . . . so—" Cartwright's eyes narrowed. "—perhaps there is something a trifle less straightforward about it than I assumed?"

"It?"

Cartwright looked at his son. "I suppose there is no reason you should not know. Come along. We'll see if your grandfather was as sly as I think he was—and we will discover just why our family solicitor made a journey into the country merely to confirm something of which I am already convinced."

"It has to do with Mrs. Runyard?" asked Steven a trifle tentatively.

"One thing I've never thought," said his father with satisfaction, "is that you are the least little bit stupid. Yes. As you have guessed, it has to do with Mrs. Runyard. Come along."

The solicitor rose to his feet as the two entered the library, looked startled that Steven was there as well, and bit his lip, a wary look in his eyes. "My lord?" He cast a quick look at Steven and back to his lordship.

"My son is aware I was once intimately involved with Mrs. Runyard," said Cartwright with only a trifling amount of hauteur. "Are you here to confirm the guess I made as to the source of the annuity paid Mrs. Runyard each quarter?"

The man cast Steven a frown, but if the father did not send him away from a situation that should have been of a private nature, then who was he to object? "It was a codicil added to his will some months before he died."

Cartwright nodded. "About the time he asked me if I remembered a little opera dancer I'd known years earlier."

Steven blinked. He stared at his father. "Mrs. Runyard?" he asked.

Cartwright smiled a rather self-denigrating smile. "I made it clear to my father what Di meant to me when I returned home to meet your mother, commenting at that time that I was not ready to marry anyone just yet." His lordship's gaze turned inward, back in time. "I was too young. He should have known. . . ."

"You . . . you suffered too, didn't you? Married to Mother?" Steven looked shocked by the notion.

Cartwright looked up. "Suffered? In a way. Yes. Not so much as she did, I suppose. I had responsibilities to take up my time and energy. Far more than she, you see. I had less time to daydream or indulge in foolish regrets for what might have been." He shook his head. "Not that anything 'might have been' between Di and me. I was heir. She was reared in the theater. A man of my birth could not wed a woman of hers. . . ." A muscle jumped in his jaw. "Something your grandfather pointed out to me in no uncertain terms."

"But he gave Mrs. Runyard an annuity? An income? Years after the affair ended?"

Cartwright looked toward the solicitor. When the man nodded confirmation, he added, slowly, "Years and years after. I don't really understand it." He turned to his solicitor. "Why did you come to tell me this when a letter would have done the same with far less effort on your part?"

The man retrieved a leather folder that he'd laid on a nearby table. He opened it and produced a document that he handed to Lord Cartwright. "If you ever asked about the matter, I was to give you this."

Cartwright's brows arched at the sight of his father's firm, wide-nibbed penmanship. "I see." The brows dropped and his eyes narrowed. "I think." He thought a moment. "Or maybe not."

For a very long moment he hesitated to take the proffered document, and then, reluctantly, he grasped it. But even when it was in his hands, he merely stared at the spot where his father's favorite signet ring had pressed deeply into the red wax melted to seal the folds of heavy paper.

Steven shifted from one foot to the other. He looked from the thick paper to his father. He bit his lip against a demand that the seal be broken and the words be read.

A muscle jumped in Cartwright's clenched jaw. "What the devil can the old man have had in his head?"

"When he asked if you remembered her?" asked Steven, attempting to make sense of his father's muttered question.

"You mean, what did I say in answer?" asked Cartwright a trifle impatiently. "That *of course* I remembered her. That a love such as we'd had for each other might mellow but never disappeared. That our feelings had been pure as the purest crystal and rang as true when touched. Even after all the years. . . ."

"But you didn't . . . ?"

"No, Steven, I didn't. I never again spoke to her until I was brought here, hotfoot, to save you from a scheming, aging actress!"

Steven grinned, but the grin faded at his father's biting sarcasm. "She isn't aging," contradicted the lad. "And she never *schemed*. Never." That thought had him hanging his head in shame. "I guess . . . I was the schemer," he said.

"Someone who knows our history said I should congratulate you on your good taste in women," said his lordship dryly, his brows arched. "He was twitting me that my son was enamored of the same woman who stole my heart, you see."

The solicitor cleared his throat. He was, the Cartwright men realized, exceedingly embarrassed by their half-serious, half-jesting banter. "Steven, ask that excuse Witherspoon has hired for a butler to settle Mr. Striker in a comfortable sitting room with a pot of tea and whatever else is appropriate at this time of day."

The solicitor promised to remain in the house until dismissed and that any questions would be answered to the best of his ability. He left the library thankful to have escaped a scene that was intriguing but, as his lordship had guessed, embarrassing.

"Now," said Cartwright when the two were alone. "Let us see. . . ."

Steven sat across from his father, who placed the packet on the table and, after one more moment's hesitation, ran his finger under the wax. He unfolded the pages and had to blink away moisture at the sight of his father's hand.

"Words from the crypt," he muttered.

Then Cartwright read. There were three sheets, the handwriting large and sprawling: the well-known penmanship his lordship had never thought to see again. He casually handed over each sheet to Steven as he finished it—except that before the last one left his hands, a muttered curse escaped him. When both had read it to the end, Cartwright looked across the table into Steven's eyes.

"She is . . . wonderful," said Steven.

"You were about to say perfect?" asked his father, a hint of a smile on his lips.

"It has been pointed out to me," said Steven carefully, "that no one is perfect. That it is not only impossible, but to expect it of someone only makes that person uncomfortable. Or," he added thoughtfully, "instills in them strong and upsetting feelings of inadequacy."

"I am sorry if something I did or said made you think I wished you to be perfect, Steven."

Steven sighed. "I didn't somehow merely think it. Mother told me it was so."

Cartwright's eyes widened. "She didn't!"

"She did. Now that I've thought about it," continued Steven, "I think it was her way of encouraging me to do my very best at everything I did—but it only made me feel you were further from me than ever." He looked up, frowning. "Could she have meant that to happen as well? She did keep us apart in other ways," he added quickly, "so it wouldn't be an impossible thought."

"I doubt she had more in mind than a wish to encourage you," said Lord Cartwright quickly. "She might have approved the second result, but I think it far more devious than she was capable of being."

"She *wasn't* devious, was she?"

Cartwright heard the hint of desperation in that. "She wasn't devious. She wasn't a bad woman at all in any way—"

*If one discounted her dislike of intimacy and her inability to accept the world as it is.* "—and she loved you very much," said Cartwright firmly.

Steven relaxed. He glanced at the papers scattered between them. "Will you tell Mrs. Runyard?"

"That my father kept an eye on her all those years? That he came to admire her? That he felt guilty for separating us, although he also felt it was necessary in that, at that time, nothing could come of our love? And that he wished to assure she would never suffer when she could no longer work?"

"And," asked Steven softly, "his last words?"

Cartwright stilled. "Would you find it a terrible thing, Steven?"

Steven blushed rosily. "I've no right to object, have I?"

"Of course you do," said his lordship a trifle testily and then, more evenly, added, "I think you are over your infatuation for her—"

A brow arched, a tacit query that was answered by a sharp nod of Steven's head along with a faint blush that Cartwright ignored.

"—but she is still an actress. It would still be social folly. You, as my son, might find yourself laughed at for your new mother. If I were to wed her, that is."

A belligerent look filled Steven's features and hardened them. "I'd black anyone's eyes who dared to—"

Cartwright laughed and relaxed. "No, you wouldn't. You'd chuckle and shrug and say that the follies of our elders have nothing to do with us."

"I wouldn't," said Steven, his chin rising.

"It would be the best way of handling your friends, my lad," said his lordship lightly. Then Lord Cartwright sobered. "Thank you, Steven. I don't know what I mean to do, but that you'd not object . . . that means a great deal to me."

His lordship stretched his hand across the table, holding it open, waiting. Steven stared at it. Then, in a rush, he put his own hand into the larger, older, stronger hand. They clasped each other and held for a long, emotional moment.

"Just remember, Steven," said his father softly. "I have always loved you. I love you now. I will love you throughout time. I am here if you need me. I will help in any way I can. If you have questions, I will try to answer them . . . and I hope very much that, in the future, we are not strangers to each other."

Steven, his heart full, his throat half-clogged with unshed tears, nodded.

The solicitor, assured the annuity should continue to be paid, departed—and wondered, off and on for the rest of his life, what, exactly, was in the letter he'd delivered to his lordship.

Late that afternoon, still another unexpected coach pulled up to the front of the Witherspoon's mansion. Miss Witherspoon, informed of the latest arrival, fretted. All the best rooms had been given to others. To move someone from the room they'd made their own would, at this point, be an insult. Yet, to give the Earl of Eldenstone a lesser room would also be an insult. She was somewhat eased by the information that she had a trifling amount of time in which to determine what she was to do.

His lordship had demanded the presence of his son and the privacy in which they could meet.

"He's in the library, miss," said Jenkins. "I've sent footmen running to find his son."

But it was Sir Cyrall who appeared soon after, having been rousted from working, again, with Lord Cartwright and Steven and their fight scene. "Father?" he asked, entering the library with quick, light steps. "An unexpected treat," he said lightly. "You cannot have received my letter yet, so what has—" He broke off. "Oh, oh. Wrong son?" he asked, still in that light manner that would have told those who knew him that he was trying hard to avoid a scene.

Lord Eldenstone frowned. "I should have told that man I wished my heir, should I not? Tell him to find Elden and send him here at once."

"Father . . ."

"No. If half of what Benningcorn wrote is true, then Elden has gone too far. How dare he—"

"Hush, Father. You know my brother's temper. I have not allowed him to make a scene." He thought of Primus's entrance that first evening but pushed *that* scene from his mind.

The door swept open, and Lord Benningcorn entered. "Thank goodness you've arrived," he said to Eldenstone. "Oh. You here, boy? Run along. I've things to say to your father."

"My lord . . ."

"He is correct, Son. You return to whatever you were doing. John," he added, turning slightly, "go with him. I want no . . . scene, did you call it, Cyrall?" He grimaced.

Cyrall turned slightly, surprised to find anyone else in the room and saw not one but two of the rather hulking footmen that accompanied his father most everywhere. "Oh, surely . . ."

"Oh, yes, *surely*."

There was no arguing with that tone, and Sir Cyrall, followed by the footman, headed toward the door.

His father's voice stopped him. "A moment. What did you mean that your letter had not reached me?"

Cyrall turned, his eyes light with emotion. "I am engaged, Father. I have asked Miss Winthrop to marry me, and she has agreed."

"Miss Winthrop!" After a moment, Lord Eldenstone's shoulders relaxed. "I begin to understand. . . ."

"Why your other son appeared here so unexpectedly?" asked Lord Benningcorn with ponderous humor. "No surprise at all, is it? You go away, boy. I want words with your father."

The rather obese form of his father's friend had once been a source of great amusement to Sir Cyrall. Now, looking at him with new eyes, he saw intelligence behind the smallish eyes, the snuff-powdered cheeks, and the spot of egg staining the older man's cravat. Cyrall nodded, wondering what it was that Benningcorn meant to tell his father.

He hoped it was not the tale of last night's attempt on Miss Winthrop's virtue. Nothing had happened, after all, and he and Maddie had decided to forget it. It was always better to ignore his brother's attempts to outrage and hurt. Had Benningcorn been in the hall last night? Cyrall thought not; very likely, it was the scene in the ballroom.

Cyrall sighed deeply at more than one thought as he returned to the music room where the Cartwrights awaited him.

In the library, Lord Benningcorn did just what Cyrall hoped he'd not do. He told Lord Eldenstone exactly both what occurred the night Lord Elden arrived and what he believed had occurred the previous night to interrupt everyone's sleep. "I believe you'll find a letter from Winthrop awaiting you when you return home. Perhaps two—one concerning the engagement, and then the sad story I've just spun for you."

"All too likely a true tale." Eldenstone sighed. "We ruined the boy, Benny, old friend. Turned him into a monster. . . ."

"Oh, no. You encouraged him to know his beauty, but you did not encourage him to believe it the whole of what he should be. I remember his years at school when you berated him for slothful work. I remember your spending a great deal of time attempting to teach him the proper handling of the reins, of a gun. Elden was interested in nothing that did not come easily, Eldenstone. If he had to work to master something, he cast it aside. That was not your doing."

The two fell silent. Benningcorn had, for years, been the recipient of Lord Eldenstone's concern for his eldest, the heir to great estates and greater responsibilities. "If only . . . ," his lordship said at one point.

"Let us not think of that," said Benningcorn, soothingly.

Another passage of time in which each sunk into the gloom of memories they'd rather forget. Eldenstone stirred, pulled his watch from his fob pocket, and opened it. "Where the devil is he?"

The door opened on the words, and Jenkins peered in. "Not here, hum?"

"My heir is not here, if that is what you are asking," said Eldenstone, rising to his feet.

"Blast the man," said Jenkins in a decidedly un-butlerish tone and disappeared.

Some moments later they heard the man's lightly humorous tones. "Now then, son, you cannot go running off before you see your papa, can you? No, no, now, none of *that*. You come along just like you oughta, now." Looking amused, he reentered the library with Lord Elden in tow. "Here he is, your lordship. Caught him stealing out the door like he was in the basket and escaping the paying of his tab. Can't think what he was thinking . . . unless he's expecting a lecture and hoped to avoid it."

Lord Eldenstone's second footman had moved instantly and now stood at the door, closing it behind the departing butler. Lord Elden cast the overly brawny footman a look of apprehension and then, lifting his chin to an arrogant angle, strutted nearer the table where his father and Benningcorn stood. "Well?" he asked, casting what he hoped was an amused glance at his father's friend. "Couldn't wait to tell tales, could you, old man?"

Eldenstone glared. "You will show respect to your betters."

"Bah," said Elden, but softly—unfortunately unable to hide the sneer that went with it.

His father sighed. "A month ago we had another long

talk, Elden. At the end of it I told you I had lost patience. You swore you would reform your ways."

Elden shrugged, pretending his fingernails were of more interest to him than anything his father had to say. "I have an appointment in Leicestershire and must leave at once, so if you'd reach your point—assuming, of course, that there is a point—I could be on my way."

"Oh, you'll be on your way," said his father, a muscle jumping in his jaw.

Elden cast him a quick look. His mouth tightened. "Then it is all right if I go now?" he asked, stepping back.

"No."

Elden froze.

"No, it is not all right. Not if you mean to Leicestershire. I warned you a month ago I would not allow you to go on as you've been doing. I would not tolerate a scandal at your hands."

"So?"

"You have gone too far."

Elden had not moved, but now something changed in him, and, although he had not shifted, he gave the impression of utter stillness. "So?" he repeated.

"I have arranged for your transport to our West Indian estates. You will go there. You will stay there. You will not return to England for ten years."

"Oh?"

"You may sneer if you wish, but I assure you that no one will take you off the island. You will live there for the next decade. Assuming you survive, you may then think about returning."

"I am your heir."

"So you are. Unfortunately."

"You have always preferred Cyrall."

"You have always believed that. I find your brother's posturing as irritating as I find your viciousness, but I do not find him ready to push the family name deep into the mud for pure perversity."

The icy note in his father's voice penetrated Elden's preoccupation with himself. "Viciousness."

"Viciousness."

Elden blinked, frowning. "I don't understand."

His father stared. "My God. You haven't a notion, have you!"

"Well?"

"I have been told that last night you entered a young lady's bedchamber, with, I'm certain, fell intent."

"If you mean I meant to seduce her, of course I did. How else could I so easily convince her she should wed me instead of Cyrall?"

It was his father's turn to become utterly still. "And her feelings?" asked his father softly.

"She is confused, obviously," said Elden airily, certain he could convince his father he was in the right and change his elder's mind about his exile.

"Or perhaps she has seen that you have no concern for how another feels, what another wants, and has no wish to spend her life trying to guess what you wish of her so that she will not rouse your temper."

Elden realized he had not explained properly. He made another attempt. And another. He began to panic. "You cannot send me to that place. There is no one there. No society. No shops. No—"

"No one about whom I care a jot," interrupted his lordship. "Therefore your behavior will not shame me. Yes. Exactly." He looked across the room at the impassive footman. "William, you and John will take Elden in hand now. If he was about to depart these premises, then his boxes are packed and ready to go. There need be no delay. The ship departs from Portsmouth in three days. The captain will have had my packet of letters that are to be passed on, some to the governor and some to my agent. When you have delivered Elden where he is going in the islands into the hands of my agent, then you and John may continue to the colonies, as planned. Good luck, William. You have both done well by me and will find I've been generous."

"Generous to servants," sneered Elden, sweat running down one side of his face. "Generous to the dirt beneath our feet! And your own son? How do you treat me?" Elden clenched his fists. "Oh, you'll be sorry. You'll be sorry," he screamed, suddenly losing all control.

He ranted and raved, paced the library, and, finally, reached out and shoved everything off a table. Water and flowers flew over carpet and furniture and spotted the books in a nearby bookcase. The beautiful vase shattered.

Feeling reluctant pity, Lord Eldenstone had allowed his heir the outlet to his temper, but the destruction of another's property was going too far. His voice firm, he said, "Enough. You are an adult. Put childish tantrums behind you. Learn to control yourself."

Elden turned to stare at his father. "Control myself?" He looked bemused. "But why? Am I not the Adonis? Am I not perfect? What can you mean, *control myself?*"

Half an hour later, subdued if not resigned, Lord Elden was placed in a traveling carriage along with John and William. The footmen kept wary watch, knowing they must have a care for themselves and not trust the young man in their charge for a minute.

Lord Eldenstone, taking leave of his heir, eyed him for a minute and then turned to the two men. "He will attempt to avoid his destiny. See that he does not. John, you have the pistol I gave you? And you, William, you are well armed? I am aware you are a genius with those knives of yours. Don't kill him if you can avoid it. But, one way or another, get him on that ship, away from England, and into exile." He looked back at his suddenly white-faced heir. "Good-bye, Primus. I am very sorry that, somehow, we failed to make a decent man of you."

He stepped back and watched the carriage trundle down the drive. He hadn't much hope for his heir's future. He knew he was very likely condemning his son to a rough and ready death at the hands of someone insulted beyond bearing. Feeling old, hating himself, he sighed in resignation.

But Primus's fate was in other hands now.

"Father?"

Lord Eldenstone turned. "Cyrall."

"Benningcorn said . . ."

Cyrall couldn't finish the sentence, but Lord Eldenstone nodded. "Your brother goes into exile. He has proven himself incapable of acting the gentleman. He has been given chance after chance and warning after warning. He cannot be allowed to go his length. I had hoped . . . but he grows worse rather than better." Eldenstone had been staring at his feet. He looked up. "Cyrall . . . ?"

Cyrall went to his father, put his arm around the older man's shoulders, and led him back into the house. "You have thought long and hard about this. I know you have. It was not a mere impulse. And if you thought about it and concluded it was necessary that Primus be sent away, then it *was* necessary." Cyrall continued speaking softly as he led his father into an empty salon in which he knew decanters held a very good burgundy and a lighter canary. He hesitated then poured two glasses of the burgundy and handed one to his father, who sat, unseeing, staring into the empty grate. "Father, I'll say one more thing." He waited.

After a moment, his father looked up.

"I am glad I no longer have to worry about protecting my back from my brother's revenge for some imagined slight. It has become more and more difficult to avoid him."

Lord Eldenstone's eyes cleared, and his gaze sharpened.

"Is *that* why you left Miss Winthrop when he showed interest in her?"

"I hoped that if I withdrew from the lists, he'd lose interest." Cyrall sighed. "It didn't work because I could not make him believe I didn't care. He could too easily arouse me where she was concerned."

"So you came away."

"So I came away."

"And he followed."

"No, no. He followed Maddy. It was impossible that he allow her to wed someone else when he had made it clear she was to be his bride. You see?"

"I see." Lord Eldenstone grew thoughtful, nodded once, and then sighed. He looked up. "Have I congratulated you on your choice of bride?"

Sir Cyrall smiled. "There has been no time for such things, has there? Would you care to meet her and welcome her to the family?" he asked just a trifle shyly.

"Yes. I'd like that. Something happy with which to end the day." Lord Eldenstone smiled. It wasn't the strongest of smiles, but it was a true one. Sir Cyrall relaxed slightly. He finished off his wine, offered his arm to his sire, and they went off to find Miss Winthrop.

# CHAPTER
# SEVENTEEN

Diane stood on the balcony, her hands on the rail, and stared at one of the fountains. The sun made rainbows through the drops swirling up into the air before falling into the basin below. She started when young Cartwright came up beside her. Then she turned, leaned against the rail, and looked at him. "Steven?"

"I must apologize," said the lad. It was his turn to stare at the fountain. "I made a fool of myself. Can you forgive me?"

"Of course," she said promptly.

"I don't deserve it," he muttered.

"Of course you do. Do you think you are the first driven to folly by unsettling emotions?" She spoke in a teasing tone, but he refused to smile at her as she wished.

"I might have killed my father." His hands clenched. "As *Oedipus* did his."

"I suppose he might have slipped, or he might not have realized you were seriously attacking him. In time, I mean." She shrugged. "Rather doubtful, though. And you knew that."

"I was . . ." He straightened his shoulders and began again.

"I *didn't* know. I thought . . ." Again he stopped. This time his shoulders slumped a trifle. "I believed her."

Diane didn't pretend she'd no understanding. "Very likely your mother believed it herself."

Steven stilled and then, eagerly, turned toward her. "Do you think so? Is it possible?"

"Steven, I never met your mother, but she obviously wanted what was best for you. She allowed you to grow, to learn, even to leave her side and go to school. And if that is true, then I cannot think she deliberately lied about your father. Very likely, at some point in your babyhood, when men usually haven't a notion what to do with such a young child, he may have appeared to her to be uninterested in you. Perhaps she decided then that he didn't care about you, didn't or couldn't love you. She was wrong, but she may very well have believed it."

"Because she wanted to believe it." Steven sighed. "I don't think I'm going to like growing up as much as I thought I would, Mrs. Runyard. It is very complicated. People aren't simple and don't do things all of a piece, do they? They aren't always logical, and they don't always even know what they do or why they do it." Another of those sighs escaped him. "I don't know. Maybe I'll never understand."

"Maybe you'll be human, you mean?" she asked, again teasing. "Someone once said that 'to err is human.' We are all human. We all make mistakes."

"Pope said that." He looked at her then down at his hands. "He also said 'to forgive, divine,' but I thought that meant a human who forgave someone was divine. You know. A saint? But now I guess he meant that God forgives." There was a pause before he looked up. "You are very wise, are you not?"

She blinked. "I am?" She chuckled, blushing slightly. "I doubt it. It is merely that I have lived a lot more years than you and have learned a bit along the way. It only seems to you that I am wise." She glanced at the position of the sun. "Are you not supposed to be at the theater?"

Steven blinked, swore softly, and, excusing himself abruptly, took off at a run.

"Very well done." Lord Morningside spoke through the windows behind her.

"You listened?" she asked, not happy to find someone had overheard that little scene.

"I was about to come out when I realized you two were reaching some sort of rapprochement and that you should not be interrupted." He shrugged, his dark, cynical features rather softer than usual. "This has been a most interesting few weeks, has it not? A great deal has happened to a number of the Witherspoons' guests." A bit of his natural cynicism returned. "I wonder if his lordship has any notion of where the true drama lies. He cannot have predicted the very human emotions his guests would experience. Not when he invited us here merely to take part in his theatrical revels."

She eyed him. "Should I know what it is to which you refer?" she asked carefully after a moment's indecision.

"You know. Or perhaps not. Not all, at least." He smiled a faint and secret-looking smile. "No, not *all*," he said complacently.

"If you refer to the fact that you and Miss Fairchild have finally managed to reach accord—" She revealed a certain amount of exasperation. "—then I am, perhaps, more perceptive than you know."

"An . . . accord?" Rafe cast a worried look around to see if she'd been overheard then turned back to her. His eyes hardened. "What makes you think such nonsense? Who else might be so foolish?"

"Anyone who has watched each of you nonchalantly disappear, *separately*, from the salon of an evening. Far earlier than *you*, at least, were ever used to do."

A suppressed chuckle shook his shoulders. "Might I ask

that you not inform Miss Fairchild we've been, hmm, bubbled?"

"Assuming that means what I think it means, I'll keep mum. I rather doubt anyone else has noticed," she added, her soft heart wishing to reassure him.

He nodded. "And you? I have been rather, hmm, *preoccupied*—" His brows arched queryingly, and she smiled. "—and have not followed your saga as closely as I might have done. Have you and Cartwright reached a new agreement?"

Diane turned back to the railing, once again letting the sparkling waters and tinkling music of the fountain soothe her. "There has been no time for anything these last days, has there?"

"Brown keeping everyone up to the mark, you mean?" He nodded. "Only a few more days, Mrs. Runyard, and his lordship will seek you out."

Miss Fairchild came out in a rush just then but slowed immediately when she saw that Diane stood talking to Rafe. She approached sedately. "There you are. I wondered . . ."

Rafe cast Diane a faintly sardonic glance before giving their excuses and walking off with his Euphrasia. Diane felt a trifling jealousy as she watched them. And then she turned her eyes back to the fountain. And returned to worrying about exactly *why* his blidy lordship might seek her out. What, *exactly*, would he want of her?

Worst of all, *did she want him to find her*?

Perhaps it was too late to wonder that. Perhaps agreeing to go with him to the Lakes when done with her work here implied that she had made a decision concerning the two of them—but she had *not*, could not. So was that not the worst?

In fact, had she learned enough of the man he was now that it was possible to decide?

That thought stopped her. Of course she had come to know him again, and he was the man she'd known he'd become. Steven's behavior when they spoke together only minutes earlier proved that all Stevie had needed was to become aware there was a problem. At least—

She clutched the rail.

—surely Steven's words meant he and his father had reached a better understanding?


Steven raced into the theater a trifle late. Roger was not pleased and made no bones about it. Lord Cartwright smiled commiscratingly and Steven grimaced, rolling his eyes as he approached the stage but careful not to do so until his back was turned to their irritable and irritating director.

Their scene went well, and Lord Cartwright was dismissed, Steven remaining to take up the last scenes in Act I. Except now Miss Fairchild had not put in an appearance.

Cartwright, halfway up the aisle, idly considered whether Brown might, in rising choler, burst a blood vessel. He rather doubted it. The actor seemed rather to enjoy his histrionics. But when Miss Fairchild did not appear within a few minutes, the actor looked around, counted noses, and went on to a later scene for which Miss Fairchild was not required. Brown was not, however, a happy man, and Lord Cartwright, knowing they were all too near the dress rehearsal, offered, quietly, to go find her.

He left by way of the front entrance . . . and then halted, wondering which direction to go. "Ah. Di," he said, as she approached. "Have you seen Miss Fairchild? She is late."

Di groaned. "She is late and Roger is being his usual impossible self?"

"Actually, no. He ranted for a bit but then went on to a later scene. *Have* you seen her?"

Di dithered.

He grinned. "You are too tactful to say that you saw her go off with Morningside, is that it? And you are not quite certain but what they would be embarrassed if found?"

"More that I, for instance, might be embarrassed to stumble over them?" asked Diane, smiling.

"I suspect Miss Fairchild would not like it either. Perhaps if we go slowly and call out to them?"

Diane tipped her head. "We? But I am due inside. I am in the Sphinx scene, you know, and that was to follow the scene between Steven and Miss Fairchild. Oh, dear. Is that what Roger wanted when Miss Fairchild was unavailable?"

"He mentioned it, but you too were absent."

Diane felt reluctance to part from Cartwright, but her sense of responsibility insisted it must be done. She passed him and then, at the door, turned. "I hope you find them. They went off toward the woods."

"I'd better find her," said Cartwright. "We have dress rehearsal day after tomorrow." He touched her arm lightly, running one finger down the back of her wrist to her knuckles. Then he looked up at her. "I will be glad when this is over, Di."

He stared steadily into her eyes, and she realized he meant they'd have a serious talk once they were no longer dealing with the play. A touch of panic rose up in her.

*I'm not ready*, she thought.

Something of her feeling must have shown. He smiled, but a touch of sadness looked out of his eyes. "Don't worry, my dear. We need not rush into anything. We've all the time in the world."

She nodded, reached out a hand to touch his cheek, and found it clasped, his head turning, his lips warm against her palm, his gaze holding hers. Diane, who was quite certain she had not blushed for years before arriving here, once again felt heat rise up her neck and into her face.

He smiled, nodded, and turned away.

\* \* \*

Lord Witherspoon fumed. Rafe, Lord Morningside, had just gone off after informing him that he and Miss Fairchild had been called away, that they would remain until after the performance of Coxwald's *Oedipus,* but then they must depart. They were the second couple to tell him they'd be leaving. Four of his guests would depart. Six, actually, since Miss Winthrop's parents would escort their daughter.

Witherspoon was exceedingly unhappy. He had counted on Sir Cyrall to take a leading role in the next play and assumed both Miss Fairchild and Lord Morningside would take roles. What could possibly be so important, he wondered. Irritable, irascible, he called permission to still another person scratching at his door.

"Yes?" he asked. He raised a scowling face toward the man who entered.

Lord Cartwright eyed his host and considered postponing what he had to say. Then he shrugged. "My lord, it has been an interesting visit, but I find I must depart as soon as this play is over. If I tell you a secret will you keep it to yourself?" he added.

"Depart! Not you as well."

Cartwright wondered who else might be leaving but didn't care enough to ask. "It seems my secret means I've even worse news for you. I will be removing Mrs. Runyard from her work as well."

Witherspoon reared back, a stubborn expression taking up residence on his face. "*No,*" he said, shaking his head. "You cannot do that. I hired her and Brown for the whole of the summer. *For three plays*. She cannot go. *I won't have it!*"

"Nevertheless, she *will* go," said Cartwright softly. Not that Diane yet knew of her imminent departure. She would soon. As soon as he had gathered the courage to ask her to wed him . . . that the journey to the Lakes would be by way of a wedding trip. He smiled at the thought.

"You think it humorous to steal away my professional

staff?" Witherspoon's voice rose with each word. "I'll see she never acts on another stage! I'll see she's never hired by anyone ever again. I'll sue you, Lord Cartwright, for theft! I'll—"

His eyes bugged out as Cartwright, uninterested in either explaining or attempting to soothe his host, walked out and quietly closed the door.

Witherspoon sat down with something of a thud. First he swore. Then he came very near to bawling out his frustration. "Why?" He raised his eyes to the heavens. "What have I done to deserve this? How can they not see the importance of it all?"

And then he recalled young Coxwald's words. Not his exact words, but the sense of them that, at the time, he'd firmly rejected. *Real life is far more important than the pretense that is the theater*. His lordship's shoulders rose and fell with a mild "humph" of sound.

He tried to remember when the theater had become so important to him, but it seemed as if it had always been the center of his life. In his youth he had played parts while at house parties and had taken major roles in school plays—including a female part in *As You Like It*, which had been great fun. Then, when he'd come down from university, after playing in still more productions, he'd discovered the magic of the London theater.

Lost in reminiscence, he didn't hear the next tap on his door. His daughter opened it an inch and looked in, breathing a sigh of relief to find her father in what looked to be a benign mood. She slipped in the partly open door and shut it.

"Father?"

"Hmm? Oh, Francine. What do *you* want?"

"Richard has arrived. He went directly to the theater but wished you informed that his grandmother is much improved and he has returned to see the play produced."

"Ah! Richard." Lord Witherspoon's mood lightened.

"He'll take a part in the next—" His eyes bugged out. "Why do you shake your head?"

"He returns to Bath once it is over. He will live the rest of the summer with his grandmother, helping her, being there for her, but his mother and father thought that, since there is no longer danger to the old lady's life, he should come and see how his play turned out. They sent regrets that they'll not be able to witness it and . . . Father?" She blinked at the bewilderment that crossed chubby features not designed to express such emotion.

"Is everyone leaving?" he asked, a whiney note in his voice. "Is there to be no one to take part in the next play?"

After a moment in which she mulled over the sense of that and found only nonsense, Miss Witherspoon asked, "Could you explain?"

Her father's expression turned morose. "Sir Cyrall and the Winthrops and, I suppose—" His shoulders slumped still more at a sudden thought. "—Lord Eldenstone mean to go. Lord Morningside intends to escort Miss Fairchild—" He waved a hand in a vague, wordless comment. "—somewhere. I don't know where and don't want to know," he added pettishly. "And last but certainly not least, Lord Cartwright is threatening to remove Mrs. Runyard directly after this play is ended and take *her* away! I won't have it!" He pounded on his desk with his fists.

Miss Witherspoon saw despair beneath the anger and took a step nearer. "If I can help . . . ?"

"Bah." He glared. "You think the theater nonsense. You don't care a jot. Why would *you* help?"

"Because you are my father and I love you?"

His anger deflated and those goggling eyes once again stared out of his round face. "Why . . . hmm . . ." His voice softened. "Francie . . . ?"

Quickly, unwilling to go further than she'd gone already,

Francine asked, "Don't I remember you telling me other guests were to arrive about now? Will none of them replace those who are leaving?"

The goggling eyes relaxed, widened. A slow smile edged around his lips. "I'd forgotten that."

"I hadn't." She spoke a touch tartly. "I wondered where I was to find room for them."

He chuckled. "Well, now you know."

She sighed and nodded. "Father, I believe Richard wished to speak to you when the two of you could find a moment." She blushed.

"Speak to me?" Soothed by the recollection of new guests, Witherspoon had returned instantly to planning the next play, thinking about what should be ordered in the way of supplies for the carpenter, who must build new sets, and for the costumes the wardrobe mistress would provide. "Anytime," he muttered. "Anytime, my dear. Now, you've things to do and I have too, so off with you."

He jotted a quick note to the bottom of the list he'd half written when interrupted by the news so many were deserting him.

Miss Witherspoon realized her father had not taken her hint of the seriousness of Richard's wishes, debated making another attempt, and then decided to leave it to Richard. She reached up and touched the ring hidden on the chain hanging unseen under her high-necked morning gown. Her eyes glistened with happiness, and, nodding belated agreement that she'd things to do, she left the room.

Miss Winthrop, wishing to be alone to savor her happiness, found her way to the orchard. She put up her parasol and strolled between the trees, a smile playing around her lips as she thought of the lovely things Sir Cyrall had said to her. She was about to turn and return the way she'd come, fearing her mother's anger if she did not soon appear, when a movement attracted her attention.

She turned back. "Mrs. Runyard?"

"Miss Winthrop." Diane nodded and let go the knee she'd been hugging, allowing her foot to return to the grass where it belonged. She rose to her feet. "You have discovered my favorite place."

"Oh. Oh, dear." Miss Winthrop's eyes widened. "Should I go? That is, I meant to go anyway—returning to my mother's side, you know? She'll look around, not find me, and will be angry with me. *Again.*" A gentle pout of frustration settled on her young features. "It seems she is always angry these days."

Diane chuckled. "Poor lady. You burst her dream, so of course she is angry. No one likes one's dream destroyed, does one?"

Miss Winthrop had to think about that a moment. "You mean she dreamed I'd become a countess?"

Di nodded. "Actually," she said, her tone dry as dust, "there is a very good chance that you *will*. I've been told that where Lord Elden was sent is not a particularly nice place. If he does not succumb to a fever, his arrogance is likely to result in someone so angered by him, they put a knife into him."

Miss Winthrop blanched. Her hand covered her eyes, and she swallowed hard. "Do not say such things. So terrible to even think that . . ."

"I am merely an actress, Miss Winthrop. I have never had the luxury of not calling a spade a spade."

The young woman grew as red as she had been white. Then she laughed. "You are correct. I should not hide my head in the sand and should admit—" She glanced around to assure herself they were alone and dropped her voice to something approaching a whisper. "—I cannot like the man at all. He is . . . he is *mean*."

Miss Winthrop's hand went to her upper arm, an unconscious movement that suggested to Diane that, at some point, Lord Elden had hurt the girl. "A very nasty man," agreed Diane. "I knew a woman he had in keeping. . . ." She shook her head. "But I should not speak of such things to you. I believe I heard you will leave immediately after the play has been presented?"

Miss Winthrop appeared to wish to ask about Diane's friend but then thought better of it. "The day following the performance. We go first to Lord Eldenstone's estate and from there to my father's. My mother is, reluctantly, inviting relatives to a formal dinner where we will announce my engagement." She grimaced. "All the worst of our relatives will come, and the ones I wish to have there will be kept away for one reason or another. I *know* it will happen that way."

Diane's laugh was freer this time. "You, my dear child, must be a pessimist. Is that not what it is called when someone is always looking for the black side of life?"

Miss Winthrop smiled, seeing the mild jest on herself. "I suppose I am. A bit. I'll try to do better." She drew in a deep breath. "I wish I'd the time to get to know you better, Mrs. Runyard. You are so sensible. I like you."

"Because I am sensible?" asked Diane, and if there was a wry touch in her tone, it was too mild for Miss Winthrop to recognize. "I too wish we might have had longer, Miss Winthrop. Will you accept my very best wishes for a happy future? I believe you will have it," she added quickly. "Sir Cyrall is a rather complicated man. There is a goodness in him that he tries to hide, but that there *is* means he will see to your comfort and care for your feelings."

Miss Winthrop nodded. "Yes. I wish he didn't feel it necessary to hide his true nature, but I'll not try to change him. I watched my older sisters." She shook her head and sighed. "It doesn't work, does it? Trying to change someone into the person you want them to be. You have to accept them the way they are, I think."

"I couldn't agree more." Diane was more than a trifle surprised at the maturity in that thought and began to see what it was about Miss Winthrop that had called to something in Sir Cyrall. What, beyond her obvious beauty, appealed to him to the point he'd fallen in love with her.

"I talked to him about you," added Miss Winthrop a bit shyly. "He says that once we are married and living in our own home, we will have you to visit. Mama would not approve, but he sees nothing wrong in it. You are, he says, known to be respectable, and quite a few people think nothing of inviting musicians and actors and painters to their smaller soirees or *at homes*." She looked up and blushed nicely. "I don't think I am saying this quite right. Not the highest sticklers, you see, but real people do it. People like Cyrall."

Diane particularly liked that "real" people and tucked it away to tell Lord Cartwright, who would appreciate it—since he too was *real*. Thoughts of his lordship returned to plague her, and, after saying all the right things concerning the rather odd invitation to visit, Diane was glad to see the back of the young lady, who, having once again recalled the existence of her disapproving mother, was reminded that that lady would not be happy at her prolonged absence. "I must go. Mother, you see, is a very high stickler indeed," she said by way of excuse.

*And therefore*, thought Diane, *not real*.

She wasn't alone for long. Rafe, Lord Morningside, and Miss Fairchild, arm in arm, were the next to discover her. "Diane," called Miss Fairchild, "there you are."

"Have I been missing?" quipped Diane, smiling a welcome she was glad to find she actually felt. "Are you not supposed to be rehearsing?"

"Rehearsal is over until this afternoon, when your Mr. Brown wishes to go over two scenes he feels are not quite up to snuff. Then we are dismissed until tomorrow for the dress rehearsal, when, finally, everyone together, we begin at the beginning and go on to the end." Eustacia grinned a quick grin. "*And*," she added, "we two are not required for the later practice, so we have planned a picnic for this afternoon. Would you care to join us?"

Diane blinked. "I . . . would like that," she said, uncertain. Never before had she so blithely been invited to a party planned by a member of the ton. Even such an informal party as a picnic. "I would, of course, have to be certain that Roger has no need of me."

"I think you will find he can do without," said Rafe, his eyes narrowed in that way he had, slightly hooded, and one brow very slightly elevated, asking you to enjoy a joke he wasn't quite expressing.

Diane turned a look his way. She tipped her head. "He will be *encouraged* to do without? Is that what you would suggest?"

Rafe grinned, his teeth momentarily white in his sun-darkened face. "I have come to realize you are an intelligent woman, Mrs. Runyard. I hope once this summer is over, you will not become a stranger to us. At least, it is our intention to issue you invitations and our sincere hope you will not turn them down."

Diane felt heat rise up into her face. "Why . . . how very kind of you." She smiled a very slightly tremulous smile. "Thank you." More firmly, she added, "I would be honored—"

Rafe's gesture had her breaking off what she would say. He nodded and looked down at Eustacia. "I ordered horses tacked up for us, Euphrasia, for eleven. If you are to be ready, I believe we must return to the house." He looked at

Diane. "Will you join us?" he asked, offering his free arm to the actress.

"I believe I'll remain here for a bit longer," she said. "Oh, by the way, I did not give you my good wishes, Miss Fairchild. Nor congratulated you, my lord, on your good fortune."

Rafe cast a quick looked at Eustacia, who blushed slightly. "Did you . . . ?" he asked.

She shook her head. "I've told no one."

Diane chuckled. "My lord, you told me yourself."

He straightened, his smile fading. "I did no such thing!"

"But you did. You asked that I not be a stranger to the both of you and then said that the two of you mean to issue me an invitation sometime in the future. I must assume that means the two of you will be married. If, however," she added, tongue in cheek, "it meant something else . . ."

The blush that had faded returned to Eustacia's cheeks, and she bit her lip to hold back a laugh. "So, *you* are at fault— for once. Not quite so discreet as you would like to think, hmm, Rafe? I must remember that."

He groaned but then smiled. "It seems I trust Mrs. Runyard as I do *not* trust many." He turned to Diane. "I am so relaxed with you I feel no need to watch my tongue."

"I am complimented, my lord, that you feel that way. I'll not tell anyone if you'd prefer I not."

"We mean to elope, Mrs. Runyard, and will wed by special license on our way to London. Once we have given orders so that we may leave everything behind for a time, we depart for Italy and perhaps Greece for a long wedding journey—and we don't mean to send a notice to the papers concerning our marriage until the date of our departure. In the meantime, we would appreciate your discretion."

"You'll have it, my lord. I will discover if I am free to attend your picnic."

A few more words and she was, once again, alone. For a

time. When she looked up, feeling his presence, Lord Cartwright stood some little distance away, watching her. She felt her cheeks heat and wondered if she had blushed so much, even when very young, as she'd done since his arrival here.

He strolled forward. "You were in a deep study, my dear."

"Hmm. Trying to find the proper words to tell you I must not go with you on that absurd journey to the Lakes. It was temper that drew that yes from me, my lord. I knew, even as I said it, that I must not." She sighed.

"Nonsense." Lord Cartwright frowned. He had meant, once he had her attention, to ask her to wed him. Now he was uncertain. Perhaps she was not yet ready for a proposal? Perhaps he should allow her a bit more time? But he wanted it settled. He wanted to know she was his, that he would not once again lose her. Would never lose her.

"What is it, Stevie?"

"Hum?" His eyes came into focus. "Oh, just a brief siege of indecision. I have been told there is a picnic and that we are invited. Will you come?"

"Depends on Roger, does it not? If he needs me, then I cannot go. You know I am being paid for my work here this summer. You would not wish me to—" Her eyes widened when he grimaced. "Stevie, what is it?"

"*Paid*. I hate it that you must earn your living as you do. I'll not have it a moment longer." He drew in a breath and, in a rush, added, "I have warned Lord Witherspoon that you'll not be here beyond this play." His tone stern and an implacable look to him, he continued, "You are mine, Di. It is time you understood that. I'll not have you working for the likes of Witherspoon. Or appearing on the stage for that matter. It is time someone, *me*, took care of you as you should be cared for." His voice rose slightly, riding over the inchoate spate of words she was trying to insert into his tirade. "I *will*

care for you. Forever. You know that. I know you know. And
I believe it is what you want as much as I want—" He broke
off, turning as she pushed past him. "Di!"

"We will talk when you can be rational, my lord, and not
before." She broke into a run and raced away from him. He
could catch her if he willed it. But she knew he would not.
Worse, she feared he'd no understanding at all of why she
ran from him. He'd think it because he lost his temper, when,
really, it was her own sense of self that drove her away. He
would try to change her. He would try to make her the person he wanted her to be. *Even Miss Winthrop knew better.*

As Diane approached the house, she slowed. Reaching
the terrace, she looked back the way she'd come, checking
that he was not in view. He was not, and she realized she was
disappointed. She sighed at her own irrational emotions. Then
she looked along the length of the house and decided the
best means of entering privately was through the open library
windows right beside her. She stepped over the low ledge.

"Mrs. Run-run-runyard."

Diane allowed one soft swear word to escape her. "Sir
George. I didn't see you there."

"N-no. Are y-y-you all ri-ri-right?"

"Not entirely. Not that there is anything *wrong*. Just a
misunderstanding that must be made straight, but nothing
that is worrying me or a danger to me or anything of that nature."

"You look harassed," he said, not a stutter to be heard.

She sighed and took the chair to which he gestured. "It
truly is nothing. Lord Cartwright seemed to think that . . .
but . . . except I . . ." She drew in a breath and let it out and
was surprised when Allingham chuckled. "Ah. It is my turn
to stutter?" she asked, and he nodded. "You see, the problem
is that I fear I cannot make him understand me. I am not entirely certain I understand myself, and that makes it difficult,
you'll agree." She shrugged. "Anyway, I ran away."

"And he allowed it?"

She nodded. "He rather lost his temper. I suspect he thinks he frightened me." She smiled. "He's never seen Roger in a temper if he thought his mild outburst would send me running in fear of my life."

"So, later, he will a-a-apol—" Once again he spoke slowly and carefully. "—o-gize."

She smiled a secret smile. "He will try, and I will tell him that's nonsense." The smile faded. "I wish I knew how to explain." She glanced up, once again feeling the heat of embarrassment. "You are a very easy man with whom to talk," she said, an accusing note in her voice.

He nodded, smiling, his eyes twinkling. "It is be-be-because I have tr-tr-trou—" His lips closed tightly for half a moment. "—ble speaking. I do not tell secrets, you see."

She nodded. "That makes sense. You also have a kind heart, and it shows."

"But is there a *real* problem? Lord Cartwright loves you, so it cannot be that."

She cast him a quick glance and looked down at her hands.

"And you love him," he added softly.

Her jaw clenched. "But is it enough?" She looked up, misery in her mien. "Can he accept that I am merely an actress? That it is my life? That I make my living that way and that I cannot simply . . . simply . . ."

"Marry him?"

Shock looked out of Diane's eyes. "That is an utter impossibility."

"Why?"

"I shouldn't have to explain. You know why."

"Because you are an actress?" He shook his head. "He has an heir. You are old enough you are unlikely to have offspring, but even if you do, I cannot see it as a problem. You are known to be a respectable woman." He shrugged. "Cartwright, I am sure, sees no impediment."

"He hasn't asked me to marry him. I don't expect it," she added quickly. "What he has asked . . ." She closed her mouth and looked back down at her hands.

"He has asked you to resume your old relationship?"

She sighed. "You too? Does everyone know of our youthful folly?"

After a moment he asked, softly, "Was it folly?"

Her head came up. "*No.*" After half a second she added, "Not for me."

"And not, I think, for his lordship. Mrs. Runyard, do not despair. And do consider whether you could give up the theater in order to marry him, because, married, I think you would have to do so."

"Yes. I see that." She was thoughtful for a long moment and then sighed. "But it is not relevant, is it? He has not asked." She rose and wandered away—and only much later did it occur to her that Sir George had not stuttered once while they conversed about her problems. A puzzle, that.

# CHAPTER
# EIGHTEEN

Richard Coxwald congratulated Roger Brown. The two shook hands, Richard smiling and Roger looking a trifle more sardonic than usual. "You have done very well with my poor effort," Coxwald said as the two strolled up the aisle. "I did not imagine it would play so well."

"For an amateur's first effort, you have done better than just *well*," conceded Brown. Slowly, very nearly reluctantly, he added, "I have wondered if it might be produced in London."

Richard felt his ears heat. "I never dreamed of such a thing."

"It may never happen," warned Roger. "I've no control over such things, but I do have the ear of one or two who might consider it. If you like, I will lay your play before them."

"I will see that a clean copy, with all changes written out clearly, is prepared before you return to London." Richard looked up and smiled broadly. "Francie, did you hear?"

"There is no assurance it will ever happen," warned Brown

once again. He nodded to Miss Witherspoon and passed the two as Richard, holding her hands tightly, explained to her.

"That is wonderful," she said slowly.

He laughed. "I see you are not entirely happy with the notion, but you needn't worry I'll let it go to my head, my love. I am still your Richard."

She smiled and shook her head weakly but turned at his urging, took his arm, and strolled toward the house with him. "You meant to talk to Father, did you not? Now?"

Hearing something in her tone, he glanced down at her. "In a snit?" he asked, his brow arched in a querying fashion. Then he grinned. "Or is he merely worrying about the play and how his neighbors will respond to it?"

She sighed. "You know him well. A snit on top of worry, in this case, I think. Several guests, guests who play important roles in this play, are leaving. So is Sir Cyrall."

"So? It was my impression that more guests arrive soon. Is that not so?"

She nodded. "That thought soothed him, but he wanted Sir Cyrall to take a leading role in the next play, you see, and he cannot understand what could be more important than that." She sighed.

"What *is* more important? To Sir Cyrall, I mean."

"Oh, Richard," she said, turning sparkling eyes up to him, "you were not here! It was quite exciting. First Lord and Lady Winthrop and their daughter arrived. And then Sir Cyrall's brother followed hotfoot."

"Cyrall's brother?" There was a sudden sharp note to Richard's voice. "You would say Lord Elden is here?"

Francine was silent for half a moment. "You do not like him."

"No." The sharp note turned harsh. "*I do not.*" He continued somewhat more reasonably. "You see, I know of a young lady, the sister of a friend, that Lord Elden . . . treated badly."

A muscle jumped in Richard's jaw. "I do not like it that he is anywhere near to you, my love."

"Nothing of the sort can happen ever again," she said and paused for a dramatic moment. "*He has been banished*."

Richard stopped. Short. "Banished?"

She told him the story—or as much of it as she knew. "So you see, the Winthrops, Lord Eldenstone, and Sir Cyrall will all depart as soon as the play is over. Family celebrations and the like. But they are not all."

"Who else goes?"

"Lord Morningside means to escort Miss Fairchild to London." Francine frowned slightly. "She received a letter by courier not long ago, so I assume there is something she must attend to. Something not *hugely* important but such that it cannot wait until the end of the summer."

Richard nodded. "I am glad they were able to remain long enough to play their parts," he said. "I presume that is all?"

"I think," she added, hesitantly, "that Lord Cartwright means to take his son and Mrs. Runyard away."

Again Richard stopped. This time his brows were arched in surprise. "But she . . . ," he began.

She nodded. "That is the thing bothering Father the most. Richard, I wonder if you should postpone . . . ?"

"Asking him for your hand?" he asked when she paused.

She nodded, her cheeks suddenly quite rosy.

Richard frowned. "Perhaps I could wait until after the play. If it is successful with our neighbors, then he will be in alt, will he not? And far more likely to look favorably on my suit."

Her chin firmed. "He has no reason to forbid the banns, Richard. None at all."

Her face took on a mulish look that always brought out the tease in Richard. "Hmm, yes, but do you think he *needs* a reason?"

Her eyes widened. "Oh, no. Surely he would not forbid the banns. Not from mere *perversity*."

He laughed. "Now that I think on it, my dear, there is one good reason."

She frowned and cast him a worried look. "I can think of nothing. Whatever can you mean?"

"Don't look like that, love. I haven't a secret wife tucked away, and I am not depraved in some particularly evil fashion." He patted her hand. "I merely meant that if you wed, who will keep house for him and see to all the multitude of details with which you deal so capably? He might actually have to make a decision now and again concerning the household."

She frowned, taking him seriously when, in truth, he'd meant to make her smile. "Father would not like that. . . ."

Richard smiled, that teasing twinkle still sparkling in his eyes. "Then I will suggest that he find himself a wife so I may have mine."

She looked a trifle shocked. "Richard! That would be a terrible reason for marrying some poor soul."

"Have you a better suggestion?" he asked, innocently.

"Yes." She nodded one firm nod. "My old governess. She received a small inheritance not too long ago and retired. From the tone of her recent letters, she is already bored to tears and not nearly so happy as she expected to be. She knows Father and would manage him very well. *And* she is far more capable than I to manage his various houses as he wishes them managed."

Richard decided his little love would not be teased into a less serious mood and altered his to match hers. "Then if she will agree to come, he has nothing whatever about which he can complain. But—" Something which had worried Richard off and on popped into his head. "—there is one very real problem. One that has concerned me a great deal. My dear, I have no desire to live under my parents' roof once we've wed. Will you dislike it very much, living in the dower house? It will seem cramped to you after all this."

"I will *like* it," she said, surprising him. "You cannot guess at the problems one faces dealing with an establishment this size. It will be a relief to have only three housemaids, two footmen, and a cook."

"Surely a housekeeper?"

"I see no reason why we should go to that added expense. I can order the work done, and what else does a housekeeper do?" she asked.

He smiled. "We'll see. For instance, if you were not there to order it all . . . ?"

"But why would I not be?"

He cast her a sideways look and then turned his eyes straight ahead. "My dear, I have hopes that this blasted war is about to end, and once it does I have even greater hopes that the two of us may travel together and explore the continent much as our forefathers did during their grand tours."

Her eyes widened. "I didn't know you wanted to travel."

"I have never spoken of it because it seemed as if it would always be impossible. The war has gone on for most of our lives, has it not?" He cast her a concerned look. "Does it bother you? Do you dislike the notion?"

"I have never thought of the possibility." She blinked. "Perhaps . . . if there were no children to worry about."

Richard glanced down at his little love and sighed softly. If that were her condition for going off with him, he rather hoped there would be no children for several years. Not if, once there were, it meant she'd no longer want to leave hearth and home. . . .


The next days were hectic, and no one among the guests had a moment free for personal problems. Most especially, Diane had no time to herself—but, in the long night watches, she came to a decision that she hoped would satisfy her Stevie. And, just as soon as they could, once the last curtain fell, she meant to tell him what she had concluded concerning their future.

Still, in the meantime, there was barely time to even reassure him that she was no longer afraid or angry. Roger, suddenly a general firmly leading his troops—or in this case, troupe—toward the final denouement of the weeks of preparation, knew precisely what needed doing and knew exactly who should do it.

Mostly Diane.

She spent hours making certain that the scenery was organized in such a way it could be moved onstage easily the moment it was needed. She spent more hours with the wardrobe mistress going over each costume to check there were no loose seams, a hem that might fall down, or decoration that could come loose—or any other of the hundred problems that might arise. The wardrobe mistress had done an excellent job, so all Diane found were three costumes that needed washing and pressing, their wearers having managed to get them dirty during the dress rehearsal.

Then came the performance for servants and tenants.

Diane peeked through the curtains as their audience filed in wearing their best clothes and in a holiday mood. She hoped they were not disappointed that there was no humor in the play or, alternately, not shocked too badly by patricide, incest, and suicide—to say nothing of the scene in which Jocasta is found dead or the one in which Oedipus blinds himself in self-imposed punishment for his sins.

She shrugged. If they *were* upset, they'd just think the gentry had, once again, provided them with something new about which they could gossip—for the next fifty years or so.

The following evening, the *real* performance ended to stunned silence. And then the audience clamored with shouts of appreciation. Diane, along with the other actors, returned to the stage for a second bow. She glanced to the side, the box where Lord Witherspoon sat with his daughter and Richard Coxwald. Witherspoon glowed with happiness.

A few minutes later, Witherspoon himself appeared on stage. The words of his little speech might have been suitably modest, but his tone was rich with satisfaction. He ended by introducing Richard as the play's author—information that resulted in another brief silence, this one ending with a buzz of gossipy voices indicating surprise. Richard refused to speak of his work, merely rising and bowing in their box.

Lord Witherspoon blinked at such modesty but next called Roger Brown on stage. Roger raised his hands for silence.

"So ends our first effort to entertain you," he said and, after regaining silence, added, "I'd like to announce that the next play will be a Shakespeare comedy and will be ready in approximately three weeks." He had remembered to tell George Allingham which part he'd have and had been surprised by the stutterer's un-stuttered and effusive thanks.

Now, looking out over the audience, he beamed, bowed, and exited—but the instant he was offstage, a frown settled onto his features as, already, he worried about whether it was possible to force his amateur actors and actresses to be ready in such a brief time . . . to say nothing of all the details of scenery and costumes.

Diane, seeing that he fumed, quickly disappeared. She had no intention of having the rest of this evening spoiled by finding herself with a list of tasks to accomplish immediately. Once she'd cleaned off her makeup and hung her last costume, she sat herself down before the excellently lit mirror and gazed at her naked face.

Now there was no excuse. Now she was not rushed off her feet, she had no reason to avoid Stevie as she'd been doing. None whatsoever. It had to be tonight, because ear-

lier, when she'd gone into her room, she'd found a maid
packing for her, an order she immediately rescinded.

She had to convince him she could not leave. Not yet. Not
until she had fulfilled the contract she'd signed. She had
never broken a contract. She would not begin a new life by
ending her old on a sour note. Her jaw firmed, and she rose—
just as a firm knock sounded at her door.

It was Lord Cartwright.

Somehow she had known it would be her Stevie. She
turned her back and returned to her seat by the mirror, letting him close the door behind him.

"We have to talk," she said.

He sighed.

She stared at her fingers, tightly wound together in her
lap. "You cannot ride roughshod over me, Steve. I will not
begin a new life with you, not ever, if that is the way you
mean to go on."

"I have, I think, come to my senses," he said quietly.
"When I learned you'd ordered that maid to put away your
garments. Tell me what we *are* to do."

She looked up at his reflection in the mirror and found
him staring at hers.

He sighed heavily. "I lost all patience, my love. I suppose
that isn't a good excuse, but I fear it is the only one I have for
what I did."

She stared at him for a moment, then nodded. "I have a
suggestion, Steve. Will you listen?"

He nodded as well but swallowed, hard, in anticipation of
her words.

"I must finish this contract. I will not end my career on
stage by avoiding my final obligations."

"I feared something of the sort was in your head," he said,
but that she meant to end her career could mean only one
thing and his mood improved instantly.

"Yes, but, Steve, there is another, even better reason to

postpone our . . . reunion." She caught his gaze with her own and held it. "You have finally begun to get to know your son. He is a good lad. He is, at the moment, ready to cooperate with you in that endeavor, the getting to know each other. You must take this time for him. Do those things with him you have always wanted to do. Ride over your acres. Introduce him to people. Take him fishing." She waved a hand, having run out of suggestions. "I don't know what a father does with his son . . . perhaps a prizefight?"

He chuckled, but a bit wryly. "I don't believe there are any scheduled in the next few weeks. Races, perhaps?"

"Yes." She nodded. "Anything where you can spend time with him doing man-things."

He sobered. "That impatience . . . I don't know if . . ." When she scowled, he sighed. "Very well, Di. Two more plays. But then . . . you are mine?"

It was her turn to swallow hard. "I am older, Stevie. I am no longer young and lovely and . . ." She trailed off, raising her gaze to meet his in the mirror.

"And worry your body will displease me? For all we know, mine will displease you—but somehow I doubt either of us will care about the changes the years have made in what the world may see. It is the *inside* of us that is important."

"*I* believe that, but men . . ."

He chuckled. "My dear, I love you."

She blinked. "Love . . . ?"

"*Love.*" He reached for her and drew her up. "May I kiss you, Di?"

She blushed but nodded, lifting her face before he need do it for her. It was a wonderful kiss. Strong but gentle. Thorough and arousing but controlled and demanding no more than she was willing to give. They separated a trifle and looked at each other.

"And that," he said, laughing at himself, "only makes me

*more* impatient." Very slowly he released her. "Very well, Di. We will go tell Steven, and then I will attempt to discover exactly when you will have finished here. Not one day longer!"

"Not even one," she agreed. And wondered what the Lake District was like in the autumn. . . .

The next weeks were busy ones. Diane, often, had to force herself to concentrate. She hadn't a part in the Shakespeare play but took a far greater hand in arranging for the necessary costumes, borrowing many from the London theater in which Roger and she worked. Then she had to see they were cleaned and altered to fit the particular characters' forms. She spent hours coaching people in their parts, working with them while they memorized their roles, tactfully showing them the proper tone and stresses to make each line best express the playwright's intent.

She was rushed off her feet from morning to night . . . as she wished to be. Only when she'd spent full days working did she manage to sleep at all. The notes and letters and small gifts that arrived very nearly daily from Lord Cartwright intrigued the household—except, of course, for Lord Witherspoon, who never noticed anything that was not directly related to his theater.

One morning late in the summer a footman entered the breakfast room as usual and began handing around the post to those guests who had received any that day. He came to where Diane sat trying hard not to show her anticipation of whatever it was her love had, that day, sent her. It included a small box, a flat envelope, and a folded and sealed letter. The last she stuffed into her pocket for a time when she was alone, and a touch of rose brightened her cheeks when she saw one of the guests grinning knowingly. She lay aside the flat package and turn the small box over and over. Finally, she opened it, and, wide-eyed, removed crystal drop earrings.

There were oohs and aahs from the ladies, and the red in Di's cheeks deepened.

"How very lovely," said one woman, who, preemptively, held out a hand.

Diane dropped the jewelry into it and turned to the flat package. Carefully she opened it, wondering what it could be. A stiff folder emerged. It was covered in red leather and tied shut with a matching velvet ribbon. There was a folded paper tucked under the ribbon that she removed and opened. Her brows arched when she discovered it was from Steven rather than her Stevie.

*Dear Mrs. Runyard,*

*I hope very much you like my small effort. I myself think it more successful than I'd any right to hope. With your help, I have come to understand that my parents' marriage was a tragedy for both. My mother needed a man who would dote on her. My father needed a woman who would joyfully give him a quiverful of young, as I think you will agree when you view the enclosed, which is only a small gesture of thanks for all you did for me.*

*With best wishes, Steven Cartwright.*

Intrigued, Diane untied the bow and set the ribbon aside. Slowly, she opened the cover—and gasped at what was revealed.

"What is it?" demanded the lady with the overweening curiosity. She was wearing one of the earrings and attempting to put the other in the other lobe.

"A drawing," said Diane, staring at it. "A truly wonderful drawing."

Diane blinked back tears. The man was her Stevie in every line. In the drawing, he squatted before a poorly dressed child, his hands on his knees. The child squatted in exactly the same fashion and was, obviously, telling him something which she felt important. His features revealed his love and understanding—and very likely that expression had helped his son to understand better all he'd missed by not knowing his father when he himself was a child. And, very likely, explained the words in Steven's letter concerning his parents' marriage.

"What is it?"

"May we see?"

Diane barely heard the spate of questions her expression roused. Indeed, she forgot the earrings as she got to her feet and walked away carrying the folder. Miss Witherspoon looked around the table, extracted the earrings from the one lady's possession, and followed after Diane.

"Mrs. Runyard," she called. "What is it? What is the matter?"

"The matter?" Diane turned, revealing a glowing face. "Nothing is the matter."

Hesitantly, since Diane had ignored other such requests, Francine asked, "May *I* see . . . ?"

Diane had not meant to be rude. She had not heard the others. Now she smiled. "Why not?" She opened the folder, revealing the drawing. "I had no notion that young Steven was an artist, but this is surely exceptional, do you not agree?" She stared, again, at the pen-and-ink rendition of Stevie. "This captures so much of who Lord Cartwright *is*."

"It is a marvelous picture," said Francine slowly, wondering that such an informal drawing could express so much. "I wonder if Steven showed it to Lord Cartwright."

"Is there some reason why he should not?"

"Well, usually, portraits aren't so . . . are more . . . don't . . ." She huffed a breath in exasperation at not finding the words to express what she meant.

"You mean most portraits aren't so revealing? I think that untrue. The very *best* artists are said to capture the soul of the sitter. I would say young Steven has done that."

"Yes. He has. But . . ." Again Francine couldn't find the words she wanted.

Diane laughed. "You would ask if Lord Cartwright wished to be revealed quite so thoroughly?"

Francine blushed but nodded.

"Since it is for my eyes, I do not think he will mind," said Diane gently. "I will not show it to just anyone, however."

"Would you like a frame?" asked Francine shyly, finding herself flattered that she had been honored with a glimpse of something so private. "I can find—" Francine stopped. "No?"

"I think it will always be my favorite picture of his lordship, but it will live in the folder in which I received it." Diane turned to continue on to her room but turned at Francine's exclamation of irritation. "What is it?"

"I nearly forgot. You left these with Lady Burton-Wright." She handed over the earrings.

Diane thanked her and, finally, was able to continue on to her room, where, with the folder open before her, she read Lord Cartwright's latest love letter. She finished and looked blindly across the room.

"Will this summer never end?" she asked the portrait of a cross-grained-looking Witherspoon ancestress.

And then, putting the missive under her handkerchiefs with the others she'd received, she firmly closed the drawer, forced herself to remember just what duties Roger had given her for this morning, and then took herself off to fulfill them.

And, of course, the summer did end.

Finally.

Diane had a part in the third play, and Lord Cartwright returned in time to watch the final production. It occurred to him to wonder if she would miss the theater but dismissed the notion. There would be no reason she could not do as she did now and take part in amateur productions whenever the urge was upon her.

The next morning, the two said good-bye to the Wither-spoons, father and daughter, and were, finally, alone together in Lord Cartwright's traveling carriage. The talk for the first stage revolved around what each had done that summer. The next stage was devoted to a discussion of Steven and the progress he and Lord Cartwright had made toward an understanding of each other.

That leg of their journey was nearing its end when Lord Cartwright cleared his throat and bit his lip.

"What is it?"

"I've planned a brief delay here," he said, his ears heating.

"It is early to stop for the night," she said, hesitating.

"This isn't for the night." He fidgeted.

"Stevie—"

His skin darkened still more.

"—you are beginning to worry me."

"You know we are only a few miles from one of my estates?"

"You intend to stop there?" she asked when he again shut his mouth and looked undecided.

"*No*. Oh blast!" He turned to her and grasped her shoulders. "I am remembering what you said about riding roughshod over you."

She reared back. "Steve . . ."

"*Damn*." His eyes flicked to meet hers. "I mean . . ."

"Blidy hell?" she asked, widening her eyes in an expression of mock innocence.

He smiled, but it faded, and he settled back into his corner. The coach slowed, stopped.

"This is a church," she said, looking out her window.

"Hmm."

The door opened on her side and Steven grinned up at her. He let down the steps and held out his hand. "Are you ready?" he asked.

"I haven't asked her," said his father from the dusky corner in which he sat.

"Well, why not?" asked his son, frowning.

"Spinelessness."

Steven chuckled. "I'll go away. But only five minutes, Father," he said warningly as he shut the door.

"Stevie . . . ," began Diane, her eyes widening.

"Will you?" he asked, turning to her and grasping her hands. "Now? Today?"

"Stevie, is this a proposal?" she asked, utterly astounded. "I can't. You . . . I . . . we . . ."

"If you are thinking of some nonsense," said Lord Cartwright, "concerning our relative statuses in life, then allow me to tell you that we have my father's permission."

"We *what*?" Diane stiffened. "What in the world can you mean?"

Lord Cartwright released her and sat back into his corner. "I told you, you'll recall, that my solicitor came to explain about your annuity. He had a letter for me. In it my father apologized to me and expressed his hope that, in the future, we would find happiness."

After a moment, her eyes wide, she asked, "And you consider that permission?"

There had been more, but he didn't know how to say it, so he nodded.

"Come now. He surely meant, if he meant anything at all other than the tritest of best wishes, that we do as we planned and come together again."

He shook his head. "No. In context of the rest of the letter, he meant that we should, if it became possible, wed."

Diane huffed out a breath of air and folded her arms. She glared at nothing at all.

"Di, don't you *wish* to wed me?"

She stilled. "I have dreamed of it."

"Then, my dearest love . . . will you? Now? With Steven to witness?"

Her arms unwound, and she turned to him. "Steven approves?"

"You saw him. You know he does."

"Has he any notion of how it will be for him that his stepmama is nothing but an *actress* off the *stage*?"

The door opened. "A respectable, well-known, and much-admired actress," said Steven belligerently. Then he grinned. "Now do be sensible," he half coaxed, half ordered, "and come quickly. The vicar awaits, and you'll be late reaching your night's lodging if we don't get this done and get you back on the road."

"You've been listening."

"I've been *waiting*. Very patiently."

Diane looked from him to his father. The hopeful look in Lord Cartwright's eyes melted her, and, almost reluctantly, fearfully, she nodded.

Steven held his hand out. "*Finally.*"

The wedding was solemn and sincere and all a private wedding should be—and soon over. Steven waved them off, telling them to have fun and not hurry home, and then, pleased with the world and himself and all around him, Steven rode back to a house he finally felt was a home. A home with loving parents who would return to live there happily . . .

. . . which, after a month among the Lakes, was exactly what Lord and Lady Cartwright did.

# EPILOGUE

It snowed that Christmas when Lord and Lady Cartwright visited Sir Cyrall and his wife, Madeline, Lady Jamison. Steven was also there, but Richard Coxwald and his Francine sent regrets, adding word that they would stop for a night or two after the New Year when on their way to London, where Richard's play was to be presented in one of the smaller theaters.

"Do you wish to see it?" Lord Cartwright asked Diane as she buttoned up his vest.

"Not particularly," she said. "I have enjoyed this house party far more than I ever expected, but . . ."

"But you are still worried about the reaction of most of my friends to our marriage?"

She nodded.

"While we've been here, has a single one of them made you feel unwelcome?" he asked sternly.

She glanced up, thought of one lady who had deliberately snubbed her, thought of one gentleman who had made an unacceptable suggestion, knew that neither was a friend of her husband's, and said, "None of your friends would care to insult you by insulting me, Stevie . . . but not all are your friends."

She finished the last button and reached for his coat, holding it to help ease it over his shoulders. His lordship had retired Franklin, his longtime valet, just before his marriage, after the man made one comment too many about designing women. He had not yet gone about the business of hiring a new.

"*You*," continued Diane, "haven't been to London since we returned from the Lakes. What you should do is escort me home and then go up to Town with Steven—" She found him, the coat half on, turning to grasp her arms tightly. "What . . . ?"

"If and when I go to London, my love, I'll go with you. Steven may come if he wishes. Or he may go without us, but I'll not leave you home and go *anywhere* without you." He gave her a tiny shake for emphasis.

She sighed. "Love . . ."

"*No.* I am not ashamed of you. I have no reason to be ashamed of you—and don't say because you made your living on the stage!" When she shut her mouth, and he was certain she'd ceased her arguing, he released her and changed the subject. "Did you read the letter Sir Cyrall received from Lord Morningside?"

That brought a smile to her face. "I am so glad he and Eustacia are enjoying themselves, but—" The smiled faded. "—do you think it was quite the thing to spend so much time with Lord Byron?"

"Are you one of those who disapproves of his lordship, my dear?"

"Of much of his behavior, one *must* disapprove. His poetry . . . *can* that excuse such depravity?" she asked.

"I will remember," he said, speaking solemnly but his eyes twinkling, "that when we go abroad next spring it will be to wherever Lord Byron is *not*."

Her eyes widened. "Abroad?"

He nodded. "You did read that part of the letter, did you not?"

"You mean where he assumes we are wed and invites Sir Cyrall, his bride, and the two of us to join them in the villa he's leased?"

"You will enjoy Italy."

"So sure of me, are you?"

"Hmm." He ignored that little jest just as she'd expected. Of course he was sure of her. "I wonder," he said, "do you suppose that Richard Coxwald and his Francine would also like to go abroad?"

Diane grinned. "Had you not better discuss this with Sir Cyrall? The way you are going on, you will next think to invite Lord Witherspoon, and the cast will be nearly complete!"

Lord Cartwright shouted with laughter—which was overheard and later questioned. When he explained, Sir Cyrall went silent and then smiled. "It was a very odd situation, there at the Witherspoons, was it not? But when I consider it all, I can think of no one who finished the summer unhappy."

"I suspect," said Diane, smiling, "that the happiest of all was Lord Witherspoon himself. His theater was a great success, just as he'd hoped. But if no one objects, I'd rather we not accept the, um, *invitation* he sent us recently concerning his plans for *next* summer."

"You call what we received an *invitation*?" asked Lord Cartwright sternly. "We will turn it down, whatever anyone else thinks to do. Where the man got the notion *my wife* might hire herself out to help Brown stage three more plays I'll never know! In fact, given how obtuse his lordship is, I think I'll keep my wife far away from *anything* he has a finger in."

"Because he'll attempt to put her to work?" asked Cyrall, that little V-shaped smile twisting his lips.

"Exactly. Any work she does in future will be for me."

Diane's eyes twinkled. "Except I don't call it work, of course." She laughed when Madeline's cheeks flew roses and laughed harder when Sir Cyrall, who might have been expected to say such a sly thing, expressed disapproval of her suggestive remark.

Lord Cartwright, grinning, took her by the elbow and, offering good night's over his shoulder, led her off for more of that *work* to which she referred.

Sir Cyrall frowned after them until his wife, a speculative look in her eye, offered, "I think I would like to go to *work* as well."

And then he too laughed heartily.

The footman on duty in the hall raised a silent prayer of thanks that he could finally fulfill the last of his duties for the night, banking the fires and snuffing any remaining candles, and, at long last, find his bed as well.